# MOONLIGHT EXPOSURE

BY

## Sheila DuGantt

# MOONLIGHT EXPOSURE

Designed by Acorn Book Services

Publication Managed by Acorn Book Services
www.acornbookservices.com
info@acornbookservices.com
304-285-8205

ISBN-13: 978-0692766804
ISBN-10: 0692766804

Cover designed by Todd Aune
Spokane, Washington
www.projetoonline.com

Printed in the United States of America

To my children who have so graciously accepted the moonlight side of me.

# FOREWORD

Sometimes, we come through a difficult time only to face another one on the horizon. We wonder if our faith will grow after each passing gale or chip away the faith we do have, leaving our soul hopeless, desolate, and frail. The storms of life can be so unpredictable. They can surface on a quiet spring day or lay low until the icy winds of winter. Sometimes, they wait just around the corner, never knowing the path they will render. The storms of life are no respecter of persons. They touch the lives of the rich as well as the poor. They do not discriminate against race, gender, or age. There is only one requirement to feel their pain. You must be a living, breathing soul on the world's stage. So, how do we face another storm on the horizon? How does our faith grow after each passing gale? We must learn to embrace them as a fact of life. Release our faith and challenge our soul to believe. The storm has come to make us strong and not weak.

*Marilyn Jantzen*

SHEILA DUGANTT

# CHAPTER 1

Marilyn opened the French doors in the family room and stepped out onto the bluestone patio. A gust of wind blew her long, auburn hair away from her face—revealing fine lines that had etched their way across her forehead in the last nine months. She squinted against the sun as if it were an uninvited guest and slipped the sunglasses over her bloodshot, green eyes. She made her way to the stone wall and stepped through the half-moon opening onto the connecting walkway where her rock garden was in full bloom with daffodils, daylilies, and crocus. She could almost hear their sighs when a gentle breeze tilted their pretty little heads her way as if they were watching, waiting, and wanting the touch of her hands to remove the weeds that had infiltrated their garden.

She gave nature's children no mind. She was no longer interested or captivated by their beauty. How could she, when the precious flower she had cultivated for five years had been taken from right out under her nose, choking the very life out of her?

On her left, a mockingbird in a flowering red maple tree screeched. Marilyn scanned the backyard and spotted the object of its ridicule prowling in the tall grass, trying its best to avoid the harassment of its predator. With one last warning the bird swooped down and attacked the back of the cat's head—taking a tuft of black fur along with it. With a victory under its wing, the bird flew back to its perch and twitched its head toward Marilyn. Squawking, it gave her a scornful look. It was letting her know in no uncertain terms that she would share the same fate if she posed a threat to her young.

*If only I had been as attentive*, she thought as the walkway gave way to gray stepping stones.

She scuffed to the white gazebo and sat down in one of the two white wicker chairs. With a sigh, she leaned back and placed the small thermos of tea on the matching table to her left. She planted her feet on the edge of the seat and stretched her baggy, blue and gold Mountaineer sweatshirt over the knees of her faded blue jeans. She gazed toward the pond where a gaggle of geese were cleaning their feathers. It brought back the time when she was six, and her dad had taken her fishing.

"Daddy, why do geese honk?" She had asked, looking up as a flock of geese flew overhead.

"Well, that's how they talk to each other." He had answered, casting his fishing line into the water.

"Oh, what do they say?" She held her pink fishing pole while watching a dragon fly skim across the water like a little spy looking for the catch of the day.

"All depends. If they're flying, the ones in the back honk to encourage the ones in the front to keep going. If one of them is lost, it helps them find their way back to the flock. But I think the real reason," he said as he sat down in the boat next to her, "is the ones in the back are really saying, 'Hey, I'm behind you, so don't fart.'"

"Oh, Daddy ..." She laughed as his big, freckled hand rubbed the top of her head.

"Are you hungry?"

"Yes," she giggled.

He opened the cooler and pulled out the traditional fishing lunch of two bologna and cheese sandwiches with globs of mayonnaise, along with a bag of Oreo cookies.

"Here you go." He handed her the sandwich and set the cookies on top of the cooler.

Together, father and daughter placed their elbows on their knees, took a bite of their sandwiches, and chased them with a bite of cookie. All of a sudden, a loud bang echoed across the sky where one of the geese fell out of formation and tumbled to the ground.

"Daddy!" She quickly stood, causing the boat to slightly rock back and forth.

"Honey, it's okay. Just keep your eyes on the geese." He gently pulled her back down and slipped his arm around her shoulders.

A tear slipped down her cheek while two geese drop out of formation to follow the goose to the ground where they stayed with it until it died.

"Remember, Mare," he had said as he pulled her close and kissed the top of her head, "sometimes the only thing we can do in life is to comfort one another."

Marilyn placed the thermos back on the table and hugged her knees to her chest. She'd give anything just to spend one more day with her father. She missed his relaxed and easy-going personality. She loved his sense of humor, especially when he made her laugh with his 'why did the chicken cross the road' type of jokes. She missed working beside him at O'Reilly's Lumber, the family business. But what she missed the most was the way he looked at her mother when they danced across the living room floor.

Her mother was half Irish and half Italian; however, it was the Italian side that was predominant. Marilyn loved the way her dark, shoulder-length, wavy hair with streaks of gray framed her soft, brown eyes—eyes that could calm all your troubles in a matter of minutes. She talked with her hands—especially if she wanted to get her point across. She was a jack-of-all-trades but a master in the kitchen. There wasn't a food group she couldn't cook.

Every time their mother was behind the stove, Marilyn's brother, Dillon, was standing right next to her with his finger in the pot to be sure it was suitable for the rest of the family.

Dillon looked more like their mother but acted like their father. He was the prankster in the family, and

there wasn't a dull moment when he was around. Even though he was five years older than her, they were very close. Growing up, she had worshipped the ground he walked on and was his constant tag-along even when he went fishing with his buddies. If they didn't like it, well, he told them they could just leave.

Several years later, after he had gone off to college, it felt like a part of her was missing. However, that moment paled in comparison to the day her parents drove him to the airport so he could live out his life-long dream.

Dillon was a history professor at Shepherd University, and all he talked about was going to Ireland. A day didn't go by that he didn't dream about seeing the glittering, white, sandy beaches, the soaring cliffs, the bogs, and the rural farmland. But she believed the real reason he wanted to go was to have a beer at The Brazen Head Pub, in Dublin. So instead of dreaming about it, he started saving and within three years had enough money to go.

Two days before he was to leave, she had a dream they were sitting in the back seat of their parent's car. Her dad was driving and her mom was sitting next to him. Out of nowhere, a grey mist rolled onto the two-lane highway with a set of headlights barreling toward them. The impact had been so great that it jolted her awake, causing her to roll out of bed and onto the floor.

The following day she had asked Dillon to postpone his trip because she had a bad feeling. He had flat out said no because he had waited too long and not even her meaningless dream was going to stop him. She had begged her parents not to take him to the airport, but they completely ignored her. The morning of the trip she made one last plea, but they had just shrugged her off and assured her everything would be fine.

Later that morning, she received a call that they had been in an accident. They were only thirty minutes away from the airport when a ten foot U-haul truck crossed the center line and hit them head on. Both of her parents were killed instantly and her brother was taken to Winchester Medical Center, where he lived for about four hours on life support and died with his dream of seeing Ireland still inside him.

The following year had been a living hell while Marilyn stumbled through the grieving process. One minute she was in denial and the next she was angry. The anger led to bargaining and she realized no matter how much she pleaded they were never coming back. Several times, she almost got to acceptance, but it always came back to the anger—anger because they ignored her warning—anger because the man that killed them lived—anger because God let it happen—and anger because her now ex-husband, Jim, hadn't been more understanding of what she was going through.

In the beginning, he had been supportive, but several months later it had all changed. One day, he just strolled into their bedroom where she was lying down, told her to get a grip and move on with her life. It only confirmed what she already knew—that he was self-absorbed, self-seeking, and self-interested.

Her assessment was reinforced fifteen months later on the day she had taken their daughter Emily to the Disney store in Tysons Corner. They had just finished shopping and were sitting on the second level of the mall eating ice cream. She thought she spotted Jim on the first level holding hands with another woman. She knew that was doubtful because he was supposed to be in Maryland  supervising a new construction site. However, the moment the man  lifted the woman's hand and gently kissed each finger, Marilyn knew it was Jim because he had kissed her the same way when they first dated.

With her heart hammering in her chest, she ran to the railing and yelled his name several times. Jim had looked up, slowly lowered the woman's hand in disbelief as his jaw dropped to the ground. On  impulse she threw up her middle finger and gave him a dirty look. She turned around to go back to Emily—but she was gone.

Marilyn dropped her feet to the ground when the memory  faded. She looked up into the heavens while a silent rage stirred inside her emptiness, receded into the pit of her stomach, and weaved its way upward.

"Why?" Her eyes flashed and closed in slits. "How much more do you think I can handle? My parents and brother weren't enough so you had to take my daughter, too? What did I ever do to  you?"

Hot, salty tears flooded down her face when the heavens gave her no answer. She slid off the chair and crumbled to the floor where deep, gut-wrenching sobs tore through her chest with the one  question she had asked herself repeatedly. Why hadn't she just walked away that day instead of confronting Jim? If she had, her daughter would still be here.

The guilt tore her apart every second of every day. She would never forgive herself for the one careless act that had cost her everything.

Marilyn wiped the tears from her face with the back of her sleeve, stood up from the deck of the gazebo, and sat down on the chair.

On the south bank of the pond, the black cat now prowled along the water's edge. It was eying several ducklings coasting peacefully under the falling canopy of the willow tree. She knew the predator had just jumped out of the frying pan and into the fire as the mama goose sailed across the water and up on the bank, hissing, biting, and flapping her wings—chasing the cat up a tree. It squawked several warnings before waddling back to her babies.

Marilyn reached for the thermos and realized nature did a lot better job of protecting their young. She took a sip of tea as a ray of light broke through the clouds north of the pond and beamed down on the field of wild flowers.

"Emily …" She gasped causing the tea to run over her chin and down the front of her shirt.

She closed her eyes and wondered if the last nine months had finally taken its toll. She took a deep breath and slowly exhaled while she opened her eyes to where the sun was still glistening upon her daughter's strawberry blonde curls.

A feeling of lightness crept across Marilyn's chest as Emily picked a daisy, placed it under her nose, and giggled. Her heart soared, causing the corners of her mouth to lift into a smile she hadn't felt in months. She quickly placed the thermos back on the table and ran toward her daughter with a vow. This time she wouldn't let go.

"No! I can't do this anymore," she collapsed to the ground and wept when the sun quickly withdrew its rays—taking Emily along with them.

Several minutes later, in the silence of her anguish, a dark shadow fell upon her and out of the ghostly rays she heard a voice.

"Marilyn."

"What?" Her muscles tensed.

"Are you okay?"

*What the hell is he doing here?* she thought, while wiping the tears off her face and trying to stand.

"Don't. I don't need your help." She jerked away when Jim placed his hand on her arm.

"Are you drinking again?" He took a step back.

"If I am, it's none of your business."

"I guess it isn't."

"Your damn right it isn't."

She got up, brushed the dirt off the seat of her pants, and stomped back to the gazebo while she glanced toward the field where she had seen Emily and wondered if it had been real.

"Jim, what do you want?" She sat down, grabbed the thermos off the table, and wished she had something stronger.

"I see the geese found their way back." He faced the pond. "Emily always loved it out here."

"Jim, I'm sure you didn't come all the way out here just to talk about the geese." She lifted her legs and tucked them under her.

"I thought I'd return the extra set of house keys." He turned around, pulled them out of his front jeans pocket, and handed them to her.

"You shouldn't have bothered. I had the locks changed months ago." She lifted her chin and glared into his blue eyes. She knew there was something else on Jim's mind when he slipped the keys into his pocket and rubbed the back of his neck. "What else?"

"What do you mean what else?"

"You're fidgeting. That tells me you have something else on your mind."

"I'm getting married." He blurted out while brushing his hand through his sandy blonde hair.

Marilyn regurgitated the bitter-taste of Jim's betrayal. He stood there with his waist tapering down to his hips filling out his stone-washed jeans in all the right places. At thirty-three, three years younger than she, he still physically took her breath away, but emotionally he had drained her.

"Married?" She smirked clenching her jaw. "I see you're not wasting any time moving on with your life."

"What is that supposed to mean?"

"Emily's only been missing for nine months, and we've only been divorced for three. So, is six months the going rate for grieving a failed marriage and a missing child?"

"That's not fair. Our marriage was going downhill long before Emily was taken."

"You're right, and it all started when I couldn't lose that extra forty pounds after having your baby." He stood there like a bump on a log so she egged him on. "Admit it! I'm right!"

"Since, we're putting it all on the table. You're right, but that's not the only reason."

"Really, why don't you enlighten me?"

"Can I be frank?"

"Sure, why not? Nothing has ever stopped you before."

"Two years ago, after your parent's accident, you became withdrawn. The only thing you cared about was Emily and your  precious café. You spent more time with your customers than your husband. After a while, I started feeling like a third wheel."

"Always looking for excuses, aren't you? I have it on good  authority you were cheating on me long before the accident. I don't know how I could've been so blind. All the signs were there—the late nights at the office, the weekend business trips. You're right. Emily and the café did become my life. And whenever I tried to include you in it, you always seemed to have more important things to do, like cheating behind my back. So I stopped asking and  decided it wasn't even worth the effort. Just like this conversation. So why don't you just go marry that little twenty-three year old slut of yours and leave me the hell alone?"

"She's not a slut. Her name is Sarah and she makes me very happy." His face started to turn red.

"Happy?" She stood wanting to smack the happy right out of him. "Your daughter is missing. How is it possible to be happy? Please, if you have a remedy that will relieve this deep, gut wrenching ache in my heart so I can move on, I would love to hear about it."

She waited for an answer, but all he gave her was an empty stare. "Jim, you don't even know what happiness is."

"Well, it's sure as hell not being with you." He lifted his eyebrows, narrowed his stance, and crossed his arms.

Several geese rustled their feathers as if the tension in the air was too much. The instant they ran across the water, spread their wings, and took flight, so did Jim.

"Well, I'm out of here." He raised his arms in the air and started to leave.

"So that's it!" She shrugged her shoulders. "What about Emily?"

"What about her? She's gone and it's your fault."

"So, you think you can ride out of here on your high, self-righteous horse." She went to where he stood and matched his stance. "If it hadn't been for the fact I saw you cheating in the mall that day, I would've  never left Emily alone."

"It doesn't matter—she was in your care. So, if anyone's to blame it's you, and you're going to have to live with that."

"Believe what you want." She jabbed her finger in his face. "It doesn't change the fact you're a lying, self-centered, deceitful, shadow of a man. I'm just thankful I can wipe my hands of you."

"I guess there's nothing left to say." He pushed her finger away.

"You're right. There isn't. I'm just glad this façade of a marriage is finally over so we can both move on." She resisted the urge to slap him across the face.

"I couldn't agree more." He stomped away.

Marilyn headed back to the gazebo and realized Jim was right about one thing. If she had paid more attention to her daughter and less to her cheating husband, Emily would still be here. She picked up the thermos and started back to the house when her cell phone rang. She reached inside the pocket of her sweatshirt to jerk it out.

"Hello!"

"It doesn't sound like you're in a good mood."

"Jim just left. Need I say more?"

"What did the scum bag want this time?"

"Dana, he's getting married." She stepped through the half-moon opening, flopped down on the teak patio chair, and slammed the thermos on the table.

"Marilyn, don't let that weasel get under your skin."

"I just don't understand." She grabbed the chair next to her, pulled it close, and propped her feet up on the seat.

"Understand what?"

"How can he just move on with his life when Emily is missing?"

"Come on, Mare. You know Jim has always been self-centered. Remember the time your car broke down and you were stranded for over an hour because he wanted to finish his golf game?"

"Yes."

"And remember the time we planned for months to go on the Women Bikers against Breast Cancer ride and you had to cancel? All because something came up on the spur of the moment, and he couldn't watch Emily."

"I get it! I just don't want to talk about him anymore."

"I'm just saying …"

"So, what's up?"

"Some of the girls are planning a bike run to Skyline Drive Saturday, and I thought maybe you'd like to come along for a change of scenery."

"Dana, I really appreciate the offer but I can't go."

"Come on, Mare, you need to get out and have some fun instead of working at the café all the time."

"Dana," she dropped her feet to the ground and sat up in the chair, "how am I supposed to have fun when my daughter's missing? I don't deserve to be happy when she's out there all alone, scared, and wondering why her mommy let go of her hand."

"Mare, I'm sorry. I didn't mean to upset you."

"No, I'm sorry." She rubbed the back of her neck. "Jim just has a way of getting under my skin and I don't mean to take it out on you. Anyway, another reason why I can't go is because Charlie invited me to a Parents of Comfort dinner party on Saturday."

"How is that old godfather of yours? I haven't seen him in a while."

"He's doing fine."

"So, what's a Parents of Comfort dinner party?"

"It's an annual party for parents who have or had a missing child. I guess it's like an AA meeting where you get to share your experiences. Only it's done in a semi-formal dinner party atmosphere where you get to dress up your depression to help make you feel better."

"Mare, I think that's a great idea. Are you going?"

"I don't know. I told Charlie I'd think about it. I'm not sure I want to play dress up and share my feelings with complete strangers."

"Well, I think you should go."

"I guess. Anyway, tell the girls maybe I'll go next time."

"Alright, I'm going to hold you to that."

"I said maybe, so it's still up in the air."

"I know, but I'm going to bug you until you give in."

"Dana, sometimes you can be a pain in the behind, but you are my best friend and I don't know what I'd do without you."

"I don't know what you'd do without me either." She laughed. "Hey, I've got to go."

"Okay. I think I'm going to go take a long, hot bath and wash off the Jim-tamination."

"Now you're talking. It's time to wash off the scent of that dirty, rotten scoundrel once and for all."

"Dana, I'll talk to you later."

"Later."

Marilyn tucked the phone back into her pocket while the sun melted behind a sheet of cumulus clouds painting the sky into a fiery red. Two squirrels played chase around the trunk of the red maple tree.

In my next life, I'm coming back as a squirrel; the only nuts I'll have to worry about are those I have for lunch.

She grabbed the thermos and went inside.

# CHAPTER 2

A classic rock radio station played in the background as Marilyn stepped into the Victorian clawfoot tub. She slipped under the lavender-scented water while the candles placed causally around the room danced shadows upon the cream-colored walls. With a sigh, she leaned back to reach for the glass of wine on the white, marble-top table and took a sip. She closed her eyes and listened to the rain lightly tapping on the skylight above her and remembered how she had met Jim.

He had been one of her clients at a marketing and advertising firm in Washington, D.C. Within three years she had made Jantzen Construction one of the greatest company's in the Tri-State area. A year later they were married and built their two-story, Victorian-style, dream house on ten acres of land on the outskirts of Shepherdstown, West Virginia. The house was over three-thousand square feet with four bedrooms, three full baths, and enough space for a family of five. Space no longer filled with her daughter's laughter. Space where the sound of her husband's footsteps still echoed across the floor to the opening and closing of the door reminding her the day he left.

She thought about the reasons Jim had given for his betrayal—she was too fat and not giving him enough attention. He sounded like a country song that always blamed everything on the whiskey. She swirled the wine in her glass and thought that if women were like fine wine and only got better with age, cheating husbands were like a bottle of Jack Daniels—the moment Jack got a hold of them, they blame Daniel for their cheating drunken stupor, convincing themselves at ninety-four proof nothing was their fault.

She circled her big toe around the edge of the faucet and wondered if it was time to put the house up for sale. It was way too much for one person to handle, and at thirty-six, the hope of having more children was doubtful. Besides, all that was left behind the four walls were empty promises and broken dreams. Yet, she couldn't bear the thought of leaving because Emily's memory was in every nook and cranny, and it would be like letting go of her hand for a second time.

"This is just great!" She tried to pull her toe out of the opening of the spigot but it wouldn't budge. She set the glass on the table and scooted forward with tomorrow's headlines flashing before her, "Woman rescued after getting toe stuck in faucet while bathing."

An episode of *The Untold Stories in the ER* where a woman gets her butt stuck in the toilet because her husband left the seat up ran through her mind. Supposedly she was stuck for eighteen hours until someone called 911, and she ended up in the emergency room with the toilet still attached. *Who in their right mind would leave their wife stuck for that long? Jim,* she thought as her toe gave way and her foot flopped back into the water.

A distant thunder began its slow grumbling roll across the sky while she scooted back and wondered when all the insanity would end. Within two years her entire family had been stripped away, and she wasn't sure where she belonged anymore. Sure, she had people who cared, but at the end of the day, they all went home to their families while she was left with an empty house that no longer felt like a home, and the silence reminded her of who she had become—a shadow in a wasteland.

She rested her head on the bath pillow, took a sip of wine, and closed her eyes. She listened to the hypnotic sound of the rain lightly tapping above her. Before she knew it, her head gently rolled to the right while the glass slipped from her fingers and crashed to the floor. Amidst the sound of shattering glass, she entered a dream that would alter her life forever.

❋　　❋　　❋

Cool air penetrated Marilyn's black, leather jacket when she entered a grove of trees on a motorcycle. She could feel every ripple and pot hole in the surface of the old country road while the sunlight streaked through the dense branches. She let up on the throttle when the rays of light reached the small brush along the forest floor creating a sense of warmth and magic. Just for a second, she closed her eyes while a gentle breeze lifted her hair off her shoulders carrying with it the scent of honeysuckle.

To her right she noticed the pink, tubular flowers growing along the road. Several feet behind them stood an oak tree where a heart was carved in its trunk with the initials R.H. and W.M. A gentle wind rustled through its bristly-tipped leaves while a woodpecker drummed nearby. The bird tapped three times and paused. It repeated this cycle several times. Then silence. The quietness was almost tangible; no rustling of leaves, no sound of gravel crunching under the tires, even her breathing slowed, and became barely audible when dusk descended like a final curtain.

In the purple mist of nightfall, a chill ran up her spine and crawled into her brain when the woodpecker began hammering non-stop. A whirlwind of leaves started dancing under her and swirled up with such force that it lifted the front tire off the ground. Her knuckles turned white while she squeezed her knees against the tank, holding on for dear life. The bike revved up its engine, plunged to the ground, and took off whipping her hair behind her. She hunched over the gas tank with her jaw flapping in the wind. Everything sped by her in a blur. She kept her eyes focused on the clearing at the end of the tunnel of trees. With a mind of its own, the bike shifted down to first gear as a large mirror descended out of nowhere and covered the opening.

The moonlight penetrated the awning of the overhead branches as she coasted toward her reflection. Suspended in the mist of dust particles, she lifted her hand and touched the mole just above the right corner of her mouth. The face was hers, but the beauty mark was not. With that observation, the bike glided through the glass causing a small current of electricity to pass through her body.

On the other side, the landscape turned into a green field of clarity as if she were looking through a pair of night goggles. On her left stood a large maple tree, its branches sheltering a walkway leading to a two story farmhouse. Cattycornered to the right back side of the house was a red barn with the advertisement slogan, "Chew Mail Pouch Tobacco, Treat Yourself to the Best," painted in big white letters on the side. Perched on top of the roof was an owl with its dark eyes fixed in a white, heart-shaped face. Its face stretched out into a blood-curdling scream and the headlight on her bike began to flicker.

She leaned forward where a broad, flat, gray head covered with scales pressed against the lens inside the headlight. It pushed until the glass erupted into a crystal shower. She jerked back when the head of a king cobra wiggled out of the socket and moved toward her. Its piercing, blue eyes got right up in her face, opened its mouth, and released a vapor of toxic fumes from its half-inch fangs.

"My sweet Rebecca," it growled a bone-chilling hiss. "I've been patiently waiting for you."

The grey mist swirled up and around her making it almost impossible to breath. She tightened her grip on the handlebars. The hard metal under her became soft and round, slithered to the ground, where the cold-blooded beast snuffed out the warmth of the engine. The back tire unraveled, inched its way forward, and wrapped itself around her body.

Sweat formed above her brow when the snake jabbed its hooded flare through the grey mist in an unmistakable warning. "So, you think you can outrun me," it smirked when he lifted her off the ground. "Well, let me give you a head start." It hurled her through the air.

She soared past the trees and through the brush before coming to an abrupt painful landing on a pile of rocks with a thump. She laid there, her nostrils filled with a mixture of damp leaves and bark while a shadow flapped across her path. She looked up through the mist of the moonlight to where the owl she had seen earlier was now perched on a branch, bobbing its head and swaying back and forth. Her mind rushed around in tight little circles at the sound of twigs snapping. She jerked back her head to see the snake rapidly slithering toward her. The owl let out a loud shriek, spread its wings, and when it took flight, so did she.

She followed the moon with her eyes, allowing it to guide her past the scattered beech and conifer trees. She moved faster and didn't look back, ignoring the briars that caught at her jeans. A branch hit her in the face causing her to fall to the ground, hitting her back on a log and losing her breath. She gasped for air, but nothing came in. She heard branches crackling under foot and knew the creature was gaining on her. She finally took a gulp of air and scrambled to her feet.

She weaved through tree after tree, through bush after bush. A cloud covered the face of the moon and left her in a cloak of darkness. A tree root snatched her ankle and she fell to the ground screaming. She ignored the pain and stood again. Before she could limp forward, the moon slid out and lit up the edge of a cliff several feet in front of her.

"Poor Rebecca," the voice hissed behind her when she leaned to peer over the edge. "Trapped like a caged animal."

The thunderous roar of a raging river below caused a painful lump to form in her throat. There was no escape. Her fate had been sealed. With a hopeless sigh she turned and faced her assailant.

In the moonlight exposure the snake dangled at the end of a tree branch above the forest floor. She could see the storm brewing in its dark blue eyes as it propelled itself upward, flattened its body to twice its normal width, captured the air in flight, and nose-dived toward her. Seconds later it sank its teeth into the side of her neck. She grabbed a hold of it, pulled, but it wouldn't budge. A burning sensation surged through her skin. She became lightheaded, and her heart began to palpitate. As the poison traveled to her extremities, paralysis started to set in.

The snake released its hold, reared back its head, and stared into her eyes. "I told you, you couldn't outrun me."

With a silent scream her body plunged over the side of the cliff taking the snake along with her. She hit the cold water as her heart raced into a panic. She flailed her arms, kicking, coughing, and gasping for air. Just when she thought she was about to die she woke up.

Marilyn grabbed the sides of the tub sputtering and pulled herself to the surface. She frantically wiped her hair out of her face and did a three-sixty in the tub looking for the snake. When she didn't see it, she glanced around the room and realized it had all been a dream. Shaking, she took a deep breath, got out, and grabbed the towel off the floor. She wrapped it around her, stepped off the rug, slipped in a puddle of water, and the next thing she knew her head was banging against the white ceramic tile.

While she lay there waiting for her bones to settle, she thought about the dream and wondered what it all meant. Was it symbolic of her already messed up life or was it … Rebecca, the snake had called her Rebecca. That was Emily's middle name. She thought about her reflection in the mirror and the mole on her face. Emily had the same blemish. What if it all was just a premonition like the one she had about her parents' accident? What if the vision in the field of wildflowers was her daughter's spirit and it was letting her know she was already dead?

Tears blurred her vision as the voice of Barry Manilow crooned "I Made it Through the Rain" in the background. She listened to the lyrics and wondered, how could she make it through the rain when it wouldn't stop? How could she keep her world protected when she had failed to protect the one thing that mattered most? Her little girl was gone, all because of her, and she didn't deserve to live.

"Emily, I'm so sorry," she whispered.

A silent tear trickled down her cheek. She stepped back into the tub. A tense heat flushed through her body while she slipped under the water. Exiting through her extremities, it left behind a trail of peace. She slightly opened her mouth, the thunder rolled across the sky as if announcing her imminent departure. The bubbles popped and burst in slow motion, as the voice of Manilow faded and the song, "Ironic," by Alanis Morissette filtered the air.

Winning the lottery and dying the next day is really not that all ironic. Now getting a death row pardon minutes after you're dead is a different story. The voice of reason began to penetrate her way of thinking. How ironic it would be if she ended her own life and minutes later Emily was found alive? The dream and vision were only circumstantial—they proved nothing. She closed her mouth, let the lyrics baptize her thoughts, and slowly emerged.

She pushed down the lever to drain the water and stepped out of the tub. She picked the towel up off the floor again, wiped herself down, and wrapped it around her head. She cautiously tiptoed across the floor to grab the white terry cloth robe off the back of the door, and slipped it on. She planted her hands firmly on the sides of the sink and gave her reflection a scornful look.

"What were you thinking? Until you know for certain Emily is ..." She couldn't even say the word. To say it might make it so.

She pulled the towel off her head, wiped the puddle off the floor, and tossed it into the hamper. She lightly touched the bump on the back of her head, reached into the medicine cabinet and took a couple of aspirin to ward off the headache. She picked up the wide tooth comb from off the sink, carefully ran it through her hair while she listened to the lyrics about life having a way of helping you out. *I hope you're right,* she thought, as she turned off the radio, blew out the candles, and went into the master bedroom.

She pulled Jim's Mountaineer t-shirt from the dresser drawer and lifted it to her face. She closed her eyes and took in the musky scent that still lingered. The scent that once was pleasant had now turned sour with betrayal. She balled it up and discarded it like an old shoe in the corner. She pulled out a pair of her black boxers, along with a Rolling Stones classic tongue t-shirt, put them on, and left. In the hallway she paused in front of Emily's bedroom. She closed her eyes and lightly pressed her ear against the door. If only she could hear the words she had silenced so many times before. Mommy can you tuck me in one more time? Mommy can you read one more book? Mommy ...

"Mommy will never give up," she whispered and made her way downstairs.

Marilyn sat in the overstuffed recliner which matched the sunroom's hues of peach and ivory. Through glass walls, the night sky was pitch-black with tiny patches of deep blue peeking through. A flash of lightening zigzagged across the heavens, illuminating the heavy clouds that hung ominously low over the mountains. She took a sip of wine and thought about her episode upstairs in the bathroom. She could never allow herself to lose emotional control like that again. From here on out, she had to live by the motto 'no news is good news,' meaning that as long as she hadn't heard anything, there was a chance her daughter was still alive.

She stared out the window and watched the dark clouds engulf the patches of blue in the sky. It made her think about the week after Emily was taken, and how she had gone into a deep depression. She went for days without eating because most of the time her stomach was tied up in knots as a constant reminder that it was upset and angry with her. Each day felt like shards of glass were poking the backs of her eyeballs. Eventually she started self-medicating with alcohol to relieve her pain, but it did nothing to fill the quietness and emptiness that fit together like a lock and key, leaving her a prisoner of her own demise.

She'd never forget the day there came a persistent knock on the French doors of her bedroom. She peeked out from under the covers where Dana and Charlie stood on the balcony and knew they would no longer be ignored. It was the day love had climbed the trellis of her shattered life and helped her breathe again. The pain was still there and sometimes it was unbearable like tonight. The strange thing was every time she thought about giving up; life had a way of intervening.

Nature decided to do its song and dance in her backyard so she got up and went into the kitchen. Lightening streaked across the tumbled mosaic accent tiles while she made her way to the oak, two-tiered kitchen island. She started to grab the bottle of wine off the light green marble counter to refresh her drink when the phone rang. She thought about ignoring it because of the storm, but changed her mind thinking it could have something to do with Emily. She darted across the floor and grabbed the phone off the counter.

"Hello."

"Hey, Mare, it's Charlie."

"Hi, Charlie." She leaned against the counter with a sigh.

"Rough day?"

"You have no idea."

"Want to talk about it?"

"No, it's late and I was about ready to go to bed," she lied. "Besides, you shouldn't be calling me in this bad storm."

"I just wanted to remind you about the dinner party on Saturday."

"Charlie, I'm not sure I want to go."

"And why not?"

"I just don't think I'm ready to go out and mingle with a bunch of strangers."

"Nonsense. I'm not taking no for an answer."

"Charlie …"

"There's no 'Charlie' about it. You're going and that's it."

"A little bossy, aren't we?"

"So, I'll pick you up Saturday at five."

"Well, if you insist."

"I insist. Now get some rest because it sounds like you need it."

"Goodnight, Charlie."

"Mare, I love you."

"I love you, too."

Charles O'Connor and her dad had been army buddies. After they were discharged and went their separate ways they had lost touch. Several years' later, Charlie contacted him looking for a line of credit so he could start a business after the banks saw him as a financial risk. So, with an Irish handshake and his word of honor, her dad gave him a break. Several years later, after Lowe's and Home Depot came into town, it hit O'Reilly's Lumber hard. If it hadn't been for O'Connor's Development, the store would've gone under. In the end, that handshake meant more than a business agreement; it became a brotherhood between two friends, helping each other live the American dream.

After her father passed away, she didn't know what she was going to do with the business. Her hands were full with the café and when she told Charlie she was going to put it on the market, he bought it from her and decided he would keep the name "O'Reilly's Lumber" in honor of the man who had changed his life.

Marilyn decided to take Charlie's advice and try to get some rest. She grabbed the bottle of wine off the counter and put it back into the fridge. She was making her way across the floor when she heard a tapping sound. She'd been hearing the same sound off and on for the past couple of weeks, but she'd never identified the source. Thunder lightly rolled across the sky and, as it sang its last grumbling tune, she did a double-take when the lid of her green trash can opened and closed by itself.

*Now I know I'm losing my mind,* she thought. First it was Emily in a field of wildflowers, a crazy dream, and now moving trash can lids.

Why did moving trash can lids seem familiar? A memory from long ago resurfaced. It was a conversation she'd had with her mother. Dana's mother had finally lost her battle with cancer and they were driving home from the funeral. Witnessing her friend's sorrow, Marilyn had been struck by fear that she might lose her own mother.

"Mom, I don't know what I'd do if anything ever happened to you," she'd said.

"Honey, I felt the same way before your grandmother passed away, and I'll tell you the same thing she told me."

"What's that?"

"Each day is a gift and we should live it to the fullest. Love those around us like it was their last day on earth. And when death unexpectedly snatches them away, we have no regrets. Sure we're going to miss them, yet, in the midst of our grief, we find joy because of the love we shared. They would want us to continue to live, to love, and to laugh because it's a testament of what their love stood for. So until we see them again, we honor their memory by allowing the joy of their life to flow through us."

"Mom, I understand what you're saying, but it's just so hard to see my best friend going through the pain of losing her mother. It's almost as if I'm going through it too, and I don't have the right words to  comfort her."

"Honey, sometimes silence is all we need. It's not the saying that counts, but never needing to have to say anything. Just be there in her cycles of grief no matter how long it takes."

"I will, but it just seems so unfair."

"I know honey." She gently patted Marilyn's hand.

"Mom, you have to promise me," Marilyn had stared into the eyes of the woman that meant everything to her. "If you go before I do, I want you to give me some kind of sign you're still with me."

"What kind of sign?"

"Well, since we spend a lot of time together in the kitchen, I want you to tap the lid of my trash can."

"Done," said her mother while she squeezed her hand with a promise.

Marilyn brushed her hand through her hair as the memory faded, went to the corner, and stood in front of the trash can.

"Mom, if it's you, please tap the lid again."

The lid swung inward and tapped twice before it closed. Marilyn leaned back against the wall, slid to the floor, and softly began to sob when the oriental fragrance of *Tabu*, her mom's favorite perfume, filtered through the air. She closed her eyes, and in the stillness of the room, she let a mother's promise comfort her with her undying love.

# CHAPTER 3

They entered the magnificent avenue of live oaks leading to the entrance of the VanWyc estate. The grounds were landscaped with a neat parterre around the house. The gardens extended right up to the house with azaleas, clipped boxwood hedges, and neat brick paths. The house consisted of a rectangular main section and two small wings. There were double galleries with six, plain, unfluted Doric columns on each level that extended across the entire front of the main house. The ground floor gallery was open to the evening breezes, and the second story provided the comfort of an airy private gallery.

A man directed them to a grassy area where at least twenty cars were already parked. Charlie pulled his black, Rolls Royce sedan behind a seen-better-days pickup truck and next to a brand new Mercedes. By the looks of the vehicles, there were no prejudices when it came to families with missing children.

"Are you ready?" asked Charlie.

"I don't know why I let you talk me into this."

"You'll be fine. Besides, I'll be right beside you." He got out and opened her door.

Wearing a black tuxedo, Charlie escorted her toward the house. At sixty-five, he still kept himself in great shape, and the suit fit his six-foot frame with a sense of class. Even his signature bald head and the fine lines around his eyes gave him a mature, sophisticated look. After her parents passed away, his role as Marilyn's godfather had evolved more into a father-figure. She couldn't imagine life without him.

Marilyn stood beside him wearing an emerald green, silk jersey, dress that she hadn't worn in years. The backless, knee-length cut fit her five-foot-eight body perfectly. Gone were the back fat, the stomach pouch, and the love handles. The stress of losing her daughter had caused her to go from a size fourteen to a size six in a matter of nine months, something she hadn't been able to do in five years.

With her hair pulled back in a classic French twist, it exposed a pair of emerald and diamond cluster earrings that belonged to her grandmother. Resting softly between her breasts was a pear shaped diamond necklace. It had once been a token of Jim's promise of till-death-do-us-part. She didn't realize at the time that death and weight gain meant the same thing. To commemorate their divorce, she took her engagement ring to a jeweler and had it converted into a necklace. She wasn't sure if it was a way of dealing with her loss or a way of holding onto the past. Perhaps it was a little bit of both.

They stepped into an entrance hallway where a double-tiered crystal chandelier hung from the ceiling. Beyond the hall there was a wide open staircase. On the right was the entrance to the  dining room where guest had already gathered for cocktails. A young waiter dressed in a white tuxedo offered them a glass of wine as they entered the room.

"Thank you," Marilyn accepted a glass and took a sip.

"Sir …" the waiter nodded at Charlie.

Charlie reached into his pant pocket to pull out a ten dollar bill that he placed on the tray.

"Sir, the drinks are free."

"That's for you." He picked up a glass.

"Why, thank you," he nodded his head.

A woman with gray hair cut into a short bob stepped through the French doors from the terrace into the dining room. Dressed in a royal-blue, cap-sleeve gown with a crepe bodice, the woman exuded elegance. The boat style neckline traced over her shoulders and down into a scooped back, then to a fitted waist where a full satin and lace gathered skirt flowed to the floor. And by the way Charlie was looking  at her; you'd think she was the only woman in the room.

"Ladies and gentlemen, may I have your attention," the woman spoke to the guests. "My name is Violet Shaw, and I'd like to welcome you. We are here tonight because, at one time or another, we have all shared the common thread of a missing child. The Parents of Comfort annual dinner party is the result of the kidnapping and return of my twenty year-old granddaughter, Sophia. Through this experience, I realized the best way to cope was to connect with those who were going through the same situation."

"Charlie?"

"What?"

"Do you know her?"

"Yes," he grinned.

"Now, without further ado, I'd like to introduce you to our host, William VanWyc. Please, give him a round of applause for his generosity in allowing us to use his beautiful estate. With no charge, I might add, for this special occasion."

A man wearing a black suit stepped from the crowd and made his way to the front. He was about six-foot-two, and had dark hair with a hint of gray on the sides.

"Thank you," the man lifted his palms toward the crowd and waited for the last clap to echo across the room. "I assure you, I'm not the hero here, but you are. Your willingness to share your courage and strength with others during the most difficult season of your life is incredible. Many of you know that, several years ago, my five-year-old nephew was taken by his father. We have yet to locate him. I watched my sister spiral into the worst nightmare of her life but, through the support and comfort of others, I watched a gleam of hope begin to sparkle in her eyes. So tonight I hope you realize you are not alone in your journey. Please get to know one another and enjoy your evening."

Applause erupted across the room while William quietly stepped back into the crowd. The atmosphere was filled with gratitude that someone had taken the time to give them a reprieve from their personal hell. The emotions in the room were so overwhelming that Marilyn's hands automatically joined in.

"The dinner buffet which our host has generously provided is now open," said Violet. "Also, the terrace is open for dancing. And please feel free to roam the beautiful gardens around the estate. Enjoy your evening, and God bless."

"You want to get something to eat?" asked Marilyn.

"No, you go on ahead and I'll catch up with you later," said Charlie.

"Okay." She watched him head toward Violet.

The classic dinner buffet consisted of several stations. The salad station was filled with a variety of field harvest mixed greens with vine-ripened tomatoes served with choice of dressing. The carving station included oven-roasted strip loin served with a red wine demi-glaze and fresh horseradish cream; the oven-roasted loin of pork was served with a sweet tangy sauce.

The entrees included island herb grilled chicken, a tilapia fillet with lobster cream, orange-soy salmon, and Tuscan pasta. The accompaniments were garlic mashed potatoes, local harvest vegetables, cilantro-lime rice, fresh steamed green beans, and a variety of freshly baked rolls. The sweet dessert trio was chocolate mousse truffle, vanilla bean cheesecake, and strawberries with a chocolate fountain.

Marilyn bypassed the entrees and headed for the salad station. She picked up a plate, and grabbed the stainless steel tongs. She dipped them into the bowl of salad greens but her hand paused at the sound of the voice behind her.

"Hello, Marilyn."

She placed the greens on her plate. "Jim, I didn't realized you were going to be here."

"Same here."

"Where's Sarah?" She picked up the clear plastic bottle of raspberry vinaigrette dressing and drizzled it over her salad.

"She had other plans and couldn't make it."

"What a pity."

"Did you come alone?"

"No, I came with Charlie."

"If I knew you were coming, we could've ridden together."

"Jim, now why would I want to do that?" She narrowed her eyes, picked up a set of silverware wrapped in a burgundy napkin, and turned around.

"Well, we are Emily's parents and I don't see any harm in trying to get through this together."

"Jim, you're the one that left, remember?" She looked up at him and rolled her eyes. "So, unless you have information about our daughter's whereabouts, we're done here."

"Please," his fingers lightly brushed her arm as she started to leave.

"Jim." She looked down at the hand that hurt her and slowly pulled it away. "What do you want?"

"Can we talk?"

"What is there to talk about?"

"Please, can we go out on the terrace away from the crowd?"

Marilyn looked around and realized they were drawing attention. "Fine, but you better make it short and sweet."

She followed Jim across the room and through the French doors leading out onto the marble terrace. It was enclosed with a black cast iron railing except for the gap on each side where a set of stairs led down to the gardens. They passed several couples slow-dancing under a pair of pink flowering dogwoods that formed a natural canopy in the middle of the terrace. A gentle breeze wisped a strand of hair away from her face. Jim stopped in front of a round table dressed in a white table cloth and a hurricane candle.

"So, what was so important that you had to drag me all the way out here to tell me?" She set down her plate.

"Isn't that the dress you wore to the captain's dinner on the Royal Caribbean cruise we took on our fifth anniversary?"

"Yes." She remembered that day clearly because it was the night Emily was conceived.

"Well, it looks just as great on you now as it did then." Noticing she had lost weight.

"Thank you." Surprised Jim gave her a compliment. "So what is it you wanted to say?"

"So … how are you doing?"

"You brought me all the way out here just to ask me how I'm doing." She raised her eyebrows and shook her head.

"Yes, you are the mother of my child. I still care about you  regardless of what you think."

"I was also your wife, and you didn't seem very concerned about me when I saw you in the mall nine months ago."

"Marilyn, I know I hurt you and I'm sorry, but there's nothing I can do to change that."

"You're right, there isn't and I don't even know why we're having this conversation."

"I miss Emily. I want my daughter back and, as a father, I feel so helpless to do anything about it." He started to tear up.

"Well, you should've thought about that before you decided the other woman was more important than your daughter."

"How does that have anything to do with Emily being missing?"

"Well, if I remember correctly, on the day she was taken you were supposed to take her to the zoo. But for the life of me I can't remember why you canceled. Oh, that's right. You had more  important things to spend your time on."

"I know, I hurt you and I'm sorry."

"No, you hurt our family."

"So you're blaming me for her disappearance."

"No, I just want you to admit that some of it was your fault and  if you had kept your promise, none of this would've happened."

"Marilyn, I didn't come out here to argue about who was right and who was wrong."

"Why did you come out here?"

"I thought we could call it a truce and work together to find our daughter."

She looked at the man in front of her and wasn't sure if she could ever forgive him for his betrayal. However, she knew without a doubt he loved his daughter. After she realized Emily was missing that day, she had run to the railing in a panic and yelled to Jim that she was gone. The silent scream that passed between them was their own rendition of the famous painting by Edvard Munch. However, the only remnant left of their daughter at the end of the scream was the security video showing Emily walking beside a man with a beard wearing a hat and sunglasses.

"You're right," said Marilyn. "It's not about us, but about  finding our daughter."

"So there you are," said Charlie as he stepped up beside her. "Marilyn, is everything okay?" He looked at Jim and protectively placed his arm around her.

"Yes, everything's fine."

"I want to introduce you to Violet Shaw and William VanWyc."

She tilted her head toward Jim and said, "I'll keep in touch. For Emily."

"Thank you."

"I didn't know he was going to be here," said Charlie as he escorted her across the terrace.

"I didn't expect you to, so quit worrying. I'm a big girl and can take care of myself."

The air was filled with all kinds of emotions when Marilyn stepped into the dining room. In the corner on her right, a middle-aged Asian couple was laughing and having a good time. Standing in front of a large hearth on her left was a young white couple with tears streaming down their faces talking to an elderly, black couple. It was here she realized the pain of this hideous crime was no respecter of persons. It did not discriminate against race, gender, or age and it touched the lives of the rich as well as the poor. Here, everyone was equal and, in a strange way, she found comfort in this room knowing she was not alone in her journey.

Charlie led her out into the hallway under the crystal chandelier. "Violet, William, I'd like you to meet my beautiful goddaughter, Marilyn Jantzen."

"Marilyn, it's a pleasure to meet you," said Violet.

"It's a pleasure to meet you as well."

"Ms. Jantzen, excuse me for staring, but have we met somewhere before?" asked William.

"I don't think so," she wondered if he had seen her when she was forty pounds heavier and just didn't recognize her.

"Well, it's a pleasure to meet you Ms. Jantzen," he gently shook her hand.

"Mr. VanWyc," she nervously cleared her throat.

"Please, call me William," he slowly let go of her hand.

"William." She nodded. "You have such a beautiful estate."

"Make sure you take a tour of the gardens before you leave. I'm sure you will find them quite exquisite."

"I'm sure I will. Thank you."

The way he was staring at her made her feel a little uncomfortable. She was relieved when his phone rang inside his jacket; he reached to pull it out and looked down at the number.

"Excuse me, but I've got to take this. Violet, I'll talk to you later. Charlie, it was great meeting you. And Ms. Jantzen, it was a pleasure." His eyes lingered on her for several seconds and he headed for the staircase.

"Marilyn, Charlie told me about your daughter. I'm so sorry for what you're going through."

"Thank you." She watched William go up the stairs and just as he reached the top, he glanced back at her and proceeded down the hallway.

"My granddaughter, Sophia, whom I mentioned earlier, went missing two years ago after working late one night at Wal-Mart," said Violet catching Marilyn's attention. "It was a very difficult time for the family, but we never gave up hope. Within six months, authorities got a lead in the case. Several days later they found her in a hotel room in Richmond, Virginia, being held captive by a twenty-five-year-old man. Later we found out he had been stalking her for months."

It had been nine months since Emily had been missing. The authorities still had no leads and the likely hood of her being found alive was diminishing. Every day Marilyn waited for the dreadful phone call that gave her the news her daughter was dead. Her eyes started to tear up in the hopelessness of it all.

"Honey, don't you give up." Violet lightly touched her arm. "Sometimes hope finds its way in the most unlikely places."

"I'm not giving up. It's just that some days are harder than others."

"Just remember you have people who love and support you."

"I know." She looked up at Charlie.

"I hate to leave such good company, but there's something very important I have to attend to." Violet slightly turned to Charlie. "Don't leave without saying good-bye."

"I don't intend to."

"Marilyn, again, it was nice meeting you."

"Ms. Shaw, it has been a pleasure."

"Please call me Violet. Now you two enjoy the rest of your evening." Her eyes lingered on Charlie's before she left.

"You want to go get something to eat?" Charlie asked, barely taking his eyes off of Violet.

"By the look on your face, I'm thinking you might be ready for dessert."

"After we get something to eat I'll tell you all about it."

A light breeze swept across the terrace with a hint of hyacinths where Marilyn and Charlie were eating their dinner at a corner table. Several couples slowed danced to the music under the Dogwoods while others just meandered around the patio engaging in conversation.

"Are you fine with Jim being here?" asked Charlie as he laid his knife across the edge of his plate and took a bite of the pork tenderloin.

"Not at first. Yet, the more I thought about it, the more I realized he had just as much right to be here as I did. Regardless of what happened between us. I know without a doubt he loves his daughter."

"Well, you're a better person than I am," he laughed. "I'm not sure I'd be so lenient."

"Well, enough about me. What I want to know is why your eyes lit up when you saw Violet." She took a bite of her salad.

"We were childhood sweethearts and deeply in love."

"Really, so what happened?"

"It's the same old story about the right side and wrong side of the tracks. She was middle class, I was dirt poor, and her parents didn't approve. So after graduation she went off to college while I stayed behind and worked at the local hardware store. At first we wrote to each other almost every day. One day her letters stopped coming. After six months without hearing from her I decided to move on with my life and joined the army."

"Did you ever find out what happened?"

"Several years later, I learned through an old college professor that her dad intercepted my letters. Afterwards her parents told her I had left town and she figured I found someone else and moved on. Later, when we both found out what actually happened, it was too late because she was married and pregnant with her first child."

"Charlie, I'm so sorry." Marilyn leaned forward. "That must've been very hard."

"It was in the beginning, but when I met Helen I realized that  sometimes life turns out just the way it's supposed to. I never thought I'd be able to love another woman like I loved Violet, but I was wrong. Helen accepted me unconditionally, regardless of what my station was in life. I never had to explain to her who I was because she already knew. When she passed away three years ago, I was comfortable being a widower because I already experienced what true love was all about."

"So are you planning on seeing Violet again?"

When he didn't answer Marilyn turned her head to see what caught his attention. She watched as Violet stepped through the French doors and when she started to glide across the terrace Violet locked eyes with Charlie.

"That's it!" Marilyn exclaimed.

"What?" Charlie scrunched his eyebrows and looked at Marilyn.

"That spark I see in your eyes. My parents had it and now you have it. I've never felt that way."

"I was hoping you'd still be here. I was wondering if you'd like to dance." Violet stepped up to the table.

"I'd love to." He pushed back his chair and got up.

"You don't mind if I steal him for a few minutes do you?" Violet asked with a gleam in her eye.

"Please, not at all. I was just thinking about exploring the gardens anyway."

While they waltzed across the floor to "Fly Me to the Moon"  by Sinatra, Marilyn finished her salad and made her way to the steps that led down to the gardens.

She followed the brick path where a wide-leafed variety of Liriope, azaleas, and live oaks were planted. It led to a secluded clearing in the south garden where a summer house constructed of fine lattice work stood in the center surrounded by three varieties of azaleas. Gracing the southeast of the house was an artificial lake with two little islands planted with poplars, cedars, and crepe myrtle.

A growing darkness spread across the water while the sun began to fade behind the mountains. The moon was already visible in the sky as she headed toward a bench under a tree so she could sit down to enjoy the view.

"Rebecca."

Marilyn caught her breath. Cautiously turned around almost expecting to see the snake with its piercing blue eyes and half-inch fangs slithering toward her, but instead William emerged from the shadows.

"Marilyn." Her name slowly rolled off her lips. "My name is Marilyn."

"I'm sorry." He stepped toward her. "It's just you look so much like a girl I used to know."

"They say everyone has a double."

"That may be true but you could past for, Rebecca Hilliard's, twin." William stepped closer. "The only thing different is she had a mole just above the right corner of her mouth and you don't."

Marilyn thought about her reflection in the mirror and the snake calling her Rebecca in her dream. "Who's Rebecca Hilliard?"

"She was a young woman who lived in Harpers Ferry eighteen years ago until she went missing. Earlier when Charlie introduced us I thought for sure I was seeing a ghost. That's the reason I answered my phone, I needed time to collect my thoughts. I'm still trying to convince myself you're not her."

Marilyn slightly jumped when her phone rang inside her purse. She excused herself, stepped away, and answered it.

"Hello."

"Marilyn, this is Detective Seitz."

"Hello, Detective." She held her breath not sure she wanted to hear what he had to say.

"I just wanted to let you know we received some more information about Emily. Are you available to come down to the office? If not we can set up a time tomorrow."

"No, I'll be there as soon as I can." She hung up the phone and slipped it back into her purse.

"Is everything okay?" asked William.

"I've got to go find Charlie."

Marilyn ran down the walkway and the only thing she could think about was Emily.

# CHAPTER 4

Marilyn, Jim, and Charlie came into Detective Seitz's office where he was talking to someone on the phone. He pointed to a table in the corner indicating for them to have a seat. Thick piles of paper and files covered his desk while a cold cup of coffee sat next to the phone. Around it you could see layers of rings on the table where he had moved it several times. In the trash can were old takeout bags that had been there for who knows how long. Marilyn wondered how he got any work done with all the clutter. Besides, what if there was a valuable piece of information about Emily hidden in all the mess?

"Hold on, Greg. I need to get a pencil." Seitz opened the drawer and searched around. "God, I hate a cluttered drawer." Finally he found a pen, grabbed a piece of scrap paper off the desk. "Go ahead. Okay, I got it. I'll talk to you later."

"I'm sorry it's been a hectic day," he said to them as he hung up the phone, picked up the file on top of a stack of papers, and grabbed the stale coffee. "Would anyone like a cup?" He raised his dark thick eyebrows.

"No, thanks," they all said in unison.

Seitz placed the file on top of the table and opened it up. Marilyn looked down at the photo of a little girls' mutilated body lying in a ravine, she took a deep breath, closed her eyes, and hoped it wasn't Emily.

"Sorry, wrong file." Seitz quickly closed it and looked up at Marilyn. "Like I said, it's been a long day."

He went to his desk and shuffled through the folders, finally found the right file, sat down at the table and opened it up. Tears filled Marilyn's eyes when she saw her daughter's picture. She was wearing a pink and white polka dot dress with a matching bow in her hair. Her toothy grin went from ear to ear under blue eyes that twinkled like the stars in the heavens.

"Okay." Seitz leaned back in his chair. "A couple of hours ago, the authorities got a call from a woman in Arizona who was visiting family in Washington, D.C., the day Emily was taken. She was getting out of her car at Tysons Corner in parking lot C, which is between Nordstrom and AMC Theaters. She noticed a girl around five years old sitting in the front seat of a silver-colored SUV, crying. The man in the driver's seat waved with a smile, backed out and left. She figured it was just a father and daughter having a little spat so she didn't think anything of it."

"Did she get a good description? Are you sure it was Emily?"

Seitz stroked his brown goatee and looked at Marilyn. "The description was pretty accurate. She had blue eyes, strawberry blonde hair, and was wearing a yellow sundress with daises and a matching floppy white hat with a big daisy on the side. It's the same thing Emily was wearing so we're pretty sure it was her."

"What about the man? Is he the same one on the mall's security video?" asked Jim.

"Yes, he fit the description—beard, sunglasses, and a hat."

"Why didn't the woman report it sooner?" Jim leaned forward and placed his elbows on the table.

"She didn't know anything about Emily's abduction until she came back to visit her family and saw Emily's picture on the news. She realized it was the same girl she saw nine months ago so she called the authorities."

"Seitz, what good is an Amber Alert when people don't pay attention to it? I mean the alert is distributed across television, radio stations, electronic traffic-condition signs, social media, the list goes on and on."

"Jim, I know people who still run their TV off an antenna and don't have a computer or access to the Internet. Hell, they don't even have a cell phone. Unfortunately, the witness was one of them."

"So where do we go from here?" Charlie ran his hand across his bald head.

"The only thing we can do is keep investigating, circulate her picture, and hope for the best."

"Amber Renee Hagerman," Marilyn stared at Seitz.

"I'm sorry?" He cocked his head.

"That's the name of the nine-year-old girl from Arlington, Texas, who was found by a man walking his dog on January 17, 1996, four days after her abduction. She was naked, her throat cut, and found in a storm drainage ditch. I was eighteen at the time, getting ready to graduate from high school and thinking about college. Amber was nine and probably in the third grade. The only thing she was doing that sunny winter's day in January was having a good time riding her bike with her five-year-old brother. Tell me, Detective, who gave that monster the right to come into this family's life and within eight minutes tear their world apart?"

"Marilyn …" Charlie lightly placed his hand on top of hers.

"No, Mr. O'Connor. I'd like to hear what Ms. Jantzen has to say."

"Detective do you have any idea what the name Amber means?"

"No."

"Precious stone. I looked it up after Emily was taken. Tell me, Detective, how did this precious, little girl's name end up meaning 'America's Missing: Broadcast Emergency Response?'"

"Ms. Jantzen, there are a lot of sick people in our society. Unfortunately, it took one more child to get our lawmakers' attention. Because of Amber and her parents, we have tougher laws in place to govern sex offenders. Since the Amber Alert was established, nearly eight hundred missing kids have been rescued. Because of this one  precious stone there are fewer parents going through this terrible  ordeal."

"One precious stone that will never be eighteen waiting to get out of high school so she can go to college, maybe get married, and have children. This child's death might have saved hundreds, but in the end she was somebody's daughter, granddaughter, sister, and friend. Her life mattered!"

"So does your daughter's and we're doing everything we can to find her and the man that took her."

"Come on, Detective, who are we kidding here? It's been nine months. I have to come to the realization that Emily is most likely dead."

"Marilyn, you can't think that way," said Jim. "Since we know what the guys driving, that could help the case."

"Jim, that doesn't mean a damn thing," she looked at him and raised her eyebrows. "The woman didn't get a license plate number. Besides, the car was probably a rental or was stolen. You don't think he's going to be that stupid and use his own vehicle?"

"Listen, I know it seems hopeless, but so did the case of Elizabeth Smart. However, nine months later she was found alive, only eighteen miles from her home. So, we can't give up on Emily yet."

"Detective, that may be true, but the reason why the biker spotted them in Utah was because the night before he had heard of the  kidnapping on *America's Most Wanted* and alerted the police. However, the network cancelled the show several years ago because of ratings. A show that helped catch over a thousand criminals and seventeen of those were on the FBI's Ten Most Wanted list. Tell me, Detective, when did ratings become more important than people's lives?"

"Marilyn, I know it's frustrating but on the bright side. CNN is airing a new show called *The Hunt* hosted by John Walsh. It's the same premise as *America's Most Wanted* and I'm hoping to get Emily's case aired as soon as we get the go ahead."

"Seitz, that's great!" said Jim.

"I don't know how long it's going to take, but it looks promising." Seitz got up from the table. "Listen, it's getting late so unless you have any other questions, why don't you folks go on home and get some rest."

"I think that's a good idea." Charlie got up.

"Detective, thank you for all your hard work and please keep us posted," Jim stood and shook his hand.

"You're welcome." He grabbed the file off the table.

"Marilyn, you ready?" Charlie lightly placed his hand on her shoulder.

"I guess," she stood and looked at Seitz, wishing he had more substantial information about her daughter.

"Ms. Jantzen, I have an eleven-year-old daughter of my own, and if I thought someone was even thinking about harming one hair on her head, they would have hell to pay. I promise you on my honor as a father, I will not give up."

"Thank you." She wiped a tear from her cheek while she followed Charlie and Jim out of the office.

The stillness in the elevator felt like the inside of a coffin being lowered into the ground. The picture of the little girl's mutilated body was still fresh in Marilyn's mind, and the thought of someone treating her precious baby like some piece of garbage was unbearable. She started to feel dizzy while she watched the round buttons on the panel light up, and she wasn't sure she could make it through three more floors without passing out.

The instant the door dinged open, she ran out and down the hallway. Her heart pounded to the steady thump of her footsteps and at any minute she thought it was going to jump out of her chest. She didn't stop until she was outside where sirens blared in the distance getting closer and closer with each ragged breath. The night air coursed through her lungs and dried her already parched throat. She leaned against the building and rested her hands on her knees while she took two deep breaths. In through her nose and out through her mouth.

"Marilyn ..." Charlie stepped up beside her.

"Can you take me home?"

"Sure," he slipped his arm around her and led her across the parking lot.

"Marilyn ..." Jim followed close behind.

"Yes?" She glanced over her shoulder.

"Are you going to be okay?" He opened the door for her while Charlie made his way around to the driver's side and got in.

"I'll be fine."

"Please, keep in touch."

The dark circles under, Jim's eyes made her realize she wasn't the only one who was losing sleep. "For Emily." She got in the car while he shut her door.

Charlie drove out of the parking lot and said, "Marilyn, are you okay?"

"I don't know," Marilyn replied as she leaned her head against the window. "After I saw the picture of that little girl, all I could think about was Emily ending up the same way."

"That's not going to happen."

"You know, I bet that's the same thing someone told that little girl's parents and look what happened to her. What kind of monster does that kind of thing?"

"I don't know, but that's not going to happen to Emily."

"Can you pull over? I think I'm going to be sick."

Charlie pulled along the side of the road, she quickly got out and stumbled to the back of the car. She threw up everything she'd eaten at the party. After she finished, Charlie offered her his handkerchief.

"I'm sorry." She took it from him and wiped her mouth.

"You don't have anything to be sorry about."

"It's just …"

"Come on, let's get back in the car so I can get you home."

As they drove away, Marilyn leaned back on the headrest and looked out the window where the moonlight filtered through the grove of trees on her right. She stared up at the bright disc in the night sky, and closed her eyes.

"Mare, I know this is very difficult, but you can't give up."

"I'm not giving up. I just don't know if I can handle anymore."

"Everything is going to turn out fine. You just wait and see."

"What if it doesn't? What if, at the end of my search, Emily is dead just like the little girl in the photo?"

"We'll cross that bridge if we come to it."

"That's a bridge you're going to have to cross alone."

"What do mean?"

"You know what I mean."

"Are you talking about what I think you're talking about?"

"Last time I reasoned myself out of it, but I promise you, if Emily ends up dead because of my neglect I won't hesitate."

"What about Jim?"

"What about him?"

"Do you think he's blameless in all of this? If he hadn't cheated  on you none of this would've ever happened."

"How can I pin any of this on him? Sure I was mad as hell when I saw him with the other woman. But after I had my little egotistical rant, turned around, and found Emily was gone, nothing else mattered. Not Jim. Not the other woman. The only thing that mattered was the bench in front of me was empty and it was my fault. And I'll never forgive  myself because those few minutes of hatred cost me everything."

"Honey, I wish I could take your pain." Charlie lightly squeezed her hand. "Make it disappear, but I can't. The only thing I can do is be here for you. Let you know you don't have to face any of this on your own. I promised your parents, I would take care of their little girl and that's exactly what I intend to do. So, you'll just have to put up with this old geezer because I'm not going anywhere."

"Charlie, I don't know what I'd do without you." She squeezed his hand. "Besides, the way Violet was looking at you tonight. You are far from being an old geezer." She decided to change the subject. "Are you planning on seeing her again?"

"Well, as a matter-of-fact, I am."

"Charlie, that's great." She could almost hear him smiling in the dark.

"You know, I almost called Violet several times after Helen passed away. But I figured that relationship had run its course and there was no sense in looking back. After seeing and talking to her tonight, it felt like everything just fell into place. And now that both of our spouses have passed on, maybe life is giving us a second chance."

"So do you think Helen would approve of Violet?"

"Yes. Helen knew the history behind the relationship between Violet and I. Right after she fell ill, she even suggested just before she passed away that I try to find her. I told her I wouldn't have any part of it that she would be the last woman I loved. Who knows maybe even beyond the grave she's managed to have the final say."

"Charlie, do you believe your loved ones can communicate with you after they die?"

"Yes, I do. I experienced it with my grandmother just after she passed away."

"Really?"

"My grandmother was half Irish and half Native American and was known as the Bird Call Lady."

"What's a Bird Call Lady?"

"Well, she had the ability to imitate any bird sound to the T. One summer we were sitting on her front porch snapping green beans when we heard the sound of a whippoorwill. Out of the blue, she says, 'Do you know legend has it that the whippoorwill can sense a soul departing, and can capture it as it flees?' All of a sudden she stopped rocking, looked me dead in the eyes, and said, 'Charlie, when it's my time to go, you'll be the first to know because I'll be sitting outside your bedroom window singing like a whippoorwill.'"

"Well, did she?"

"That night, after going to bed, I heard the gray and brown bird singing outside my window. Several minutes later the phone rang and it was my aunt letting us know that grandma had just passed away. I know it sounds crazy, but it really happened."

"I don't think it's crazy."

"Why, did something like that happen to you?"

"Do you remember the night during that terrible storm you called to remind me about the dinner party?"

"Yes."

"After we got off the phone, I heard this tapping sound I've been hearing for weeks. When I glanced around the kitchen the lid of my trash can was moving."

"It moved by itself?"

"Yes."

"Who do you think it was?"

"It was mom."

"Why do you think it was her?"

"Well, the day we were driving back from Dana's mother's funeral. I made her promise that if anything should happen to her she would tap the lid of my trash can. You know, I waited for weeks to hear that sound after the accident when I needed it the most. What I don't understand is why now? Why two years later?"

"Did she give you a time frame after she made the promise?"

"No."

"You know your mother was always on time and never late."

"That's true."

"So, as far as I'm concerned, her timing is perfect. Besides, maybe she thought your garbage stunk to high heaven these past couple of years and couldn't stand the thought of being near it, much less touching it."

"You're real funny Charlie," she chuckled.

"Well, I got you to laugh."

"I guess you did."

As Charlie turned into Marilyn's driveway, his cell phone rang. He looked down at the center console where he recognized Violet's phone number and smiled.

"Don't you think you should answer that?"

"I'll call her back later. She probably wanted to know what we found out about Emily." He pulled up in front of her house.

"Do you want to come in?" she asked, grabbing her purse and not wanting to be alone.

"No, I'm going to go on home."

"Okay, I'll see you later."

"I'll call you tomorrow to see how you're doing."

"I love you, Charlie." She kissed him on the cheek. "Thanks for always being there."

"Honey, I love you, too."

Marilyn got out of the car, waited until Charlie got to the end of the driveway, waved, and went inside. She made her way to the stairs and with each step dreaded the thought of spending another night alone. When she got to the top she made a right and paused in front of Emily's room. Overwhelmed with the need to be near her, she opened the door and stepped inside.

The room was exactly the way Emily left it. Her pink ballet slippers and tights along with her black leotard she had worn that morning to dance class still lay on the floor next to her bed. The board game, Candy Land, sat in the corner waiting to be finished. The only difference was the candles she had placed in the windows. It represented the hope that someday soon the ballet slippers would be dancing with her little girl's laughter and the game would be finished and put away.

Marilyn made her way over to the canopy bed in the corner and sat down. It was decorated in the floral quilt her mother had made Emily the day she moved into her 'big girl' bed. Under the pile of stuffed animals she pulled out the buried treasure and lifted it to her face. The scent of her daughter still lingered in the white, tattered fabric of the blanket Marilyn had wrapped her in the day she had brought Emily home from the hospital. After she tucked her in at night, Marilyn would soothe Emily by rubbing the edge of the fabric against her nose until she fell asleep.

In the silence of her own breathing, she pressed the blanket to her face and lay down. She closed her eyes surrounded with the sweet scent of her baby girl, and in a matter of seconds she drifted off to sleep.

"Mommy ..."

Marilyn's eyes jerked open and her heart quickened at the sound of her daughter's voice. She sat up, looked around the room, and waited to feel the small arms slip around her waist. The touch never came because it was merely a memory of better days gone by. She slowly stood, gave the room one more glance, and left. After she changed into her pajamas, she headed downstairs to the kitchen, made herself a cup of chamomile tea and headed outside to the front porch.

Marilyn rocked back and forth on the porch swing as the trees swayed under the countless stars that dotted the night sky. A dark, wispy cloud eclipsed the moon and, for a few shadowy moments, it shined with a halo. A shooting star streaked across the heavens, carrying with it the memory of Emily lying under the dome with her sweet little voice reciting the nursery rhyme. *Star light, start bright, the first star I see tonight; I wish I may I wish I might, have the wish I wish tonight.* Marilyn closed her eyes to make a wish for her daughter's safe return when the haunting picture of the little girl in Seitz's office flashed before her.

She rushed to the edge of the porch, grabbed a hold of the railing, with her stomach tied up in knocks. Tortured sobs ripped through her chest as she collapsed to the floor. She laid there huddled, lost and afraid. A light breeze came whispering out of the east and with it the sound of a hiss. She glanced to where a snake was curled up in the corner of the porch basking under the moonlight. It slithered its head toward her a few inches and flicked out its forked tongue, as if considering her for a late night snack. The air becomes strangely still as she gets up and makes her way to the door. She stares at the snake and remembers William calling her Rebecca at the dinner party. That's when she realized her dream had just crossed the threshold of her reality; to wreck havoc on her already messed-up life .

# CHAPTER 5

Marilyn sat under the green awning of The Natural Springs Café, the street lights still dimly lighting the rain-soaked streets of Shepherdstown. Last night all she did was toss and turn, thinking about the little girl's mutilated body. When she did fall asleep, it was only to dream of finding the girl's body lying face down in the ravine. However, when she turned her over, it was Emily's dead eyes staring back at her. So she got up, took a shower, and came into the café.

The café had always been a dream of hers. The second she had laid eyes on the two-story, red brick building for sale in the middle of town, she decided to quit her job and make the dream a reality. The renovation took almost a year but, when it was finished, it was well worth the time and energy. Luckily, she had the foresight to renovate the upstairs into a small, one bedroom apartment, which had become a place of sanctuary whenever her big, empty, lonely house became too much to handle.

She took a sip of coffee, inhaling the invigorating aroma, and catching a whiff of lilac filtering through the air from the planter next to the table. She watched the neighborhood's black cat, Twilight, prowl along the sidewalk across the street in front of Dana's Flower Shop. It paused, glanced toward her as if she were a sidebar, and moved on while the street lights automatically turned off. Several minutes later, she heard the sound of a door opening and people chattering, so she got up and went inside to get ready for the day.

Marilyn was pouring herself another cup of coffee when someone banged on the door. She looked up where Dana's nose was scrunched against the window. Her hair was two tones, bright red on top and black underneath. With her hair pulled back, you could clearly see the word *rebel* written across her face. She wore a silver, captive bead ring in her left brow, a pair of black glass plugs in her ears, and a diamond stud on the right side of her freckled nose. With her tattoos and motorcycle, she definitely fit the profile.

"What are you doing here so early?" asked Marilyn after she opened the door.

"I've got a big garden wedding this weekend, and I'm meeting the bride this morning about the flower arrangements."

"Anybody I know?"

"Nope, they're from out of town and it's a no expenses spared ordeal. I tell you, being a part of the Bridal

Fair at the Clarion last year was one of the smartest things I've ever done. If my business keeps booming like this, I'm going to be able to open my one-stop-shop sooner than I thought. I can see it now, Dana's Extravaganza, all your needs under one roof, from wedding to honeymoon."

"Well when you get rich and famous, make sure you don't forget your friends in low places."

"Never."

"You want the usual?"

"None other." Dana followed her to the counter and sat down.

"I don't know how you drink this stuff." Marilyn grabbed a biodegradable cup, placed it under the hopper named Chocolate Monkey, and pressed the button.

"There's nothing like the sweet taste of chocolate and a refreshing hint of banana to start your day. Besides, don't you think it fits my personality?" She placed her hands under her arms and made the sound of a monkey.

"Yes, now that I think about it." She placed the cup in front of Dana. "So how are you and Jason doing?"

"Great." Dana lifted her left hand and flashed it in front of her.

On her finger rested a white gold, cool carat trilogy engagement ring with a Malawian teal sapphire stone that sat in the middle decorated with two diamond side stones.

"It's beautiful."

"I know," Dana beamed.

"So when did he pop the question?"

"Yesterday, after we hiked up Maryland Heights." Dana pulled out a piece of paper from the pocket of her jacket.

"What's that?" asked Marilyn.

"It's Jason's proposal," she laughed. "He wrote it down so he wouldn't forget what he wanted to say."

Marilyn sat across from Dana where a vivid glow kindled in her face, took a sip of coffee and said, "Okay, let's hear it."

"Well, we were enjoying the spectacular view of Harper's Ferry from the main overlook and Jason pulls out this paper from his pocket." Dana straightened her shoulders, cleared her throat and began to read.

> *Dana, for the first time in my life I have met a woman that can see my heart and I see hers. Something I have never experienced in any previous relationship. You satisfy me heart, soul, and body. With you, I feel complete and whole as a man. You are my friend, my lover, and I want you to be my wife.*

"Jason, the biker guy wrote that?" Marilyn raised her eyebrows surprised he had it in him.

"Yes, and that's not all. He got down on one knee, pulled out this ring, and read,

> *Dana, this ring represents our past, present, and future. The sapphire is a token of our commitment while the two diamonds symbolize the trust and respect we have for one another. This ring is the timeless symbol of my love and I want to spend the rest of my life with you. Will you marry me?"*

"What did you say?"

"For the first time in my life I think I was speechless. So, I quietly offered him my hand and said yes."

"Congratulations. I am so happy for you."

"Thank you."

"When is the big day?"

"Not until sometime next year. Anyway, enough about me I want to hear about the party."

"It was good, until I got a call from Detective Seitz's."

"What did he want?" Dana took a sip of her cappuccino.

"Dana, I don't want to spoil your good news with the details."

"No, I want to hear what he had to say."

Marilyn knew there was no since in arguing so she recapped the conversation with the detective about the woman from Arizona who was visiting family in Washington D.C.

"Dana, I don't know what I'd do if Emily ended up like the picture of the little girl I saw in Seitz's office."

"What picture?"

"Seitz's mistakenly picked up a file he thought was Emily's and when he opened it, there was a picture of a different girl ... one who didn't make it. Dana, her naked little body was covered with bruises along with dirt and leaves. Her hair was matted in mud and her throat ... was slit ..." Unable to finish the words, Marilyn made a gesture across her own throat, extending from one ear to the other. She caught her breath and blinked back tears. "What kind of monster does that to an innocent little child?"

"Mare, why didn't you call me?"

"I don't know. Maybe I didn't want to ruin your day like it ruined mine."

"Mare, you're like a sister to me, and when Emily was taken it hurt like hell. Sure, I don't show it most of the time because I want to be strong for you. Do you know I still listen for the bell to ring above my door every Saturday morning waiting for Emily to walk through? I love your daughter like she is my own, so the next time you think you're going to ruin my day, I want you to remember that."

"Dana, I know you love Emily. If I needed you I would've called."

"Next time something like that happens. I want to know. Understood?"

"Yes."

"Good, now I've got to go potty."

After she left, Marilyn decided to go ahead and open up the café. She made her way to the door, thankful Dana was her best friend. She had been there for her when her parents and brother were killed. She had been the dumping ground of all her tears of rage after Emily was taken. If it hadn't been for her, Marilyn would've died in the quicksand of her misery a long time ago. She flipped the sign on the door to open and picked the welcome mat off the floor. She stepped outside knowing her day was a little brighter because of her.

"Good morning Ms. J."

Kyle leaned against the brick wall dressed in a skull and bones t-shirt which tapered down to a pair of black skinny jeans. Kyle wasn't just your typical college student from Pennsylvania; he was also the neighborhood watchman. If you wanted firsthand knowledge of what was going on around town, he was the one to talk to because nothing ever slipped by him.

"Good morning, Kyle." She dropped the mat on the porch.

"Ms. J., have I told you lately how beautiful you are?" He crossed his arms and flipped his straight black hair out of his eyes.

"Yes, just last week, and the flattery will get you absolutely nowhere."

"Come on Ms. J., just one date."

"Unless you can add twenty years on to your age like the speed of light, my answer will always be …"

"No." He finished her sentence while a young girl with a streak of blonde through her dark hair came toward him. By the look she was giving Kyle, she didn't like the way he was flirting with the much older lady.

"Kyle, you have a nice day and try not to give the professors a hard time."

"You too Ms. J." He slipped his arm around the girl's waist.

Marilyn went back inside grateful to be a part of this quaint little town. After Dillon had died, the support of the faculty and student body at the university had been overwhelming. After Emily was taken, the community had rallied around her with such love and compassion as if she were family. The saying 'good things come in small packages' was so true especially when it came to the wonderful people of Shepherdstown.

Marilyn grabbed her coffee and sat down across from Dana at the counter. "Do you want to have dinner later on at the Bistro?"

"Sure, what time?"

"How's five-thirty?"

"That sounds good." Dana looked down at her watch. "Hey, I've got to go."

As Dana was getting up to leave, the door opened and William VanWyc stepped inside wearing a pair of jeans and a denim shirt.

"Oh my, who's that?" Dana whispered as she looked him over from head to toe.

"Good morning, ladies."

"Dana, this is Mr. VanWyc. I met him the other night at the dinner party."

"You didn't tell me there were Chippendales at the dinner party," Dana muttered from the corner of her mouth as she raised her eyebrows at Marilyn.

"Dana, it's a pleasure to meet you," said William.

"Oh, I assure you the pleasure is all mine, Mr. VanWyc," Dana replied, throwing a charming smile on her face.

"Please call me William."

"William, are you from around here?"

"I live on the outskirts of Sharpsburg, but I'm originally from Harpers Ferry."

"So what do you do for a living?"

"I'm a real estate developer. I buy abandoned buildings and convert them into commercial properties."

"Well, I may be looking for some commercial property sometime in the near future. Do you have a business card in case I want to contact you?"

Marilyn could see Dana's wheels turning as William reached into his wallet and pulled out his card. Ever since Jim had cheated on her, Dana was always trying to fix her up with someone new. If it wasn't one of Jason's buddies, it was one of her customers. And, no matter how many times Marilyn told her she wasn't interested, Dana never gave up.

"Thank you, William." She took the card and slipped it into her pants pocket. "Well, I'd like to stay and chat but I've got to get to work."

"I'll see you tonight," said Marilyn giving her the eye.

"Absolutely, and you two have a nice day." She nodded at William and left.

"Mr. VanWyc, can I get you something to drink?" asked Marilyn.

"Black coffee would be fine. And, please call me William," he repeated as he sat down at the counter.

"And you can call me, Marilyn." She said with a sly glance as she poured his coffee, hoping he'd take the correction as a joke and not a reproach; even though something about him still made her uneasy.

"I guess I deserve that one."

"So what brings you to this neck of the woods on a Saturday morning?"

She placed the cup in front of him as the door opened and Carmen stepped inside.

"How's it going Ms. J.? Sorry I'm a little late. I got caught in traffic." She took off her backpack, set it behind the counter, and made her way over to the cappuccino machine.

"The hoppers are filled."

"You got to be kidding. Are you telling me Tyler actually remembered to fill them last night?" Carmen placed her hand on her forehead, pretending to faint.

"I guess all your nagging paid off."

"I guess so."

"William, this is Carmen Lombardi, a full-time student at Shepherd University and one of my part-time employees."

"Hey, you're Mr. VanWyc, owner of VanWyc Enterprises." Carmen leaned against the counter. "You're the one who donated ten thousand dollars to the women's and children's shelter last year."

"It's nice to meet you, Carmen."

"I volunteer at the shelter and believe me, your contribution was a blessing."

"I'm glad I could help. The shelter has a special place in my heart."

"Mine too. My mom and I lived in the shelter for several months. Without it, I don't think we would've survived. After we left I decided to volunteer in a way to give back. Well, I guess I better get ready for the morning rush."

"Carmen it was nice meeting you."

"Likewise." She picked up her backpack and headed for the kitchen.

"Marilyn is there some place we can talk privately?" asked William.

"Now's not a good time."

"Ms. J., you go ahead." Carmen glanced over her shoulder. "I've got everything under control."

"Are you sure?"

"Yes, if I need you I'll come and get you."

Marilyn knew there was no sense in arguing with an Italian, so she grabbed her coffee, looked at William and said, "Follow me."

She stepped out from behind the counter to her left where a door with a transom half-moon window was stenciled with the words, "Shh ... He who enters this door takes the oath of silence. He who breaks this oath will be asked to leave."

"So, are you going to throw me out if I'm not quiet?"

"Not this time." She opened the door.

In the small foyer, a bronze, scrolled-metal table with gold accents stood right of the entrance archway that led into the sitting room. Above the table hung a matching mirror decorated with two candle sconces. In the corner stood a bronze coat rack and umbrella holder with curlicues on the base echoing the curved accents on the top. To the left of the archway hung a, sunburst-shaped clock, a product of S&H Green Stamps from the sixties. It originally belonged to her grandmother. After her mom's death, it automatically passed down to her. In honor of the two special women that had meant the world to her, she decided to make it a part of the café.

Stenciled in a freestyle script above the archway was another warning that read: "Warning! Enter at your own risk. Peace and Quiet can be Contagious."

They stepped inside the room, warmly lit by a light-honey, Tiffany chandelier. Under the chandelier stood six, lovely, mahogany-finished, circular dining tables. Two windows facing the front of the café were decorated in burgundy, faux, jacquard drapes which were drawn back with a pair of Cedric holdbacks in antique gold revealing a pair of cream-colored sheers. In front of the windows stood two, leather, burgundy, wingback chairs connected by a mahogany pedestal table with a honey-locust, Tiffany lamp. The left side of the room was a mirrored-image of the right, minus the windows. Two chess tables stood against the backdrop of a large hearth where a picture of the library on the old market square in Shepherdstown hung above the mantel.

"This is amazing." William exclaimed as he took in his surroundings. "To look at the café from the outside, you wouldn't think something like this existed on the inside."

"That's what everyone says." Marilyn stepped further into the room.

"So, how did you come up with the name, *The Natural Springs Café*?"

"Well, what most people don't realize while they are casually walking or exploring the oldest town in West Virginia is that, right underneath them, are over twenty natural springs silently meandering along with them."

"Really? I didn't know that." He narrowed his forehead. "But I thought Romney was the oldest town in West Virginia?"

"Well, that's been a long-running dispute, one which probably will never be resolved. However, they say just like beauty is in the eye of the beholder, so is age in the mind of the resident."

"I couldn't agree more." William's blue eyes stirred up a spark of turquoise as he stared into her green ones.

"Do you like to read?" She cut off the fluttering in the pit of her stomach and stepped to her left where a library of books lined the back wall.

"Yes, when I get a chance."

"When the café first opened, I made a deal with the community." She grabbed one of Dillon's favorite books about Ireland off the shelf. "If anyone donated a book to the library, they would get a coupon for a free cup of coffee and a pastry of their choice. Before I knew it, the library grew with leaps and bounds."

"That's very innovative. If you had bought these books yourself, it would've cost you a small fortune."

"Well, thanks to the bartering system, the books that were once covered with dust, dying to be read in some attic, can now be shared with the community."

"These are magnificent." He stepped to the tables under the chandelier. "Who did the art work?"

"Some of the students in the art department at the university did it for extra credit." She placed the book back on the shelf and followed him to where each table was painted with an historical landmark in Shepherdstown.

"I noticed this house when I drove through town."

"It's the little, two-story house on Princess Street built in 1929. It has five rooms and measures ten-feet high by nine and a half feet wide, with five and a half foot ceilings. They say it was built so student teachers could observe children playing in a laboratory setting."

"You've certainly managed to capture the essence of this quaint little town in this room."

"Well, Mr. Van … William, what is it you want to talk to me about?" She pulled out one of the chairs and sat down.

He sat across from her, reached into the front pocket of his shirt, pulled out a picture, and slid it across the table.

"This is a picture of Rebecca. Now do you see why I thought you were her?"

Marilyn picked up the picture of a young girl wearing a pair of jeans and a red tank top standing in front of an oak tree. The resemblance was unbelievable and if it hadn't been for the mole on the girls face she would've sworn it was her.

"You said she went missing eighteen years ago." She laid the picture back on the table. "What happened?"

William told her Rebecca was the daughter of a well-to-do family in Harpers Ferry, how they met, and had fallen in love. However, when her mother found out she was dating the son of the town drunk, they put a restraining order on him and two weeks later she disappeared.

"Were there any suspects?"

"You're looking at him. However, when the authorities didn't have enough evidence they let me go. Still her parents and others in the community thought I was guilty. I started getting death threats, so I left town and Rebecca became a cold case."

Marilyn had a suspicion William wasn't telling her everything. It didn't make sense Rebecca's parents putting a restraining order on him without good reason. There were always two-sides to a story and she wondered what parts he was leaving out.

"Hey, Ms. J., Jim's here to see you." Carmen peeked into the room.

"Tell him I'll be there in a minute."

*Wonder what he's doing here,* she thought. He hadn't shown his face in the café since the divorce. She specifically told him she would contact him at the dinner party, not the other way around, unless he had some news about Emily.

"William, I've got to go."

"Before you go, I was wondering. Would you like to go to the Harpers Ferry Festival with me on Saturday?"

"I'll think about it. Why don't you give me a call here at the café on Wednesday, and I'll let you know."

"Fair enough," said William.

"Well, enjoy the rest of your day."

"Thanks, you too."

Marilyn left the room a little unnerved. What if her dream was warning her about William? Even though he seemed like a nice guy it didn't mean he was. Sometimes appearances were deceiving. Yet, if she wanted to know where the dream was leading her and her connection with Rebecca she had no choice but to go.

# CHAPTER 6

Spring had finally arrived in Madison, Wisconsin, but, to look at Kathryn Rubin, it might as well have been the dead of winter. She stared out the bay window where the sun's rays shone fully upon her face. It did nothing to lift her spirit as its warmth bounced off the dust particles of the shattered, frigid pieces of her broken heart, left over from last spring's tragedy. Her eyes darted to where a honey bee swarmed around the yellow petals of a dandelion. It was there to barter for its nectar and in return, it would give the flower the pollen it needed to reproduce. However, the worm a robin was having for breakfast a few feet away didn't share the same fate. In the end, she knew the worm would have the last laugh when the lyrics of "The Hearse Song" ran though her mind.

"A big green worm with rolling eyes, crawls in your stomach and out your eyes," she hummed to herself, watching the bird gulp down the worm.

A year ago today, the big green worm of death rolled its eyes, crawled into her life, and required her to do the unspeakable. To  identify her children's bodies under a big white sheet on a cold hard gray slab. A week later, she put them both in a big black box, lowered them in the ground, and was left with one question; *Who was she now?* For five years she had been known as 'Mom.' She wondered what she would become when the unbearable pain that continued to rip and tear at her every waking minute eventually faded into a chronic, dull, lifetime ache. She knew she would never be the same because losing her children was an experience so profoundly disorienting that she felt totally lost in a vortex of nothingness.

Kathryn scuffed across the wooden floor in a pair of Richard's worn out bedroom slippers, headed to the stone fireplace and grabbed the family picture off the white, wooden mantel. She pressed it lightly to her chest and sat down in the old, burgundy recliner in the corner. And remembered her husband's reaction the day she decided to get rid of the old piece of junk.

"No! What do you think you're doing with my favorite chair?" Richard had screamed, running over to the truck in the driveway and planting his hands on his hips.

"Sir, all I know is that I was told to haul it away." The man loaded the chair on the truck.

"You wait right here. I don't want you to move another muscle." He jabbed his finger at the man and darted into the house.

The memory faded as she curled up in the over-stuffed chair and buried her face into the fabric where the traces of Richard's *Old Spice* cologne still lingered. She was so glad he was adamant that day about  not getting rid of it because now it served as a point of comfort.

She stared at the photo that had been taken the year they had been on vacation in Emerald Isle, North Carolina. On this particular day they had visited Black Beard's house in the adjoining town of Beaufort. After the tour, Richard had brought the kids pirate outfits and they insisted they wear them to the beach that afternoon.

"Come on! Let us bury you in the sand." Ricky and Rachel, their five-year-old twins, had pleaded.

She could still see Rachel's auburn curls tinged with gold, bouncing in the sun as she ran toward an old man sitting on a bench feeding the seagulls, causing the birds to scatter.

"Hey, mister, can you please take our picture?"

"Why, sure, honey." The man sprinkled the rest of the bread crumbs on the ground and got up.

Kathryn and Richard had been buried up to their necks in the  sand while the kids knelt behind them dressed in their pirate suits.

"Okay, repeat after me." The old man held up the camera. "Ho, ho, ho, and a bottle of rum."

"Ho, ho, ho, and a bottle of rum," they repeated in unison.

Just before the old man pressed the button, Ricky grabbed a fist-full of his dad's dark hair, identical to his own, while Rachel grabbed her mom's auburn hair. With a smirk on their faces, they drew their plastic swords into the air.

With a sob, she closed her eyes, pressed the picture to her chest and relived the terrible day that had altered her life forever.

"Honey, it's time to get up," whispered Kathryn, rolling over in bed and cuddling against Richard's back.

"Just give me a few more minutes," he grumbled.

"You promised to take the kids to school today and pick them up, remember?"

"Why don't we just play hooky and let the kids sleep in?" He reached for her arm, placed it around his waist, and drew her close.

"Richard, you're an orthodontist. You can't cancel your patient's appointments—their teeth depend on it. Besides, I've made plans to go out to breakfast with some of the girls before I go to work. So get your butt up while I get the kids ready for school."

"Fine, but not until I hold my wife and tell her how much I love her." He turned over and pulled her close.

"Well, in that case you can be a few minutes late." She placed her lips softly upon his.

Later that evening, she stood in the kitchen while the little bird came out of his house and coo-cooed on the half-hour. It was already four-thirty and she was starting to worry. Richard and the kids should've been home by now. She picked up the phone on the kitchen counter and dialed his cell phone, but there was no answer.

*He probably forgot to recharge his battery again,* she thought.

Kathryn turned off the water in the sink when the doorbell rang. She grabbed the front of her apron and wiped her hands while she made her way out into the hallway. She froze. Two officers stood on the other side of the front door. She wanted to run back into the kitchen and hide because she didn't want to hear what she now  already knew. Instead, she took a step forward and with each step, the ticking of the grandfather clock grew louder. About half-way down the hallway she paused, opened its door, and gently stopped the brass pendulum. From now on the phrase, its five o'clock somewhere, would have a different meaning.

She stared out the window and searched one of the officer's eyes. By the look on his face she knew he didn't want to be here and have to tell her the bad news. She briefly closed her eyes, took a deep breath, and opened the door.

"Good evening Ma'am." The male officer took off his hat. "Are you Mrs. Kathryn Rubin?"

"Yes." She slowly exhaled while her heart pounded against her chest.

"Mrs. Rubin I'm sorry to inform you there's been an accident."

One year later, Richard still lay in a coma in room 213 at St. Mary's Hospital while her children rested in Sunset Memorial Gardens.

Several weeks after her children's funeral, Kathryn finally decided to read the police report. Richard had only been about ten minutes away from home when the accident occurred. It was the result of a high speed chase by the state police with speeds exceeding 100 miles per hour. They had been chasing a car northbound, driving erratically. During the pursuit, the suspect ran other drivers off the road before finally striking Richard's car from behind. They determined the driver's blood alcohol level was elevated and cocaine was found in his system. He suffered a broken neck along with other injuries, but made a full recovery.

Kathryn reached into the pocket of her robe and as she pulled out a tissue the doorbell echoed through the house.

*Who in the world is that,* she thought, wanting to be left alone. The bell rang non-stop and she knew whoever it was, wasn't going to be ignored. She wiped her nose, got up, and answered the front door.

"Honey, you've been crying." Lillian stepped in and hugged her daughter.

"Mom, Dad, what are you doing here?"

"Your dad and I thought it was best if you weren't alone today." Lillian took off her jacket and hung it on the coat rack in the corner.

"I'm fine," she sniffled.

"If you're fine, why are you crying?" Garth closed the door, stepped around Lillian, and gave his daughter a peck on the cheek.

"Dad, I don't need you and Mom babying me." She balled up the tissue in her hand.

"Nonsense, by the look of your swollen, blood shot eyes you need us." He wrapped his arms around her and kissed the top of her head.

"Honey, why don't you go and take a nice hot long bath?" Her mother lightly rubbed her daughter's back. "While your dad and I go into the kitchen and fix something for lunch."

"Mom, there's not much to fix. I haven't been to the grocery store." She stepped away from her dad, unfolded the used tissue, and blew her nose.

"And it shows." Lillian looked at her daughter's frail body. "Now, run along. I'm sure I'll find something to whip up in your kitchen."

Kathryn started to leave when her parents step into the family room. Her mother grabbed the picture up off the chair and glanced at her father. He slipped his arm around her waist while they placed it back on the mantel. Kathryn made her way toward the stairs and realized she wasn't the only one hurting. They had lost their beloved grandchildren and a son-in-law they adored. Even though Richard wasn't dead, he might as well be. She knew if he didn't wake up soon, she would have to abide by his wishes and pull the plug.

About an hour later, she came into the kitchen dressed in a pair of jeans and a red t-shirt. "Mom, Something sure smells good."

"I made your favorite, beans and dumplings. Now sit down so I can fatten you up."

Kathryn sat down across from her dad in front of the steaming hot bowl of soup while her mother grabbed the corn bread off the kitchen counter.

"Garth, would you like to say grace?" Lillian sat down and reached for their hands.

It was the voice of her father that brought her comfort, not a prayer to an absentee God who stood back in silence while he watched the innocent die and the guilty live. The day her children were killed, her faith detonated like a time bomb and pierced her heart with the shrapnel of betrayal. As far as she was concerned, God was just as dead as her two children. Out of respect for her father, she waited until he finished and took a bite of her soup.

"Mom, you still haven't lost your touch. I believe these are the best beans and dumplings you've ever made."

"I agree, and the cornbread isn't bad either," said Garth.

"Thank you. I must say they are pretty tasty."

"Dad, are you still teaching the glass-blowing class on Saturdays?" Kathryn took a bite of her cornbread.

"Yes, I wish you were there to help out."

"I've been really busy at the flower shop. I haven't even had time to find someone to replace Julian."

"You lost Julian?" Lillian took a sip of her ice tea.

"Yes, he finally graduated from the university and moved on to bigger and better things."

"Some of the students have been asking about you," said Garth. "They really miss your work and are wondering when you are coming back."

"Dad, I don't know. I'll just have to wait and see."

Kathryn had loved teaching the Saturday class at Oates Glass Studio for her dad. It gave her a sense of great satisfaction to create something beautiful just by inflating a blob of molten glass by blowing through a tube. However, she no longer felt the creativity inside of her after the loss of the two masterpieces of her own body. The bright colors of her palette had turned dull, and she was afraid the murky air in her lungs would only inflate the blob of glass into the image of her own heart; beaten, bruised, and with wounds that would never heal.

"Old woman, you've out done yourself!" Garth patted the small pouch around his middle, leaned back in the chair until its front legs came off the floor. "Now I know why I've kept you around all these years."

"Dear, you know as well as I do, if it hadn't been for my cooking, you would've starved to death by now."

The word death lingered in Kathryn's ears causing a lump to form in her throat. She knew her mom didn't mean anything by it, but her emotions were always sitting on pins and needles. Just the smallest thing could send her over the edge.

"Oh, honey, I'm so sorry." Lillian looked at Garth while he raised his eyebrows.

"Mom, I'm fine." She held back the tears.

"I should've watched my words."

"I know you didn't mean anything by it."

"Honey, we've all suffered a big loss and the only way we're going to get through this is to be there for one another." Garth set the legs of his chair back down on all fours.

"And one way we can do that is to remember all the love and joy those two beautiful children brought into our world," said Lillian.

"I know, but when I think about them it hurts too much. Some days it's all I can do just to make it through this empty house. You know, sometimes I'll be standing in the kitchen and I swear I can hear Rachel and Ricky's footsteps running in the hallway. But when I go to look, nothing is there but the grandfather clock reminding me of the time my world fell apart."

Lillian stacked the bowls on top of one another, got up, and put them in the sink while she gazed out the window at the dandelions covering the backyard.

"Kat, do you remember how every spring Rachel would pick dandelions and put them in every room in the house?"

Kathryn sniffled, looked up at her mother and stared off into space remembering. "At the first sign of their little yellow heads, she was out the door, carrying her basket, and wouldn't come back in until it was filled to the brim."

"Remember when Ricky use to go into my sunflower garden and pretend they were radar dishes? He thought for sure he was going to make contact with ET," said Garth.

"I bet that boy watched that movie a thousand times." Lillian said as she went back to the table.

"Yeah, actually, I made up a bouquet of dandelions and sunflowers to place on their graves. I think they'll like that, don't you?" asked Kathryn as she stood up.

"Honey, I'm sure they will love it." Lillian place her hand on her daughter's arm.

"I hope you don't mind, but I made a three foot cross to place along the roadside as a memorial."

"Dad, I think …" She gently touched the Saint Jude pendant around her neck they had given her, after her life became a lost cause.

"Oh, honey." Lillian placed her arm around Kathryn as she began to sob.

Garth gathered his family into his arms. In the midst of her circle of pain, a father's strong embrace and a mother's gentle touch brought her a sense of comfort. After the accident, they had been her soft place to fall. Their unconditional love never relented, giving her the strength to face another day in her living hell. While the ache in her heart succumbed to their warmth, the words Richard use to quote from the book of Ecclesiastes ran through her mind.

*Pity the man when he falls and has no one to pick him up.*

❋    ❋    ❋

David Sawyer turned off the alarm on the nightstand and pulled the blanket over his head for just a few more minutes of shut eye. Several minutes later, the Carly Simon song, "Anticipation," started playing in his head. He sat up on the edge of the bed, ran his hands through his sandy blond hair, and willed it to stop. However, the lyrics kept playing over and over again so he got up and went into the bathroom.

After David took a shower, he stood in front of the mirror and stared at his reflection; remembering the first time he discovered the voice in his head. He was around twelve and had woken up in the middle of the night, on a park bench, down town, with no recollection of how he got there. He had been so afraid to go home. He knew if his mom had found out; there would've been hell to pay. Luckily, when he did get home she was still asleep in bed.

His mom was a very controlling and narcissistic woman. Yet there were times she could be sweet. It all depended on what type of mood she woke up in. If he smelled a hint of hickory bacon wafting in the air, nine times out of ten, it was going to be a good day. If not, he would have to walk on eggshells because anything could set her off.

Like the day she found out he got a C+ on his report card in math. She had planted her hands on her hips while the veins on her forehead popped green. She screamed so loud that his ears rang. She told him he was stupid, lazy, and ignored him for days. She instilled so much fear of failure in him, in fact, that he cheated on his math tests by hiding a calculator under his desk. Yet, that didn't stop her because she would always find something else wrong; which is probably why the voice showed up as a coping mechanism.

Several weeks after the park incident, the voice reemerged and they had the battle of the voices. One minute they liked each other and, in the next, they couldn't stand to share the same space. In time, they learned to tolerate one another. Through the years David had managed to stay in control most of the time. He was the alpha dog; so to speak. Until one day last summer he couldn't account for lost time and found himself in a different place from where he had originally been. He had no idea how he got there. One day he discovered what the voice had been up to. He had done something so outrageous that he silenced him and had barely spoken to him ever since. He was still trying to figure out how to clean up his mess without incriminating himself.

David grabbed the musk aftershave off the counter and sprinkled it on his hands. He rubbed his palms together, lightly slapped the cologne on his face, causing his pupils to pulsate with the song that still played in his head. In the center of his dark pupils a green light flashed signaling the voice was getting stronger and stronger. David tried to push it back, but to no avail.

*"Miss me?"* The words rushed out of the right corner of David's mouth and slapped him on the face.

"How can anyone miss a pebble in his shoe?"

*"Fine, I'll leave."*

"Go ahead, and while you're at it, lose the song."

*"I'm just letting you know, I'm tired of you making me late and keeping me waiting."*

"Yeah, well I'm tired of you doing stupid things behind my back."

*"If I didn't do stupid things behind your back nothing would ever get done. Besides, I was only trying to give you what you always wanted and this is the thanks I get."*

"I didn't ask for your help, especially when you act stupid. I'm in charge. So leave, and don't come back." David demanded.

His face began to soften as his pupils started to retract. Just before his eyes went back to normal, David changed his mind.

"No! Wait!"

In an instant his pupils widened. *"You know you need me."*

"Maybe." David raised his eyebrows, shrugged his shoulders, turned on the faucet, and washed his hands.

*"I'm glad we got that out of the way, but I promise the next time you ignore me, I'm leaving and never coming back."*

"You know I had no choice." David grabbed the towel and wiped his hands while he stared at his reflection, barely recognizing himself. "I had to pull the plug on you because you became reckless. What were you thinking? You can't do whatever the hell you want without consulting me first. I was here before you, so I have seniority."

*"Just remember, if it wasn't for me you wouldn't even have the balls to step up and be a man."* The capillaries in his face began to pulsate. *"Maybe your mother was right. If you had become a lawyer instead of some sissy chef in the kitchen, maybe you would've grown a backbone."*

"Don't you dare bring my mother into this!"

*"That's kind of hard to do when she's the reason for my existence. So quit wasting my time and let's get on with the plan."*

"Fine!" David relented.

*"First and foremost, she has to be a true redhead. Not brown, black, or blonde wannabes that dye their hair. That's a sign of insecurity. Second, she has to be a confident, phenomenal, strong-willed woman. We don't need any weak or inferior prey. Remember, once you break the will of the woman into submission so she stays sweet, the curse of your controlling mother will be broken."*

"I know what I need to do." He growled at his reflection, already getting irritated with his know-it-all attitude.

*"And just for the record, the next time you make me wait, we're through."*

David's pupils slowly retracted and he knew he was being dismissed. *Good,* he thought, *because in one more minute I would've told him where to stick it.*

David went into the bedroom and gently lifted the white, tailored, imperial chef coat with black piping off the bed. He slipped his arms through the sleeves which were made with underarm vents. This allowed him to stay cool in the kitchen and also gave him plenty of room for movement. He buttoned up the black fabric-covered buttons and touched the chef's knife embroidered on the left side pocket. The initials *TC* engraved in silver on the black handle were the logo of his business, Temporary Chef.

After finishing culinary school and eating food at restaurants that were unfit for man or beast, he decided to start a business where he would go in and help restaurant owner's revamp or create a new menu. He'd stay on for at least two weeks to help train the cooks and follow-up a month later to be sure everything was running smoothly. Within ten years, his business became very successful and now there was a possibility he could be a guest chef on one of the food networks.

Today he was attending a two-day Culinary Conference in Madison, Wisconsin. It was designed to provide culinary arts instructors with the skills and knowledge to reach the highest level of culinary standards in their classrooms. He would be one of the guest chefs, leading one of the breakout sessions and assisting in the hands-on, lab time to help students learn the latest culinary trends.

He looked at his reflection in the mirror that hung on the back of the door. He had to admit the jacket with his black jeans looked pretty sharp, but what caught his attention the most was the gleam in his eyes. David knew the voice was antsy while he waited in the shadows. He would love nothing more than for him to skip the conference altogether. However, he took a deep breath, reined in its compulsion, calmly picked up his black briefcase, and left.

David sat in the lounge of the hotel in a tan, wing-back chair. He had just finished a traditional breakfast of eggs, bacon, and toast. He felt calm, cool, and collected on the outside, but on the inside it felt like he was about to bungee jump. He grabbed the complimentary newspaper off the table, crossed his legs, and snapped it into place while he scouted out a potential victim without being too conspicuous. After fifteen minutes, only three redheads had entered the hotel. One was too short, the other too old, and the third was a wannabe. With a sigh of boredom, he closed the paper and was about to put it down when the front page headlines grabbed his attention. "State police agreement reached in pursuit that left a father in a coma and two children dead." He caught his breathe at the picture of the woman next to the article as he began to read.

*Kathryn Rubin, wife of Dr. Richard Rubin and the mother of Ricky and Rachel Rubin, agreed to*

*a one million dollar settlement with state police this
week. Mrs. Rubin received the settlement, which included a denial of liability or fault from Wisconsin
state police, one year after the incident. The terms
of the suit effectively closed the civil action against
the state police. Rubin said she will continue to fight
for changes in police procedures in high-speed chases.
"Many mistakes were made that night, and I want to
keep them from ever occurring again," she said.*

She had the same auburn hair and the beauty mark
just above the right corner of her mouth. She had the
same green eyes that had defied him when she escaped
over the cliff and into the river. For months he had
searched for her, but everyday had left him empty
handed and he came to the conclusion she was dead.
The more he stared at the picture of Kathryn Rubin,
the more he was convinced it was his beloved, Rebecca.

He picked up his briefcase and carefully tucked the
paper inside. He took a deep breath and slowly exhaled.
With a spring in his step he headed down the hallway to
the conference. Anticipation is making me wait … the
lyrics ran through his mind. *Not anymore*, he thought.

# CHAPTER 7

Kathryn picked the yellow daylily up from the table and thought about the roadside memorial. After she and her parents placed the bouquet of flowers on her children's grave, they had gone to the site of the accident. She was so overwhelmed with emotion when she saw her community, along with complete strangers, placing flowers and stuffed animals along the road in her children's memory. However, when the mother of the seventeen-year-old boy who was responsible for why she was there showed up, it was too much to handle.

"Mrs. Rubin." A woman in her late thirties dressed in a pair of jeans and a black sweater touched her arm. "I'm deeply sorry for your loss. My son is so devastated by what he did and wishes he could take that night back. For whatever it's worth, he wanted you to know that he is so sorry and hopes that someday you will be able to forgive him."

Blinded by her own suffering, Kathryn looked into the eyes of the woman who rocked the cradle of the monster who stole her life. She recognized the pain in her eyes for it was a reflection of her own. Yet the barrier of her loss had been too wide, too deep, to allow forgiveness, so she jerked her arm away and left in silence.

"Excuse me."

Kathryn looked up from the table while she wedged the daylily into the vase. "I'm sorry. I didn't hear you come in." She wiped her hands on her apron and stepped to the counter.

"No need to apologize. I've only been waiting for a couple of minutes." The man smiled.

"How can I help you?"

"I'd like to order a fresh bouquet of flowers for my daughter."

"What kind of arrangement would you like?" She grabbed an order form from off the counter and reached for the pen behind her ear.

"Anything is fine, just as long it's wrapped up in a pink bow."

"How old is your daughter?"

"Jenny would've turned eight tomorrow but she died two years ago from leukemia."

"I'm so sorry for your loss." She laid the pen on the counter.

Kathryn knew all too well what he was going through. However, she didn't know what was worse. A child dying unexpectedly or watching them suffer day in and day out while they dwindled down to nothing.

"Thank you. It's taken its toll, but I'm managing."

"Does it get any easier?"

"So you've lost someone?"

"I lost my two children in an automobile accident last year."

"I'm so sorry. You and your husband must've been devastated."

"My husband was the one driving when a drunk driver hit his car. He's been in a coma in St. Mary's Hospital ever since."

"Again, I'm so sorry."

"If it hadn't been for family and friends, I don't know what I would've done."

"My wife, Ellen, had a difficult time when Jenny passed away. Eventually she left me because the memories we shared with our daughter were too painful."

"What made you keep going?"

"Jenny. The last thing she said to me was, 'Daddy, don't be sad because all the love we shared together will always be with you.'"

"Your daughter was very wise for her age, Mr ..."

"Sawyer, but you can call me David."

"David, you can pick up your bouquet any time after three o'clock."

"Thank you, Mrs ..."

"Rubin, Kathryn Rubin."

"I have a few errands to run, so I'll pick up the flowers around four."

"That's fine. If I'm not here, my assistant Nancy will be able to help you."

"Kathryn, it was so nice to meet you." He started to leave.

"David."

"Yes." He looked into her haunting green eyes.

"If you don't mind, I'd like to give the flowers as a gift in the memory of your daughter."

"You don't have to do that."

"I insist."

"Jenny would be greatly touched by your kindness."

"You have a good day."

"Thank you, and you too."

David turned to leave and Kathryn had a moment of déjà vu. She swore she had known him from somewhere. The minute he walked out the door a room with a fireplace and a two-tone, antique, bronze-colored, chandelier flashed before her. The snapshot was short-lived by the phone ringing on the counter.

"Hello, Rubin's Florist. How may I help you?"

"Hey, honey."

"Hi, Mom."

"I just called to see if you wanted to come over for dinner tonight."

"What time?"

"I was thinking around five-thirty."

"Could you make it around six-thirty? I wanted to stop by the hospital after work."

"That's fine dear."

"Do you want me to bring anything?"

"No, just bring yourself. And give our love to Richard."

"Okay, I'll see you tonight."

Kathryn hung up the phone, went back to the table and thought about the flashback after David had left. Somehow, the traumatic loss of her family had opened the gateway to her forgotten memories. Little by little, she was starting to remember things. Like a barn with the sweet smell of hay, riding across the field on a chestnut mare, and now a room that meant nothing to her. She picked the daylily off the table, slipped it into the vase, and hoped the memories would fill in the missing pieces of her forgotten past.

❈   ❈   ❈

David parked across the street from Rubin's Florist and watched Kathryn through the window. He knew going into the shop earlier was risky, but he had to get a closer look. Once he got up close and personal, he knew it was Rebecca. The way she moved, the way she talked, the way her long, silky, auburn hair framed the beauty mark just above her soft full lips. However, she never gave any indication she recognized him. Sure it had been eighteen years since the last time she saw him, but he hadn't changed that much or had he?

He caught a glimpse of his reflection in the rearview mirror and ran his hand through his hair. It was still sandy blond except for a few strains of gray here and there. A few more extra lines had etched their way across his forehead, and the corner of his blue eyes showed faint signs of crow's feet. Besides that … He watched as the pin holes of his pupils grew wider with a question.

*"Why are you still sitting here?"*

"I have to be sure."

*"Sure of what?"*

"That she's Rebecca."

*"You're procrastinating again."*

"No, I'm not." He gripped the steering wheel.

*"Yes, you are. You always do that when you're scared."*

"I'm not scared." He glared into the mirror.

*"Then, let go of the wheel."*

"No, this time I'm in charge. I'm not going to let you jeopardize this operation. It's too important.

*"You know you need me!"*

David stared into his eyes and almost surrendered to the hypnotic darkness. Instead, he took a deep breath of insubordination. "Not this time."

His pupils quickly retracted and he knew the voice was pissed, but he didn't care. He wasn't going to give that egotistical bastard another chance to destroy everything he had worked for. He had his business and the reputation of being a well-respected chef. The more he thought about it; maybe he should just forget this whole thing. However, a glimpse of Kathryn through the bay window superseded his logic, so he grabbed the keys out of the ignition and went inside.

"I see you made it back." Kathryn placed the broom in the corner.

"My errands took longer than I thought, and I didn't think I was going to make it back in time."

"I don't close for another thirty minutes."

"I guess I'm better off than I thought."

Kathryn grabbed the bouquet of daylilies, tulips, daisies, and stargazers accented with a single white rose out of the refrigerator. He could barely take his eyes off of her, and it took everything he had not to kidnap her right there. She set the flowers wrapped up in a pink bow on the counter as he reigned in the urge and decided to save it for the right moment.

"Beautiful." And he wasn't talking about the flowers.

"Thank you. I'm glad you're pleased."

*Women can be so gullible,* he thought. All a man needed was a little information about some tragedy they had endured and relate to it. The story of his imaginary daughter dying of cancer was brilliant because she bought it hook, line, and sinker.

"Kathryn, thanks so much for your generosity." He picked up the bouquet.

"You're welcome." She thought about the déjà vu moment she had earlier. "David, have we met somewhere before because you seem vaguely familiar."

"I don't think so. If we had, I would've never forgotten someone so beautiful."

Kathryn blushed.

"Sorry, I just thought I knew you from somewhere."

"Well, if you have some time to spare, I noticed there was a café down on the corner. Would you like to go get a cup of coffee, and maybe get to know one another better?"

"Thanks, but I'm going to the hospital after I close."

"Maybe some other time."

"Maybe."

"To 'maybe,' then." He lifted the flowers as if making a toast and left.

David got back in his car and threw the flowers on the backseat, disappointed she had ruined his plans. He had already paid her empty shell of a husband a visit earlier. He distinctly told Richard his wife was no longer going to waste her time on him because, after tonight, she would be his. He turned on the ignition and started to pull away to go back to the hotel when he caught his reflection in the rearview mirror. He felt the shift when his hands clutched the steering wheel and his foot pressed against the brake. The gravitational pull of the two black holes snared him. The voice emerged and took absolute control.

He stepped into the dimly lit hospital room, past the comatose elderly man on his left, and made his way to the bed next to the window. He placed his hands on the railing where Richard was surrounded by gadgets and equipment playing the symphony of buzzing, clicking, and air whistling.

*"Hello, anybody there?"* The voice knocked twice on the comatose man's head where tubes were coming from his mouth and nose. *"I guess not."*

He sat down in the brown leather chair next to the bed, crossed his legs, placed his fist under his chin, and drew his breath. He let it back out with a sigh and David resurfaced. He glanced around the room with his brain in a fog wondering where he was. The instant Richard's face came into focus, he quickly stood up, almost knocking the chair onto the floor.

"What the hell are we doing here?"

*"I thought we'd get a little closer to the situation,"* the voice gave his best imitation of an Italian mobster.

"It's too risky. Kathryn could be here at any moment."

*"See, you're still not convinced she's your beloved Rebecca."*

"Maybe, but if she shows up and finds me here I'll never get a chance to find out. So I'm leaving."

David's eyes darted toward the door where he heard footsteps in the hallway. "Now what are we going to do, Sherlock?"

*"Hide behind the curtain."*

The split second David pulled the curtain around Richard's roommate, Kathryn entered the room. He faded into the shadows against the wall and watched her silhouette take off the jacket, gave it a few shakes, and hung it on the coat rack next to the bathroom.

"Honey, it's raining like cats and dogs outside." She bent down and kissed Richard on the cheek.

She grabbed the arm of the leather chair and pulled it closer to the bed. Just the thought of her sitting in the exact same place he had been moments ago made David's heart race. He closed his eyes and thought about the first time he had touched her. He could still feel the heat of that moment and before he knew it, he took a step forward. Just when he was about to pull back the curtain, his eyes shifted.

*"Stop!"* the voice screamed in his head.

"Why?" David echoed back.

*"It defeats our purpose. So quit acting like a school boy in heat or you're going to blow our cover."*

David knew the voice was right so he receded back into the shadows while he stared at Kathryn and eavesdropped on the pitiful one-way conversation she was having with her husband.

"Hey, honey." David sensed the tired and repetitious sound in her voice. "I thought I'd stop by for a few minutes before I headed to mom and dad's for dinner. Oh, by the way, they send their love."

*Now that's just lovely, she's going to her parents,* he thought. Her parents weren't from Wisconsin. Maybe he had a case of mistaken identity. Perhaps it wasn't Rebecca after all, but someone who just looked like her.

"A man by the name of David Sawyer stopped by the shop today." She gently took Richard's hand in her own.

David's attention snapped back to the conversation when he heard his name mentioned.

"The funny thing was, after he left I got this sense of déjà vu. It was like that time we went skiing and passed that old deserted barn on the way to Devil's Head Ski Resort in Merrimac. Remember, I swore I'd been there before."

*I knew it,* he thought. That's where he had taken Rebecca when he had kidnapped her eighteen years ago and kept her prisoner for six months until she escaped. The day she slipped through his fingers was one of the worst days of his life, and still haunted him after all these years. David suddenly turned his head toward the door at the sound of footsteps. A nurse with short blonde hair stepped into the room. He sighed with relief as she passed right by the curtain without even a glance.

"Hey, how are you?"

"Janet." Kathryn scooted back the chair and got up.

"I thought I'd come in and see how you were doing."

"I'm doing okay."

"I also wanted to let you know Richard had an unexpected visitor earlier today."

"Do you know who it was?"

"I don't know. I've never seen him before."

"What did he look like?"

"I really didn't get a good look at him because I had an emergency with another patient, but he did have a goatee and was wearing one of those little round caps that Jewish people wear."

"It's a kippah. Must've been someone visiting from the synagogue. Janet, do you have a minute so we can go somewhere to talk?"

"Sure, let's go out into the hallway."

David held his breath until they passed by and exhaled with relief when he went unnoticed. He couldn't believe the voice had placed him in this predicament. What if he got caught? Maybe he should just forget about this whole harebrained idea. He had his business and his reputation as a chef to think about. Maybe, instead of kidnapping her, he should just kill her husband. Allow her some time to grieve and step into the picture as a suitor.

*"Why are you standing there with your thumb up your butt?"* The voice whispered from the right side of his mouth. *"Go see what they're up to."*

"Just hold on to your britches. Maybe we should rethink this whole kidnapping thing."

*"And miss the thrill of the ride? Not on your life."*

David heard Rebecca's sweet voice out in the hallway. The thought of having her and breaking her into submission to his every whim was too much to resist. So, he headed to the doorway and eavesdropped on their conversation.

"Janet, I've been thinking about letting Richard go."

"Are you sure?"

"No, I'm not sure about anything. It's just Richard and I promised we'd never let one another live in a vegetative state."

"How long has it been since you made that promise?"

"It's been almost ten years."

"Listen." She placed her hand on Kathryn's shoulder. "Sometimes we make promises we can't keep, especially in a case like this."

"Richard didn't agree to any of this. The only reason I've kept him alive this long is because I've been selfish."

"What do you mean?"

"I lost my children for God's sake! The thought of losing him too was unbearable. It didn't matter if he laid there like a zombie day in and day out. All I was thinking about was me and what I wanted. I thought if I kept him on life support, maybe there was a chance he would come back to me, but it's been a year and nothing has changed."

"Who says he won't? I've been in this business for a long time and I've seen quite a few miracles."

"Miracles!" she cried. "It would've been a miracle if my family had walked away from the accident alive. Where was God when that boy plowed into my life and turned it upside down?"

"I don't know. Sometimes we don't have any answers and the only question we have left is how do we move on?"

"Move on! How do you move on when you have nothing to move on to?"

Kathryn stepped to the window at the end of the hallway and watched while the sun glided out from behind a dark cloud and danced with the rain. The silver lining made her think of her roommate, Mingxia, from college whose name meant "bright glow through clouds." Whenever Kathryn would have a bad day, she would always say, "Kat, the sky will be blue again after the rain," and she was right. But having a bad day because you flunked an exam and losing your children to a drunken and stoned driver were two totally different things.

The dark clouds recaptured the rays of the sun leaving the rain to dance alone. David watched Janet walk up behind Kathryn and place her hand on her shoulder.

"Listen, I've got to make my final rounds before my shift ends. What are you doing tomorrow morning?"

"Nothing, I just have to be at the shop around four to close up."

"Why don't you put a pot of coffee on around ten, and I'll bring those delicious homemade donuts from The Sally Shop."

"That sounds good." She turned to face Janet.

"Everything is going to be fine. You just wait and see."

"I hope so."

"I'll see you in the morning." She gave her a hug and left.

David stepped back into the room and, as he slipped behind the curtain, Kathryn came back in, got her jacket, and went over to Richard.

"Honey, I'm going to leave. I'll see you tomorrow."

She grabbed a tissue out of the box on the table, taking several others with it. She stuffed the extra ones back in, wiped her nose, and gently kissed Richard on the lips. She lingered quietly above him for several seconds, hoping true love's kiss would awaken him. Gently she placed the palm of her hand against his cheek and searched his face for some response. When the magic of what fairy tales were made of failed, she captured the sob coming out of her mouth, and ran out the door.

"Johnny boy ..." David patted the elderly man on the shoulder, thankful it wasn't him lying there. "You've been very accommodating, but I've got to go and rescue a damsel in distress." He pulled back the curtain and stepped over to Richard.

He looked down at the empty shell of a man and almost felt sorry for him. However, Richard's loss was his gain. If it hadn't been for the accident, he would never have known his Rebecca was still alive. He was sorry her children had died, but if things worked out the way he planned, hopefully they would have a family of their own someday. He grabbed the tissues Kathryn had stuffed in the box earlier and lifted them to his nose hoping to get a whiff of her scent. When there was no trace, he slipped the tissues in his pant pocket with the mere satisfaction that she had touched them.

"After tomorrow, your wife will be mine." David smirked. "You should be thankful. First thing Monday morning, she was planning on pulling the plug on your sorry ass. So, for what it's worth, consider it saving your life—what life you have."

# CHAPTER 8

Kathryn stepped into the foyer, went over to turn off the alarm and realized it wasn't on. She thought for sure she had activated it this morning before she left for work. Who knows? The way her mind had been working lately, she probably forgot. She set the alarm, took off her jacket, and hung it on the coat rack in the corner. Exhausted, she dropped her purse on the console table by the door, and decided to go to bed.

She glanced over at the grandfather clock where its hands still rested at five o'clock. Each day it waited for her to open its door, reach in, and restart its pendulum so it could fulfill the purpose of its creator. However, she decided if her children's hearts didn't tick than why should it? She reached the stairs and the phone rang. She looked down at her wristwatch and wondered who was calling her this late at night. She thought about ignoring it and realized it was probably her mom calling to see if she made it home okay.

"Hello." The dark, half-moon circles under her eyes smiled back at her in the mirror above the table.

"Kathryn, it's Janet. I just wanted to call and see how you were doing. You had me a little worried at the hospital earlier today."

"I'm doing fine. I had dinner with my parents to-night, and they always have a way of putting everything in perspective."

"Good. I know it's late so I'll just see you in the morning at ten."

"Janet thanks for calling."

"You're welcome."

Janet Reed had been Richard's nurse ever since the accident. Eventually they had forged a friendship, and if it hadn't been for her, she probably would've pulled the plug six months ago. It was hard watching her husband lay there day in and day out with the gadgets buzzing and clicking. It was one of the loneliest sounds she had ever heard. She knew she should let him go, but there was always that 'what if' in the back of her mind. What if the moment she let him go would have been the moment he woke up? That is why she agreed with her parents to give it another couple of months.

She made her way up the stairs that led to nothing. There was no Rachel waiting in her bedroom for her to tuck in. No Ricky waiting to hear one more adven-ture of Huck Finn. No Richard snoring in the bedroom waiting for her to nudge him in the sides to wake up. The home that she loved had become a place of solitary confinement where her children's laughter had stopped in the back seat of a car and Richard's voice lay dormant in a cold hospital bed.

She stepped across the walkway that overlooked the foyer and glanced toward the alarm. She couldn't believe she had forgotten to set it before she left this morning. Several years ago, there had been a couple of break-ins in the area and Richard was adamant about making sure it was armed. Satisfied the red light was on, she made her way to the master bedroom.

She flipped on the light and trudged her way to the dresser. She pulled out a pair of silk, green pajamas and pushed the drawer shut with her knee. She looked past her reflection in the mirror and gasped. Sitting on the night stand in a vase was the bouquet of flowers she had arranged for David Sawyer. The only difference was the white rose had been replaced by a red one. Calmly, she laid the pajamas on top of the dresser and slowly backed out of the room. She scanned the area below while she made her way to the top of the stairs. Cautiously, she tiptoed down the steps and, once she reached the bottom, she ran to the front door.

"Going somewhere?" David stepped out of the sitting room on her right as she fell into his arms.

"Let go of me!" She pushed against his chest, causing him to stumble backward.

"Is that any way to treat someone who's brought you flowers?"

"Those flowers were for your daughter."

"I lied." He laughed.

Kathryn ran to the phone on the table, picked up the receiver, and started dialing 911.

"Go ahead. It won't do you any good. I cut the line after you talked to your friend, Janet." He took the receiver from her and placed it back on its base.

"How did you get in here?" She took a step back realizing he had somehow disarmed the alarm.

"Rebecca, let's just say I'm a jack-of-all-trades."

"My name is not Rebecca!" She glared at him. "You've got the wrong woman!"

"Feisty! I see after all these years you haven't lost your spirit."

"What are you talking about?"

"Don't you remember who I am?"

"Yes, you're the man that came into my shop today and bought flowers for a daughter you don't even have."

"That was quite clever, don't you think?" He raised his eyebrows and grinned.

"No, I think you're one sick …" Her cell phone rang inside her purse.

"Answer it!" He twisted her arm behind her back, grabbed the gun out of his waistband, and pressed it against her temple. "I swear if you give any indication I'm here, I'll kill you along with your so-called parents and your empty shell of a husband. Understood?"

"Yes!" Her nostrils flared.

"That's my girl." He bent down lightly, kissed her neck, and slipped his arm around her waist pressing her body against him. "Now, you'd better act normal."

"Okay." She curled her lips and rolled her

shoulders.

"Remember, no stupid stunts."

Kathryn grabbed her purse off the table and took out the phone. "Hello."

"Hi, honey."

"Mom ..." David tightened his grip, reminding her not to do anything stupid.

"Kat, did you know your house phone is out?"

"Yes. I called the phone company on my cell. They said there was an accident in the area and it should be out of service for a couple of hours." She decided to play along with his sick little game, afraid he would follow through with his threats.

"Honey, are you okay? You seem a little nervous."

"Mom, it's been a long day." She closed her eyes and took a deep breath. "As a matter of fact, I was getting ready to go to bed when you called."

"Then I won't keep you. I'll give you a call tomorrow and see how you're doing."

"Mom ..." David pressed the gun against her back with a warning. "I love you."

"I love you, too, dear."

"I'll talk to you later." She turned off the phone and tried to slip it in her pants pocket.

"Oh, no you don't." He put out his hand. "Hand it over."

She tightened her grip on the phone as he jerked it out of her hand and slipped it into his pocket.

"Rebecca, I need you to cooperate and if you keep giving me a hard time ... Well, let's just say it wouldn't be in your best interest." He pushed her toward the stairs.

"How many times do I have to tell you my name isn't Rebecca?" She clinched her jaw and narrowed her eyes. "Just let me go! You've got the wrong woman."

"Let you go." He stepped behind her, drew her close, and whispered. "Why, I just got you back."

David's voice, his smell, his touch caused the memory of the sweet smell of hay to resurface. This time a young woman in her late teens was going up a set of stairs leading to a loft in a barn. Kathryn felt sick to the stomach the instant she reached the top step. Something told her evil lurked behind those four walls, so she slammed the door shut on the memory.

"I swear if you do anything stupid, you'll be begging to be six feet under with your children when I'm through with you. Understood?"

"Yes," she whispered.

"What? I didn't hear you."

"Yes, I understand." She tightened her lips.

"Good, I'm glad we're on the same page." He placed his hand on her lower back and guided her to the bottom of the stairs.

"Where are we going?" She grabbed the banister.

"It's a surprise. Besides, I can show you better than I can tell you." He nudged her up the steps.

She glanced over at the flowers on the nightstand as they entered the bedroom. How had she been so gullible to believe his lie about having a daughter who died from leukemia? After the pain of losing her children, she didn't understand how anyone could make up such a heartless, narcissistic story for such a sick, ulterior motive. Just thinking about it made her angry.

"You have to admit, the flowers do add a special touch." David gave her a wink and pushed her toward the master bathroom.

Candles were placed strategically around the garden tub where they flickered upon the water dappled with red rose petals. The sweet fragrance should've given the room a more relaxed atmosphere. If the situation had been different and Richard was here, it would have. However, the only thing it did was make her furious. If this moron thought she was going to bathe in front him, he was sadly mistaken.

"I've prepared for you a cleansing bath which will wash away all the impurities and prepare your body for the next stage of our night of intimacy." David tucked the gun back into his waistband and gently guided her to the tub.

"I'm sorry, but I can't!"

"Oh, and tell me why not?"

"I can sing it better than I can tell you." She threw a slightly different version of his own words back in his face.

S.I.N.G. Solar plexus, she elbowed him in the stomach. Instep, she stomped him in the foot. Nose, she brought up her left fist and nailed him in the face. Groin, her right fist came down and slammed him between the legs with a vengeance. Caught off-guard, David grabbed his crotch and fell to his knees.

*Oh my God, it worked,* she thought, glad Richard had let her practice the self-defense techniques on him that she had learned from the movie *Miss Congeniality.*

Kathryn darted out of the bathroom, into the bedroom, and out into the hall. She ran across the walkway and flew down the stairs to the front door. She fumbled with the lock while she heard the sound of David's footsteps gaining on her. She started to open the door when he grabbed her from behind and pulled. The knob slipped from her hands, they both fell to the floor and she landed right on top of him. The fall caused him to release his hold, so she scrambled back up, ran to the door, and just when she was about to open it, David tackled it with his shoulder.

"Oh, no you don't." He turned her around and slapped her hard across the face. "I told you not to do anything stupid."

"Yeah, and I told you to let me go." She spit in his face.

David slammed her against the door, pinned her arms over her  head, and drew back his fist. Kathryn lifted her chin to dare him when his eyes began to shift and dilate until there was nothing left but a thin blue line around the edges of his dark, empty pupils. A deep, commanding voice filtered out through the right side of his mouth and she knew he was crazy.

*"I believe we have a strong-willed, confident, woman on our hands. No weak or inferior prey here. I'm going to enjoy breaking this one."*

Kathryn knew she was dealing with a narcissistic, schizophrenic  psychopath and somehow had to diffuse the situation or his fist was going to plow right into her face. So, she lost the attitude and gave him what he wanted.

"David, I'm sorry." She whispered.

His eyes softened to a bright blue the second he heard the sound of his name sweetly coming from her lips. He lowered his hand, placed his finger under her chin, and gently examined her face.

"Good, it didn't break the skin, but you'll probably have a small bruise and some swelling."

Kathryn wanted nothing more than to spit back in his face, yet she knew she had to lose the attitude and play it smart.

"David, do you think we can go to the kitchen and get some ice for my face?" She thought about the knives tucked away in the kitchen drawer next to the refrigerator.

"First, we're going upstairs. I'm sure your bath has gone cold by now. Once I refresh it, I'll come back down and get you some ice."

David led her back upstairs. Once again she glanced toward her children's bedrooms on the left. On a stretch of highway, they weren't given a choice as they were caught between the crossfire of the cat-and-mouse chase at the rate of one-hundred miles per hour. She decided she wasn't going to let one more person waltz into her life and take what didn't belong to them. She was going to put up one hell of a fight and, if she failed, at least she had the satisfaction of knowing she didn't go down easy.

"Sit!" David pointed to the toilet and reached for the handcuff dangling from the towel rack.

"Please, don't handcuff me."

"Sorry, you can't be trusted."

"I promise I won't give you any trouble."

"No, you won't." He handcuffed her, went over, and placed his hand in the tub. "See, due to the shenanigans you just pulled, your water has gone cold." He turned on the hot water and released the stopper. "I'm going to let that run while I go get you some ice."

"I don't need ice. What I need is for you to leave!"

"Your needs or wants are no concern of mine. It's about my wants and my needs." He grabbed her by the chin, slipped his hand around her throat, and squeezed. "Understood?"

"Yes." She nodded her head with a cough.

"Now, I'm going to go get that ice." He softly kissed her bruised cheek and left.

Kathryn rubbed the disgusting kiss off her face and brushed her hand through her hair. She wondered how she was going to get out of this predicament when her fingers ran across the buried treasure. She pulled out the bobby pin, straightened it, and inserted it into the key hole of the cuff. She wiggled it back and forth, but it wouldn't give. Quickly she stuck the pin back in her hair when David entered the room.

"I couldn't find an ice bag, so this will have to do." He tossed her a bag of frozen peas.

She pressed the bag against her face while he turned off the water and pushed down the stopper. He stepped to the double sink, grabbed the tray off the counter and set it down on the edge of the tub.

"You have everything you need for your cleansing ritual. There's a bar of sage soap that is one hundred percent vegetable-based and contains pure sage oil. It's blended with cocoa seed butter to moisturize your skin and also has antibacterial properties. I've also provided you with a loofah sponge to exfoliate any dry skin and a washcloth to bath your most intimate parts. Once you are finished, drain the water out of the tub, rinse off in the shower, and wash your hair. I want you to pull your hair back from your face, so I can gaze into those beautiful green eyes of yours that have haunted me for years. Now, do you have any questions?"

"No."

David picked up the wooden egg-shaped timer off the sink, twisted the top, and placed it back down.

"You have thirty minutes. After you're finished, go into the bedroom and put on the gown I've laid out for you. Once you're dressed, tap the bell on the nightstand three times, go to the center of the room with your back facing the French doors which lead out to the balcony and wait."

He pulled a key out of his front shirt pocket and unlocked the handcuffs. She hoped he wasn't planning on staying and watching her bathe. If so, she wasn't sure she could maintain her temper and follow through with his sadistic, egotistical plan.

"Now, I'm going to leave. If you try anything stupid, you will be drowning in the tub, instead of bathing in it. Do I make myself clear?"

"Yes."

"I expect you to follow my instructions down to a T and keep sweet while doing it. Now, do you understand the plan I've laid out for you?

"Yes," relieved he wasn't staying.

"Excellent." He bent down, lingered for several seconds above her lips, kissed her on the forehead and left.

She waited for several minutes; tiptoed over and peeked into the bedroom to be sure he was gone. When she didn't see him, she quietly made her way to the linen closet next to the sink. She opened the door and pulled the rope ladder off the bottom shelf that Richard had placed there in case of an emergency.

Richard, always cautious, was always thinking ahead, especially after they had children. He was adamant about safety, which is why there was a ladder in every room on the second floor just in case a fire broke out. Four times a year he would have a fire drill to coincide with the seasons. He said escaping from a fire in the summer was totally different than in the winter, which is why every closet was equipped with everything including coats, boots, gloves, shoes, and socks.

In the beginning, the drills were all planned. Richard would make everyone go to their bedrooms and wait for the signal. After they heard the whistle, each one would grab their ladder, hang it out the window, climb down, and meet on the front lawn. After several months, he got this big idea to have a surprise drill in the middle of the night. When he reached the front lawn and saw Ricky and Rachel waiting for them, he had been one proud papa.

She smiled at the memory as she stepped up on the edge of the garden tub and pulled back the cream colored lace curtains from the window.

"Damn it!" She slapped the window pane because he had nailed it shut.

Disappointed, she got down and placed the ladder back in the closet. With no choice but to follow his instructions, she grabbed the edge of her green sweater, pulled it over her head, and waited for her next opportunity.

Kathryn made her way to the full-length mirror in the corner with her hair pulled back in a classic, French twist, just as David instructed. She slightly ran her hands over her hips and knew this wasn't the first time she had worn the bias cut, backless, emerald, silk gown. She just couldn't remember the why, when, and where. She gently brushed a loose strand of hair away from her face when the fine lines on her forehead began to slowly disappear. The flashback she had earlier in her shop, of the fireplace and chandelier, reappeared behind her younger reflection in the mirror. From the shadows, a much younger David dressed in a dark suit stepped behind her image with a sinister look on his face. The memory slowly began to fade so she closed her eyes and willed it to stay. However, the gateway to her memories slammed shut, leaving her with only a fragmented piece of her forgotten past, of the man waiting for her out on the balcony.

She took a deep breath while her finger lingered above the bell on the nightstand. What if David was right and her name was Rebecca. She thought about the day she washed up on the bank of a river eighteen years ago with no recollection of who she was. She had searched for several years to find her true identity, but with no details of her past, she ended up empty handed. After she met Richard, got married, became Mrs. Rubin and had children she decided to let the past go so she could move on with her future; a future that no longer existed.

She looked out the door into the hallway, briefly thought about  escaping, but knew it was a bad idea. She tapped the bell three times, slowly made her way to the center of the room, and waited.

The French door screeched open with a reminder that Richard had never gotten around to oiling it. Many times after the accident she thought about doing it herself, but decided not to in the hope he would wake up and do it for her. However, after a year of waiting she knew that was unlikely. A gust of wind quietly swept through the room and softly caressed the skirt of her gown. She held her breath at the tapping sound of David's footsteps crossing the hardwood floor. She cringed when he softly touched her shoulders, turned her around, ran his fingers down her arms, and gently took her hands in his.

"Rebecca, you're just as beautiful as the first time you wore this dress."

"Why do you keep calling me Rebecca? My name is Kathryn Rubin."

"Because that's who you are and from now on, that's who you  will answer to or suffer the consequences. Now, let's go downstairs and out on the patio where I've prepared a late-night romantic snack."

"I'm not hungry."

"Very well, perhaps we'll just stay here and I'll have dessert." He stepped behind her, slipped the right strap of her gown over her shoulder, and lightly kissed the nape of her neck.

"Maybe I am a little hungry." She pulled the strap back up.

"I thought so." He turned her around, gently placed his finger under her chin, and stared into her eyes. "Rebecca, I'm not the same stupid young man you knew eighteen years ago. I'm older and wiser and I assure you I will not make the same mistakes over again."

By the look in his eyes, she knew he meant every word he said. For now, she would try to stay sweet and play along until she figured out a way of beating him at his own game.

"Shall we?" He extended his elbow.

He escorted her downstairs where they entered the sitting room through an archway on the right. They made their way across the floor, through another set of French doors, and out onto the stone patio. He led her to a corner where a table was covered in a white lace tablecloth, accented with a single white tapered candle, and two wine glasses.

He pulled out her chair and as she sat down he leaned forward. "You smell like the fresh scent of windswept silk sheets. Your obedience has pleased me."

He seated himself across from her, grabbed the bottle of chardonnay chilling in the silver ice bucket and poured them each a drink.

"I'd like to propose a toast." He lifted his glass.

Kathryn picked up her glass, tempted to throw its contents in his face.

"Rebecca, to the one who was lost and now is found. To thee I pledge my love."

He lightly tapped her glass while she scanned the patio trying to figure out a way to escape. She looked at the French doors and knew going back into the house was not an option. The only thing left was to jump over the railing into the backyard and run. Now all she had to do was wait, until the opportunity presented itself.

"I know you already had dinner, so I prepared us a variety of cheeses, fruits, and crackers for a little snack." He lifted the silver lid off the tray next to the ice bucket.

"Thank you." She reached for a strawberry and slipped off her black, high heel shoes.

"Oh wait." He lifted his finger. "I forgot something."

He glided across the patio to the French doors where he had placed a CD player on one of the teak patio tables, and pressed play.

"The First Time Ever I Saw Your Face." David stared at Kathryn while he did a two-step back across the patio to the Johnny Mathis song.

The second he sat down, Kathryn stood, grabbed the edge of the table and turned it over on him. The cheese and fruit platter landed on top of him while the flame from the candle set the sleeve of his jacket on fire. She climbed over the black railing, jumped to the ground, and sprinted across the yard toward the grove of trees at the end of her property. The second she entered the wooded area, she stepped into the twilight zone of a forgotten memory. She was no longer thirty-six, but eighteen. Gone was the emerald green dress and in its place was a pair of dirty blue jeans and a grimy red t-shirt. Tree branches slapped her in the face as if to awaken her from a deep sleep. The ghostly sound of a night owl filtered through the air while the moon sailed out from behind the clouds. Just before she stepped into a clearing, the rest of the memory faded when David grabbed her from behind.

"Rebecca, this time you won't get away." He slipped a handkerchief over her mouth with the pungent smell of chloroform.

She put up a fight trying to get away but she was no match for his strength. Her body became numb, but before she lost consciousness, she remembered.

*My name is Rebecca Hilliard and David Sawyer has come back to finish what he started eighteen years ago.*

# CHAPTER 9

Marilyn's hair flowed from underneath the half-helmet like a chestnut mare running on an open range. The black, wrap-around sunglasses shielded her eyes from the sun while it kissed the spray of freckles across her nose. The open, country air had a way of clearing her mind and allowing her to get lost in the moment. It was freedom of her own space and she was totally in charge, which is why she had the inscription "Light like a feather and feeling the breeze" airbrushed on a bed of white feathers on her gas tank. She found that nature and the price of a few gallons of gas were more effective in dealing with her pain than a small, white pill and a glass of water.

She stared at the man in front of her riding his Harley, dressed in a black, leather jacket with matching chaps over a pair of jeans. He looked more like a rebel without a cause than an entrepreneur. His dark hair with a hint of gray on the sides, blue eyes, and strong jaw line with a five o'clock shadow gave him that bad boy look. If she had any sense, she would just turn around and hightail it out of there. The night he called her Rebecca in the gardens at the dinner party, it had unnerved her. But when he came into the café with the picture it had freaked her out. If it hadn't been for her dream, she would've thought he was a stalker who had taken her picture; photoshopped it and made up the whole cockamamie story just to get close to her. *Who knows? He still could end up being a snake in the grass.*

Several miles down the road, William shifted gears and turned on his left blinker. The cabin-like structure on her left stood against the backdrop of nothing but wide open spaces. She read the wooden sign in the shape of a wagon wheel while she followed him into the parking lot.

## Millie's
### (come home to country cooking)

She pulled up alongside him as he hopped off his bike, pulled off his helmet, and hooked it on the black, saddle bag.

"This place has the best breakfast in town, and I promise you will not leave here hungry."

"Good, because I'm starving." She took off her helmet, hung it on the handlebars, and followed him to the cafe.

An old man dressed in a pair of overalls rocked back and forth on one of the six rockers lined up on the wrap-around porch. Puffs of smoke floated above

his corncob pipe while the sweet smell of cherry tobacco filled the air.

"It's a great day for a ride," he mused as they
walked towards the porch.

"Yes, sir," said William.

"Where you headed?"

"To the Harpers Ferry Festival, but we thought
we would stop by and have some breakfast first."

"My missus and I used to ride. Oh, how I miss
those days when she would ride behind me with her
arms wrapped tight around my waist. They were the
best days of my life." The rocker stopped in mid-
stream and he looked at Marilyn. "Little lady, if I were
you, I'd get off of your bike and hold onto your man
like it was your last day on earth. Time doesn't wait
on anyone, before you know it, old age creeps up on
you, and the only thing left is a rocking chair with a
trough full of memories to keep you warm."

Marilyn looked up at William. This time, the spark
of turquoise was a little brighter than the one at the
café and the slight flutter in her stomach had become
stronger.

"You two have a nice day." The man rested his head
on the back of the chair and rocked with his memories
of better days long gone, disappearing as quickly as the
puffs of smoke coming from his pipe.

"Thanks, you too," said William.

Marilyn stepped inside the diner with the flutter
still lingering in the pit of her stomach. She knew she
had made a huge mistake and should've never agreed
to come on this trip. She couldn't afford to compli-

cate her life and be distracted like some giddy-headed school girl. She vowed once this day was over, she would let William VanWyc crawl back under the rock he came from.

A petite gray-haired woman stood behind a mahogany wooden bar with a brass foot rail encircling the base. At the end of the bar was a big, brass spittoon with a sign that read, "Give us your tips not your tobacco." The moment the woman saw William, a smile spread across her face as she threw the dishrag in the sink.

"Oh lordy! Look what the cat dragged in," she stepped out from behind the bar, "It's about time you stopped by to see this old woman."

"Millie, how have you been?" William grabbed her around the waist, lifted her up off the floor, swung her around, and kissed her on the cheek.

"Fair to middling." She placed her hands on the sides of his face and pecked him on the forehead. "You can let me down now."

"I see you haven't grown an inch since the last time I saw you." He set her back down.

"Don't let size fool ya' buster." She punched him on the arm. "I might be seventy-two and four-foot-eleven, but I can still whoop your butt any day of the week."

"I don't doubt that one bit." He laughed. "Millie, I'd like you to meet Marilyn Jantzen."

"What the ..." Her jaw dropped to the floor. "If she's not Rebecca Hilliard, she sure as hell could pass for her twin sister."

Millie's reaction gave Marilyn the confirmation she needed that Rebecca Hilliard had actually been a real person.

"Well, they say everyone has a double," Marilyn slightly smiled.

"That's true. I get mistaken for Raquel Welch all the time." She laughed.

"Yeah, and I'm Elvis about to die of starvation if I don't get something to eat." William placed his hands on his hips.

"I swear that boy eats like a horse and never gains an ounce." She looked at Marilyn, grabbed two menus off the bar, and waved her hand. "Come on."

They entered through a pair of swinging saloon-style doors where a five foot wagon wheel chandelier accented with ten hurricane globes hung from the ceiling. It gave light to the rustic tables scattered around on the hardwood floor in no specific order. Weathered copper lanterns hung on each wall, illuminating pictures of infamous Wild West figures like Wyatt Earp, Wild Bill Hickok, Doc Holliday, Annie Oakley, Calamity Jane, and Bell Starr. In the left corner of the room was an old upright piano. The only thing missing were gunfighters, dancing girls, and brawling cowboys.

"Your favorite spot." Millie set the menus on a table in front of a limestone fireplace where a portrait of John "The Duke" Wayne graced the wall above the mantle.

"Allow me." William pulled out Marilyn's chair.

"Thanks."

"Okay, what will it be?" Millie propped her hands on her hips.

"I'll have the Chuck Wagon breakfast with black coffee." William sat down across from Marilyn without looking at the menu.

"What about you young lady," asked Millie. "God, I can't believe how much you look like Rebecca," she said as an afterthought.

Marilyn glanced at William and said, "I guess I'll have what he's having. Only I'd like cream and sugar with my coffee, plus a glass of water."

Millie picked up the menus from off the table and said, "I'll have Troy bring your drinks out shortly." She patted William on the back, and left.

"If I didn't know better," said Marilyn as she glanced around the room. "I'd think we stepped back into a saloon from the Wild West."

"Millie and her husband, Chester, are in love with the old west," said William as he leaned back in his chair. "They even used selected reclaimed lumber to build this diner over forty years ago."

Marilyn knew from her father being in the lumber business that reclaimed lumber was recycled wood taken from regional barns, out buildings, commercial buildings, and grain elevators dating back from the turn-of the century.

"You and Millie seem really close." She took off her black, leather jacket and hung it on the back of the chair.

"She's like a second mom to me. If it hadn't been for her, I don't think my family and I would've survived."

"What do you mean?"

"Well," he set his elbows on the table, "I grew up on the outskirts of Harpers Ferry in a rundown shack with my mom, sister, and alcoholic father. Every day I watched my old man squander what little money he did have on booze and gambling while his family starved to death. Sometimes the only decent meal we got during the week was the one at school. On weekends, we were lucky if we got one meal a day. I remember when I was around fifteen and my younger sister, Abbey, was so hungry because she hadn't eaten all day. So I got on my bike and started peddling. The next thing I knew, I end up behind Millie's digging in her dumpster."

"Digging in her dumpster?"

"Yes. I couldn't believe all the good food that was being wasted. I thought I had come across a gold mine. Anyway, after about two weeks of dumpster diving, Millie caught me.

"Really, what did she do?"

William took off his jacket and hung it on the back of the chair. "I thought for sure I was going to get in trouble, but the next thing I know, Millie takes me inside. She gives me this big container of fried chicken, mashed potatoes, green beans, and a whole apple pie to take home. Plus, she gave me a job as a dishwasher. This place became my family's salvation. She became my second mom, and Chester became the dad I never had."

Marilyn couldn't imagine growing up in a family under those circumstances, where love was wasted in a bottle and gambled away by the hands that were supposed to make you feel safe. Her parents had always been loving and caring, even when she was a rebellious teenager. If she disobeyed their rules, they would sit down and talk about it so she would become a part of the solution and not the problem.

"So, where are your parents and sister now?"

"Well, after I left for the military, my mom finally decided to leave the bum. She and my sister moved to Savannah, Georgia, where she had relatives. Eventually, my mom remarried a good man and my sister became a kindergarten teacher. She met her ex-husband, Seth, and had Zach. Now, most days her time is tied up in trying to find him and unfortunately, her efforts are turning up empty-handed.

"Do you mind telling me why he took their son?"

"They had a nasty divorce and Abbey ended up getting sole custody of Zach, which didn't set too well with Seth. Two years ago, when it was his turn to have him for Thanksgiving, he was supposed to have him back the following Monday, but he never showed. Abbey decided to check his apartment and when she got there everything was cleaned out and they were gone."

"So do the authorities have any idea where he took him?"

"They believe he's taken him out of the country."

A tall, slender, dark-skinned boy around sixteen stepped up to the table. He balanced the two cups of coffee, the glass of water, and a small container of creamer on a tray, and deftly passed them out.

"My name is Troy and I will be your server today. Your breakfast should be out shortly." He set several packets of sugar on the table.

"Thanks, Troy," said Marilyn.

After he left, William took a sip of his coffee. "Violet tells me your daughter, Emily, went missing nine months ago at Tysons Corner."

"Yes." She picked up the cream and sugar and put them in her coffee.

"Do you mind talking about it?"

"Well, frankly it's quite simple. My daughter and I were at the mall eating ice cream when I saw my husband with another woman. I got up and yelled to get his attention, when I turned to go back, Emily was gone. In a matter of seconds, she had vanished into thin air. The only trace we have of her is a security video of her leaving the mall with an unidentified male."

"Have there been any new developments in the case?"

"Recently the authorities got a call from a woman in Arizona who was visiting family in D.C. the day Emily was taken. She thought for sure she saw her with a man in a gray SUV in the parking lot. Other than that, there have been no other leads."

"So I'm assuming you and your husband are divorced or otherwise you wouldn't be here with me."

"I must say you're quite observant. Actually, the same day Emily was taken, he came home, got some of his things, and without a word left. Next thing I know, he's moving in with his girlfriend, filed for divorce, and now he's getting remarried."

"I'm sorry, that must be very difficult."

"Difficult?" She leaned back, took a sip of coffee, and looked him in the eyes. "Difficult is an unsatisfied customer. Your car breaking down on a highway leaving you stranded. Losing a job and wondering where the next meal is going to come from. All these things can be resolved by giving the customer what they want, getting your car fixed, and get assistance until you find another job. When you lose a child, it reaches in, rips you apart, and steals a piece of your soul you'll never get back. Plus, knowing you're responsible, that your inattentiveness is the reason they're gone, causes your heart to bleed with guilt, and it continues to bleed until there's nothing left. Losing a child is beyond difficult—it's heart shattering."

"I understand."

"How can you understand?" She took a sip of water. "You've never lost a child."

"I lost my nephew, whom I love very much, and the day he was taken a part of my world shattered. Plus, I watched my sister spiral into a world of depression and wondered if she would ever recover. There were times I was even apprehensive about visiting her because I was afraid of what I would find. The day she met Violet Shaw was like a breath of fresh air. It was a turning point in her life when she got involved with the Parents of Comfort Organization. It gave her hope and the determination to never give up until her son was safely home."

"I'm sorry, and I know it's been very difficult for your family."

143

"Difficult, it's beyond difficult—it's heart shattering."

She slightly smiled when he made her eat her own words.

Millie and Troy navigated their way through tables filled with other customers. Millie opened the stand while Troy set down the tray.

"I hope you guys are hungry," said Millie."

Troy picked up the two plates with pancakes, scrambled eggs, sausage, bacon, hash browns, and a side order of biscuits with chip beef gravy and set them on the table.

"Oh my, maybe I should've gotten the Little Chuck Wagon."

"I told you, you wouldn't leave here hungry."

"I can't stay and chat." Millie gave William a wink. "So, make sure you say good-bye before you leave."

"Yes, ma'am."

"Okay, Troy, let's go before I have a stampeded of hungry customers on my tail looking for their breakfast."

After Millie left, William grabbed his fork and dipped it into the biscuits and gravy. They ate in silence for several minutes when William asked, "So, are you originally from Shepherdstown?"

"Born and raised." Marilyn picked up a piece of bacon off her plate and took a bite.

"What about your family? Do they still live in the area?"

"My parents and brother died in a car accident several years ago."

"I'm so sorry." William put down his fork. "You don't have to talk about it if you don't want to."

Marilyn slightly turned her head to the crackling sound of the fireplace where the residue of ashes began to accumulate as a reminder of what her life had been reduced to.

"My parents were taking my brother, Dillon, to the airport so he could catch his flight to Ireland. On the way there, a truck crossed the center line and struck them head on. My parents were killed instantly and Dillon was taken to the hospital where he died four hours later."

"Marilyn, I'm so sorry. That must've been very hard."

"If only they had listened, they would still be here." She blurted out.

"What do you mean?"

"Never mind, it doesn't matter." She shook her head, regretting she had said anything.

"No, tell me."

"I said never mind. I shouldn't have brought it up. Besides, if I tell you you're going to think I'm crazy anyway." She took a sip of her water.

"No, I really want to know."

Marilyn searched his eyes and realized these weren't Jim's eyes. These eyes were warm and inviting. Eyes that made her feel safe to share this part of her. So she told him about the dream she had about the accident. How she begged Dillon to postpone his trip, but he wouldn't listen. How she pleaded with her parents not to take him to the airport and how she blamed herself because she didn't try hard enough to stop them.

"Marilyn, it wasn't your fault. Sounds like your brother already had his mind made up and no matter what you would've said or done, you never would've changed his mind."

"You're probably right, but it still doesn't make it any easier."

"So, have you always had dream premonitions?" He leaned back in his chair.

Surprised by his question, Marilyn thought about the time when she was around eight and her neighbor's cat went missing. That same night, she had a dream it had fallen down in an old well on the neighbor's property. The next day she told her parents, they checked it out and, sure enough, there he was alive and well. Afterwards she had dreams, like finding her dad's extra set of store keys under the driver's seat of his car. Knowing what she got on a test before she got it back. The night she dreamt about finding her mother's wedding band in the drain of the kitchen sink. For some reason when she reached puberty her premonitions just stopped. However, in 2002 they resurfaced when she had a dream about the D.C. sniper.

In the dream, she was pulling into the Berkeley Plaza Shopping Center off Warm Springs Avenue in Martinsburg. All of a sudden, she scooted down in the seat as the car went into slow motion. After passing several buildings she observed a dark-skinned man on the front passenger side of a car pointing an assault rifle out of the window. She woke up wondering if the sniper's next target would be in a shopping center. The next day, when she heard on the news that a forty-seven-year-old FBI intelligence analyst was shot dead in the parking lot of the Seven Corners Shopping Center in Fairfax County, Virginia, she couldn't believe it.

She never told a soul about the premonition because if she couldn't have control over the outcome for the greater good it wasn't worth repeating.

"You didn't answer my question." William took a sip of his coffee.

"Yes, I had dream premonitions when I was younger, but most of them were small like finding a lost cat or a set of keys. However, they stopped when I got older and after I had the one about my parent's accident two years ago, I haven't had another one since." She lied, deciding she wasn't ready to tell him about the one she had about Rebecca.

"So are you telling me you didn't dream about me before we met?" He laughed.

"I'm afraid not. Anyway, enough about me. I want to know more about this Rebecca Hilliard who looks so much like me." She took a bite of the pancakes drizzled in maple syrup topped with a pat of butter.

"Actually, we met right here at the diner. It was a Friday night, and she had come in with some of her friends after a football game. I was cleaning off this very table when I noticed her sitting at the table right behind you. She smiled and I smiled back. I figured that would be the extent of the relationship but, the following Friday, she came in again, this time alone. We ended up talking and the next thing I know we're dating. We dated for about six months and when her mother found out, she put a restraining order on me."

"So did you see each other after that?"

"Yes, we found a way to see each other behind their backs. However, one weekend her mother decided to have this dinner party and everything changed. The next thing I know, Rebecca is telling me she doesn't love me anymore and no longer wanted to see me. Two weeks later, she's gone without a trace."

"Why do you think her parents blamed you for their daughter's disappearance?" she asked wondering if they had a reason to suspect him.

"I don't know. I loved Rebecca. I would've never hurt her. The day she came into my life I thought it was too good to be true. I never expected to find someone to love the way I loved her, and she felt the same way. So after she told me she didn't love me anymore, I knew she wasn't telling the truth. Something happened to her the night of the dinner party, I just don't know what. A day doesn't go by that I don't think about her."

Marilyn didn't know what to say because she never felt that way about anyone, not even Jim. For that matter, if he had felt that way about her, he would've never cheated. Perhaps they were both just in love with the thought of being in love, because if it had been something deeper, they would still be together. She envied what Rebecca and William had, and it made her sad she had never experienced it.

"So, how's everything?" Millie stepped up to the table.

"Delicious as always," said William.

"So where are you two young'uns headed off to?"

"To the Harpers Ferry Festival. Where's Chester?"

"He's home working in the flower garden. You know how that man can't sit still and relax. He's always got to be doing something. You think at seventy-five he'd slow down."

"I'm sure he thinks the same thing about you."

"Yeah, we're like two peas in a pod, which is the reason why we get along so well. Anyway, I better get back to work or they're going to fire me. Oh, that's right. I'm the boss." She laughed. "Marilyn, it was nice meeting you. Make sure you come back and see me."

"Millie, it was nice meeting you."

"William, next time don't wait so long to come by." She kissed him on top of the head and left.

"Well, I guess we better eat up so we can head on out to the festival." William picked up his fork.

Marilyn took a sip of her coffee realizing she was letting down her guard. She didn't know if it was the warm atmosphere of the diner or if sharing her thoughts with someone else besides Dana and Charlie made the difference. Whatever it was, she knew she had to proceed with  caution because sometimes things weren't always what they seemed.

# CHAPTER 10

The historical streets of Harpers Ferry were filled with wall to wall people. There were women dressed in corsets, hoop skirts, and bonnets. Some men smoked cigars, dressed in tail coats and top hats, acting as if though they owned the day. If it hadn't been for those dressed in jeans, shorts, and tank tops, it would've been a perfect day from the 1800s.

The smell of fried chicken and funnel cakes filled the air while the sound of children's laughter and babies crying echoed through the streets. It brought back memories of the first time Marilyn had brought Emily to see the historical town. She had begged Jim not to go to work that day because they were in much need of some family time. However, he made the decision that work, or the other woman, was more important than family. Instead of staying home and pouting, she decided to go anyway. From the moment they stepped into the John Brown Museum, Emily had been so fascinated by the way the voice, music, and animation told the story of the raid of Harpers Ferry that it made the trip worthwhile.

Marilyn spotted the Swiss Miss store while they strolled down Potomac Street. It was the same place she and Emily had stopped that day to get ice cream. When she saw a little girl eating a raspberry and vanilla cone, her daughter's favorite, she knew she had to get some.

"Do you want some ice cream?" she asked William.

"No, you go ahead. I'm still full from Millie's breakfast." William sat down on the bench in front of the store.

"Okay, I'll be right back."

The mom and pop shop was loaded from head to toe with Coca-Cola merchandise, pictures, toys—you name it and it was there. She made her way to the counter, passed by the life-size replica of the Coca-Cola polar bear and thought of Emily. The last time they were in here, she had sat down on the bear's lap, wrapped her tiny arms around its waist, and asked if she could take it home. Marilyn scanned the menu behind the counter and wished her little girl was here jumping up and down with excitement because she was getting ice cream. Ice cream, that's it, nothing more. If only she had held onto her ...

"May I help you?" A boy around ten with blond hair, slightly crossed eyes, and wearing thick glasses, stepped up to the counter.

"Yes, I'd like a vanilla and raspberry swirl in a waffle cone." She knew if she got a regular cone the ice cream would end up down the front of her shirt.

"One vanilla and raspberry swirl coming up." He stepped over to the ice cream machine.

Marilyn turned, leaned against the counter, and watched William through the window. She thought about the flutter she felt at Millie's when he looked into her eyes. She had to admit she was attracted to him, but under the circumstances she couldn't allow herself to go there. Besides, she was carrying around too much baggage to even think about another relationship. He caught her staring at him so she quickly turned around and reminded herself of the reason why she was here— to find out more about Rebecca.

"Ma'am, here you go." The boy handed her the cone.

"How much do I owe you?" She slipped her hand inside the pocket of her jacket.

"Five dollars."

"Keep the change," she said as she handed him a ten dollar bill.

"Thank you!" A big smile spread across his face while he ran into a back room. "Look, that lady just gave me a five dollar tip!"

Marilyn smiled when she heard someone say, 'See, all your hard work paid off.'

"Do you want to go to the footbridge?" asked William the instant she stepped outside.

"Sure." She dipped her spoon into the ice cream in her waffle cone and took a bite.

They made their way to where the Potomac and Shenandoah Streets met at an intersection next to John Brown's Fort. The one-story brick building was where the abolitionist and several of his followers barricaded themselves during the final hours of their ill-fated raid. She thought about the man who had been captured and hung for treason. Perhaps one of the reasons he was willing to sacrifice his life was because he saw too many children stripped from their mothers while they held out their arms begging not to be taken from them. The turmoil she suffered the day Emily was taken put a whole new perspective on the evils of slavery.

She stepped upon the footbridge realizing that even though slavery had been abolished, it still reared its ugly head in the modern world. Where a child was snatched away—against their will—from a bicycle or from a mall, stripping away the dignity of a human soul who had the right to choose who they were and what they wanted to be. Abraham Lincoln was right when he said, "Those who deny freedom to others deserve it not for themselves." If she ever caught the man who had taken her child, she would see him behind bars or, better yet, dead.

Halfway across the footbridge Marilyn stepped to the guardrail. There was not a cloud in the blue expanse stretching above the river. She lifted her face to the sun where its pearly rays played on her eyelids. This was the same river where she shared the love for rafting with her parents and brother. A love she promised she would share with Emily the spring she turned six. A tear slipped over her cheek when she realized this would've been the spring of that promise. A promise that would never be fulfilled and a spring that had left her numb in a world she no longer recognized or wanted to be a part of.

William stepped up beside her and leaned against the railing as the floodgate of her tears opened up and a sob escaped her trembling lips.

"What's the matter?" he asked.

At the sound of William's voice the ice cream cone slipped from her hands. She watched as her daughter's favorite ice cream plunge into the water and disappeared. The same silent scream she had felt that day Emily was taken resurfaced. It weaved its way upward and caught in her throat. Not giving William a second thought she blindly ran across the bridge and several seconds later she came to a complete stop. On her right next to the railing stood a little girl with strawberry blonde curls who looked exactly like her daughter.

"Emily." She stepped over, knelt down, and turned her around.

"Mommy!" the girl screamed.

"Hey! What do you think you're doing?" A woman attending to a baby in a stroller stood up and gave her the eye.

Marilyn covered her mouth, backed away, realizing what she had done and said, "I'm so sorry." She shook her head.

All eyes were on her as she ran to the end of the bridge sobbing like a baby. She flew down the black iron spiral staircase toward the C & O Canal where she bumped into a woman wearing hiking boots. Faintly she heard the woman say 'watch where you're going.' She reached the bottom and ran down the path until she was out of breath. She stopped, planted her hands on her knees while she hyperventilated. With tears streaming down her face, she felt a strong, gentle touch on her shoulder. She looked up, stared into William's calm blue eyes, fell into his arms, and wept.

It had been a long time since anyone had held her this way. It was a touch she had longed for from Jim after Emily's disappearance, but it never came. Just for a moment, she allowed the warmth of this man's arms so she could feel another heartbeat besides her own.

"Marilyn," he whispered while he stroked her hair.

"I'm sorry." She stepped back at the sound of his voice to regain her composure.

"Why are you apologizing? You have nothing to be sorry for."

"I just made a complete idiot of myself." She brushed her hair out of her face.

"Okay, you looked a little bit like a wild woman, and people probably thought you were a little crazy." He gently lifted her chin. "You certainly caught me off guard."

"Thanks, that makes me feel a lot better." She rolled her eyes.

"Marilyn, you're not the only one who's lost it in public." He let go of her chin. "Come on, let's take a walk and get away from the noise of the crowd."

William pointed to a bench along the river as the sounds of the festival started to fade. "Do you want to sit down?"

"Sure."

In silence they watched the water dance across the rocks, glistening like a million sparkling stars that had fallen from the sky. Marilyn took a deep breath, closed her eyes, and tilted her head toward the sun.

"Feel better?" asked William.

"Better." She sighed.

The wind rustled through the trees while the sound of a small animal scurried nearby. In the background, she could faintly hear the laughter of the festival and thought about the girl on the bridge who looked so much like Emily. This is why she didn't like leaving the comfort zone of her own home or the café. It seemed every time she did, something always reminded her of the day her world fell apart. Just like the mockingbird that now squawked nearby. She wondered if the bird in her backyard had followed her here just to remind her; if she had been vigilante, her daughter would be next to her and not a complete stranger she had just met.

"Rebecca and I used to come here all the time." William said out of the blue. "Just so we could be together. Sometimes, I come here on her birthday. If I'm real quiet, I can almost sense her next to me. I guess you never really forget your first love."

"When's her birthday?"

"May thirteenth."

"Well, I guess that's something else we have in common besides looks."

"You have more than looks in common. Even your mannerisms  are the same. The way you talk, walk, and the way you just tilted your head toward the sun. I just find it a little bizarre that both of you only lived miles apart eighteen years ago and never ran into one another."

"I don't know. I guess stranger things have happened. I read this  article once where a pair of twins who were adopted by separate families as babies got married without knowing they were brother and sister."

"That's not bizarre, that's a nightmare." His stomach growled. "I think Millie's breakfast is starting to wear off. Are you up to going back to the festival and maybe getting some of that fried chicken?"

"Sure, I might even get another ice cream cone." She slightly grinned and got up.

Marilyn did a double take when she reached the tow path and saw the oak tree several yards on her left engraved with the initials R. H. and W. M. on its trunk.

"That tree was in my dream," she whispered making her way toward the oak.

"Where are you going?" asked William as he followed behind her.

"Do you have any idea whose initials these are?"

"Yes, they are mine and Rebecca's. It's the same tree in the picture I showed you last week at the cafe. You couldn't see the initials because she was standing in front of them."

"If that's the case, why does it say W.M. and not W.V.?"

"Because I changed my name after I got out of the military from Will Mitchell to William VanWyc. I knew if I didn't, people would  always remember me as the son of the town drunk who got away  with murder. Marilyn, there were no other suspects in the case and people needed to blame someone. Even though I was cleared of doing anything wrong, in the community's eyes, it didn't mean I was innocent. I knew if I wanted to move on with my life, Will Mitchell had to die.

She glanced at William and wondered if he was telling the truth. What if his love for Rebecca, was a devotion bordered on obsession. After she realized his need, to control her every move, she decided to break it off. So he determined if he couldn't have her; nobody else would. It didn't make any sense to change your name because you were a suspect. Now, changing your name because you were guilty was a whole different story.

"You think I had something to do with Rebecca's disappearance don't you?" William asked when she just stared at him.

"I didn't say that."

"You don't have to. I can tell by the way you're looking at me."

Marilyn decided to let her suspicions go, but in the mean time, she would keep her guard up just in case he was lying and trying to pull the wool over her eyes.

"William, I barely know you. To make that assumption would be premature. So, why don't we just go back to the festival and get some of that fried chicken."

Marilyn's thoughts began to wind down to a complete halt as they made their way back to the festival. Suddenly, she felt disconnected to her surroundings when a man appeared out of nowhere carrying a body across his shoulders. He slightly glanced at Marilyn with piercing blue eyes and as he dumped the body into a boat the woman's head flopped toward her and she stared into her own eyes. She edged toward the river to get a closer look and with each step the riverbank rose up to meet her until she was standing on top of a cliff. At the sound of pounding feet she jerked her head over her shoulder and saw a man running towards her. The closer he got, the more she felt threatened, so she turned to jump.

"What are you doing?" William grabbed her before she made the plunge.

Marilyn stared at him in a daze, not sure what was going on. She closed her eyes and rubbed the back of her neck where she felt a migraine coming on. The sounds around her began to amplify, causing her head to throb even worse.

"Do you want to tell me … ?"

"Is everything okay?" a female voice interrupted.

They both looked toward the trail where a young woman around twenty with blonde hair was straddling a bicycle with her hands on her hips.

"Everything's fine," said William.

"Ma'am, are you okay?" the woman asked as if she didn't believe him.

"Yes, I'm fine."

"Do I need to call someone?" She raised her eyebrows, quickly looked at William and back at Marilyn.

"No, I'm just not feeling well. Must've been something I ate, but thank you for asking."

"Okay, you all have a nice day." She hesitated than pedaled down the trail.

After the woman left William asked, "Do you mind telling me what just happened? It was like you went into a trance. If I hadn't stopped you, you would've jumped right into the river."

Marilyn looked into his blue eyes and wondered if the man she saw carrying the woman's body was William. She couldn't see the rest of the man's face because it was obscured by shadows. Was she being warned that he had something to do with Rebecca's disappearance? To err on the side of caution she decided not to tell him about the vision."

"I don't know what happened?" She lightly rubbed her right temple.

"Well, something happened, because you scared the hell out of me."

"I don't want to talk about this right now. I have a splitting headache so I'm going to call it a day." She started to leave.

"Rebecca, please." William gently grabbed her arm.

"I'm not your beloved Rebecca." She jerked her arm away. "Can't you get that through your thick head?"

"I'm sorry. It's just that …"

"I'm leaving." She stepped around him.

Seconds later William stepped up beside Marilyn. She gave him a side glance feeling a little uneasy. For all she knew he was a murderer. They reached the spiral staircase and headed up to the footbridge. Once they got to the top she felt a little more at ease. Without a word they mingled through the crowd until they reached their bikes.

"I'll give you a call," said William.

"Listen, I'm going to be honest with you." Marilyn put on her helmet. "I don't know if I trust you. So I think it best if we just part ways until I figure this all out."

"Marilyn …"

"Good-bye, William." She got on her bike and drove away.

Once Marilyn reached the main road she opened up the throttle and headed home. With the wind on her face she knew, William wasn't the type of man to be ignored and was sure she hadn't seen or heard the last from him.

# CHAPTER 11

A tiny haze started on the horizon, rose little by little while bright streaks of red, pink, and orange slowly overcame the dark blue sky. From the comfort of her sunroom, Marilyn watched the sun take its rightful place, carrying with it the torch of a new day. She thought about the festival and the vision she had on the C & O Canal. After she got on her bike and left William in the parking lot, she got an overwhelming urge to follow the river. For the next several days it only grew worse, so she took the day off from work and decided to go canoeing just to get the feeling off her back.

Marilyn picked up the eight-by-ten photo of her and Dillon off the table next to the chair. It was taken the summer they had gone fishing, just before he went off to college. He was holding his twenty-five inch red bass, next to her sixteen inch flounder, with this big grin on his face. He had taken the picture for bragging rights. Just so he could show his friends, he had finally caught a bigger fish, than his little sister. It was one of the best days of her life and wished he was still here. Just to be near him, talk to him, so he could put everything that was happening to her into perspective.

"I miss you," she whispered as she placed the picture back on the table, drank the rest of her coffee and went inside.

She placed the cup in the kitchen sink as a burst of cool air brushed against the nape of her neck and the tapping sound vibrated across her skin. She placed her hands on the edge of the counter and was surprised she felt anger instead of comfort. She closed her eyes, took a deep breath, turned around, and stared into the corner.

"Mom! Just give me one good reason why I should listen to you?"

When her question was left unanswered, she stepped to the trash can and placed her hands on her hips.

"That's right your dead! If you had listened, you, daddy, and Dillon would still be here. So, just leave me and my trash alone!"

She kicked the can across the floor, stomped out of the kitchen, through the rotunda, and headed for the stairs. Half-way up, she heard a noise in the family room so she went to investigate. She stepped inside the room where she found her mom's rustic oak chest lying on the floor. She didn't question how it got there because she already knew. It was her mother, trying to get her attention but this time she didn't care. She picked

up the chest that had been passed down to five gen-
erations of daughters. Inside was a treasure of some
special memory they had left behind. After her mom's
death, it had passed down to her. Where it would end
up collecting dust and no longer travel the passage of
time with her daughter.

She placed the chest back on the mantle above the
fireplace where it belonged. She stepped away and this
time it flew across the room, spilling the entire contents
on the floor.

"Mom, if this has anything to do with me going
canoeing, you can forget it. I'm going and nothing you
can do is going to change my mind, so you can just take
your ghostly self and leave. What am I doing? This is
insane! I'm talking to a ghost!"

She grabbed the chest and started to pick its contents up off the floor. She noticed the bottom had
come loose so she pulled out the fake panel. Inside was
an envelope addressed to her, along with her mom's
gold wedding band. Now she knew why the ring wasn't
among her mother's belongings after the accident. She
slipped the ring on her finger, sat down on the couch,
slowly pulled the letter out of the envelope, and began
to read.

*My Dearest Marilyn,*

*I'm writing two days before your brother's trip to
Ireland. So, if you are reading this letter that means
only one thing—your dream or premonition has
become reality. I know you don't understand why we
had to go against your wishes. Darling, no one should*

*have to live their lives in fear and you know what fear is. False Evidence Appearing Real. I know it's a cliché, but fear keeps us from living our dreams, and you know how much Dillon wanted to go on this trip. Regardless, come hell or high water, you would not have stopped him no matter how much you begged. Now, having said that, there are a few things I think you should know.*

*First I want you to know I loved you the moment you were placed in my arms. You were my diamond in the ruff. You were everything a mother would want in a daughter and I love you deeply. However, there is something I should've told you a long time ago. I am sorry. I hope you can forgive me for what I'm about to tell you. There is no easy way to say it, but the truth is your father and I are not your biological parents.*

Marilyn leaned back against the couch and remembered the conversation she had with her mother in the kitchen when she was around sixteen.

"Mom, are you sure I'm not adopted?" she had asked taking a bite of her apple.

"Honey, why do you ask?" She rolled the pie dough out on the counter.

"Well, I have red hair and green eyes. Dad has … Well he has no hair at all. You and Dillon have dark hair and dark eyes. Plus, I act totally different than the rest of this family."

"You're a teenager, you're supposed to act different. Besides, your father's great grandmother had red hair, so you probably get it from his side of the family."

"Okay, but I still think I was adopted."

Marilyn had known then something was off and her mother flat out lied about it. *I wonder what else she's lied about,* she thought. She got up, stood next to fireplace, and continued to read.

*After Dillon was born, I found out I couldn't have any other children, which was a great disappointment because I wanted a girl. When your brother was around five years old, we had the opportunity to adopt. Your father's relatives in Ireland told us about a young girl who was pregnant and was being forced to put her baby up for adoption. It was a closed adoption and under no circumstance could anyone know about it except for the parties involved.*

*Several months after we brought you home, we discovered the young mother gave birth to twin girls. Marilyn, you have a twin sister. I'm so sorry. You're father and I would've taken you both if we had known.*

*I'm writing this letter because upon my death I am no longer bound by a living oath. Darling, I loved you as if you were my own. I am your mother and always will be. I just hope someday you will find the courage to forgive me.*

*If I have passed over from this life, remember my promise to communicate. Take care of my grandbaby. Now use your God-given gifts and go find your sister.*

*Love Always, Mom*

Marilyn made her way back to the couch and sat down. She tossed the letter on the coffee table and ran her hands through her hair. She questioned how her life could possibly get any worse when the doorbell rang. She thought about ignoring it, but changed her mind. So she got up, opened the door and there stood her answer.

"What are you doing here?" Marilyn took a step back.

"I haven't heard from you since the festival," said William. "So, I thought I'd stop by and see how you were doing."

"I thought I told you I didn't trust you and I didn't want to see you again, until I figured out what was going on."

"I know and I'm sorry but I just couldn't let it go."

"Listen, now is not a good time." She started to close the door.

"Wait." He stuck out his foot keeping it from closing. "Are you still mad because I didn't tell you my real name?"

"I don't know." She held onto the door.

"Obviously you're upset about something. So what is it?"

"It doesn't matter. Besides, it has nothing to do with you."

"Do you want to talk about it?"

"No, it wouldn't do any good because it won't change a damn thing."

"It might make you feel better."

"I don't think anything is going to make me feel better at the moment." She started to close the door again.

"Marilyn, please." William pleaded.

"Fine, suit yourself." She turned and went back inside not wanting to argue."

"So what's going on?" He followed her into the family room.

"Here, read it for yourself." She picked up the letter and handed it to him.

After he took the letter, she went to the bar in the corner and poured herself a scotch. She knew it was too early but she didn't care; she needed something to calm down her nerves. She took a sip while William stood by the fireplace and started to read. She grabbed the bottle off the counter and made her way to the sunroom.

Minutes later William stepped inside the doorway.

"You want a drink?" She downed the rest of her scotch and reached for the bottle on the table.

"No, thanks."

"Good, that leaves more for me." She refilled her glass.

"You want to talk about it?" He stepped further into the room where she was sitting and noticed the picture on the table of a much younger Marilyn, standing next to a young man with dark hair.

"What is there to talk about? My whole life has been a lie." She rubbed the back of her neck, got up and went to the window.

"Marilyn, I know you're upset. I would be, too."

"I'm more than upset. I'm furious. How could they possibly have kept something like this from me?"

"I'm sure they had their reasons." He stepped to the window and handed her the letter. "But you can't ignore the fact that Rebecca could be your twin sister."

"Is that all you care about? Your beloved Rebecca?" She snatched the letter from his hand. "This means my parents were impostors, and Dillon, whom I adored, is not my real brother. At this point, I don't care if I have a sister or not. Why should I? Everything I've ever cared about is either dead, missing, or a lie."

She turned and threw the glass against the wall, where it shattered into little pieces. Just like her life. She dashed out the door and didn't stop until she reached the weeping willow tree. She sat down, pulled her legs to her chest and, when she gazed out over the pond, the poem she wrote for Emily, "Willow's Lullaby," ran through her mind:

*Lay down your head under the willow*
*Count the stars on the soft green pillow*
*And when your eyes are fast asleep*
*Know you are safe in my keep*
*While I stroke your moonlit hair*
*And the whippoorwill sings in the night air*
*May your dreams always come true*
*And know forever I love you.*

The willowy branches swayed above her while the lyrics kept running through her mind. She missed those full moon nights with her daughter under the evening sky, counting the stars while the nightjar bird would chant its whip-poor-will namesake song. It was magic seeing nature through her little girl's eyes. She'd never forget the time Emily skipped to the willow, wrapped her tiny arms around its trunk, and gave thanks for allowing her to hear the wind. It was so simplistic, yet so profound. And now those moments were gone forever because she had failed to keep her safe.

"Are you okay?" William sat down next to her on the ground.

She was so tired of everybody asking her if she was okay. Hell no, she wasn't okay and probably wouldn't be for a long time. Instead of answering the redundant question, she turned her attention to the one thing that mattered most.

"Emily and I spent so much time out here, especially in the spring. The moment she heard the geese honking, she was out the door heading to the field, picking wildflowers and chasing butterflies."

"Tell me about her," said William.

"You would've loved her. She had strawberry blonde curls, a little turned up nose, bright blue eyes, and a smile that would light up any room. She could waltz into your life and bring an oasis right into your desert. She never met a stranger, which is why whoever took her knew she was easy prey."

"Well, I'm looking forward to meeting her someday."

"What if I never see her again?" She started to tear up. "What if she is … ?"

"Don't." He lightly touched her arm. "You can't think that way. I tell my sister all the time. If you give up on hope, you have no power."

"I'm trying to stay hopeful but, ever since I saw Emily's spirit several weeks ago, it's been hard."

"What do you mean you saw her spirit?"

"I was sitting under the gazebo when a ray of light broke through the clouds and I saw Emily in the field of wild flowers. The instant I started running toward her, the sun withdrew its rays and she was gone. I'm starting to believe it was just an omen letting me know she was already dead. What I'd like to know is; who gave this black hole permission to snuff out every point of light that ever mattered to me?"

"I don't know." William picked a dandelion and twirled it between his fingers. "If you can tell me why a man will beat up his wife and neglect his children, causing them to dig in a dumpster like scavengers looking for something to eat, or why a father will take his child away from his mother, maybe I could make some sense out of your life. Bad things happen to good people and the only thing we can do is find a way to make the best of it."

"Make the best of it!" She raised the letter in her hand. "I don't even know who I am anymore. I wouldn't even know where to start to make it better."

"So you had no clue you were adopted?"

"Oh, I had my suspicions, but I was told it was all in my head."

"So where did you find the letter?"

"I didn't find the letter—it found me."

"What do you mean it found you?"

She quickly recounted the tapping trash can lid, and the wooden chest flying off the mantle, leading to her discovery of the letter.

"So you're saying the chest flew across the room all by itself?"

"No, my mother did it."

"I thought you lost your mother in a car accident?"

"I did."

"So you're saying she's communicating with you beyond the grave?"

"Yes, I guess now that she's gone, she's not such a coward. You know, I can understand keeping my adoption from me when I was a child, but not as an adult. What did she think I was going to do, leave them? Plus, my dad, who I completely trusted, was in on the whole thing. I wonder if Dillon knew I wasn't his real sister. My life has turned into such a web of lies that I don't know what to believe anymore. You know, I wish the dead and the living would just leave me the hell alone. I'd be better off."

"Marilyn, I don't want to change the subject, but do you mind telling me what happened at the festival, when you almost jumped into the river?"

"You're never going to let that go, are you?"

"No, and while you're at it, you might as well tell me about the dream."

"What dream?"

"The one you mentioned when you saw the oak tree with Rebecca and my initials."

Marilyn wasn't sure she could trust William. However, she couldn't ignore the fact that something had brought them together so she threw caution to the wind and decided to tell him.

"After I saw the tree with the initials and found out your real name everything went into slow motion. That's when I saw the man carrying a body across his shoulders. After he dumped it in a boat I realized it was me. The next thing I know I'm on top of this cliff. I hear someone behind me. So I turned to see who it is and the man is running toward me. I felt threatened so I decided to jump in the river. If you hadn't stopped me, who knows what would've happened?

"Are you sure it was you in the boat and not Rebecca?"

"I don't know." She closed her eyes and focused on the woman's face. "You're right. The woman had a mole on her face, so it had to be Rebecca."

"What about the man. Did you get a good look at him?"

"Not really. The only thing I saw was his blue eyes. The rest of his features were hidden in the shadows.

"Well, perhaps he's the one who kidnapped Rebecca, and maybe he used the river as a way to escape afterwards."

"What about the man I saw coming toward me on the cliff?"

"Well that's about as clear as the nose on your face—it was me."

"Well, if that's the case, maybe you're the one carrying the body along the river and something is warning me that you had something to do with Rebecca's disappearance."

"Marilyn, I don't blame you for being suspicious. I would be too. I left town after Rebecca went missing, even changed my name which only made me look guilty. I was just a young kid and if I had to do it all over again I would've done things differently."

Marilyn thought about the day Emily was taken. Afterwards she became the prime suspect, it had been devastating, to be accused of kidnapping her own daughter. So, she decided to give William the benefit of a doubt.

"I understand. If I could go back to the day Emily was taken I would've never left her alone for one second."

"Why don't you tell me about the dream," said William.

Marilyn looked across the pond toward the mountains and recapped the dream about riding a motorcycle down a country road, where she saw the oak tree with the initials. How everything went into slow motion as a large mirror descended out of nowhere and she saw her reflection with the mole on her face. Afterwards, the bike glided through the mirror to the other side where there was a farmhouse and a barn. She shivered involuntarily at the memory of how the bike turned into a snake, called her Rebecca, and chased her through the woods until forcing her to jump off a cliff and into a river.

After she finished several moments of silence passed between them.

"Well," William finally began. "The tree with the initials is pretty self-explanatory, and the reflection in the mirror is Rebecca, so that's a no brainer. She also lived in a farmhouse, but it was sold several years ago. Now, the bike turning into a snake and calling you Rebecca probably represents whoever took her."

"You know, at first I thought the dream was about Emily because her middle name is Rebecca, plus she has the exact same mole on her face."

"Are you kidding?"

"No, ironic, isn't it?"

"Yes, it is.

Marilyn looked down at her watch and said, "Well, it's getting late and I have an important errand to run this morning."

"Could that errand have something to do with the canoe I saw strapped to the top of your SUV when I pulled up this morning?"

"Yes, as a matter of fact it does," said Marilyn. "After I left you that day at the festival, I had this sudden urge to follow the river. Maybe it's just my imagination or maybe it has something to do with Rebecca's disappearance. I don't know, but whatever it is I have to find out."

"Do you mind if I come along?"

What would it hurt? She thought. She was probably just chasing the wind that led to no particular destination. The worse that could happen was she ended up back where she started; empty-handed, frustrated, and alone. Just like the last nine months.

"What the hell. Let's do it."

# CHAPTER 12

Marilyn sat across from William while they drifted through the natural avenue of trees. The sunlight filtered through the overhead canopy causing the water to glimmer with shades of blue and green. On her right, a dragonfly in its metallic blue finery caught her eye as it landed on a cattail along the bank of the river. About ten feet from the shore were lily pads surrounded by water lilies. In the midst, a turtle sat on a log with no cares in the world. From the corner of her eye, she saw a shape move in the water. She looked back and realized there was a school of fish. One of them broke the surface and plopped back in.

She placed her hand in the river and let the cool water flow through her fingers. She took a deep breath, closed her eyes, and thought. *What if Rebecca is my sister and the man across from me is responsible for her disappearance, or even worse, death? What if getting on this river alone with*

*him is one of the stupidest mistakes I've ever made? What if I
need to escape and there was no place to go?*

"Penny for your thoughts."

"It will cost you more than a penny to unscramble
the mess in my head."

"How about a quarter?"

"Make it a dollar and we have a deal." She slightly
smiled.

"Oh, did I see a smile?"

"If you did, you'll have to pay for that, too."

"Okay, double or nothing?"

She thought about the 'what if's' running through
her mind and decided she was better off keeping her
suspicions to herself.

"Well, if you must know," she lied with an off the
wall thought rattling through her head, "I was thinking,
what if they had a computer chip that could be embed-
ded in your brain so it could sort out the mess in your
head and put everything into perspective?"

"That sounds great, but what if it released a virus
deleting every memory you've ever had, and replaced
it with the mind of a serial killer? The next thing you
know you would have blood on your hands and you
wouldn't know why. No, I think it would be best to
leave it to humans to figure out their own messed-up
lives."

A light wind blew across Marilyn's face while the
sunlight streamed through the tree branches, softly playing on her hair. She wanted to ask him if he spoke from
experience but instead opened the cooler next to her

on the floor, pulled out a bottle of water, and handed it to him.

"Thanks."

She pulled out one for herself and asked. "Do you have any theories of what could've happened to Rebecca?" She placed her feet on top of the cooler.

"Like I said, two weeks before Rebecca's disappearance, her parents decided to have a dinner party. She didn't want to go because she knew they invited a son of one of the guests. Her mother was adamant about pushing me out of the picture and hoping they would hit it off. She hounded her for weeks about going, so to get her off her back, she decided to go. After that night, everything changed and she became withdrawn. When I called and asked what was wrong, she told me she didn't love me anymore, and to just leave her alone. Two weeks later, she disappeared. After eighteen years, all that is left of her is in a cardboard box, collecting dust in some basement until they get new evidence to reopen the case."

"Did they question anyone at the party?"

"I don't know. Once my name was cleared, I left, joined the army, and tried to move on with my life."

"And have you?"

"I guess to a certain degree. Once I left the military, I got into the real estate business. Invested in empty buildings and turned them into commercial property. I wasn't expecting a profit for at least a couple of years, but the next thing I know my bank account was growing and growing. I never dreamt of having that kind of money, much less making it. I was born dirt poor and figured it was just a foreshadowing of what the rest of my life would be. I must say, having money has made my life easier. However, I would give it all back if I could find out what happened to Rebecca."

Marilyn grabbed her green fleece jacket off the floor and put it on.

"Chilly?"

"A little." She shivered as she zipped it up.

"So enough about me. Tell me about you and Jim."

"Well, he was one of my clients at a marking and advertising firm in Washington, D.C. Four years later we were married, built our dream house and I got pregnant. About two years after Emily was born things started to change. We stopped communicating and then came the late nights at the office and weekend business trips. I found out he was cheating on me the day Emily was taken, and the rest is history."

"I knew your husband."

"You mean my ex-husband. So how did you know him?"

"I had met him several years ago at a real estate conference."

"He never mentioned you."

"Why would he? We only met briefly one evening at a restaurant."

"Oh really, was he with anyone?"

When William ignored her question she said, "Hey, you brought him up, not me."

"Well, it sure wasn't you cuddled up against him at the table."

The wind began to pick up when they sailed out from under the trees into a wide, flat stretch of the river. Dark, threatening clouds were approaching at an alarming rate of speed.

"Put on your life jacket," yelled William.

Marilyn reached for the jacket behind her while the wind came in short bursts, each gust more intense than the last. It changed directions, hitting her in the face and hindering her progress before spinning around and shoving her on the back. The boat began to spin out of control, tossing the jacket overboard. Skeletal fingers of lightening flashed down to the earth. Thunder roared across the sky. Marilyn held onto the edge of her seat for dear life. Huge raindrops began to pound the river, rapidly becoming an impenetrable curtain of water. William reached out for her hand and, just when their fingers touched, the wind caught the boat and lifted it up on edge, tossing them both into the water.

The water pressed down on her from all sides. The more she struggled, the more disorientated she got. She pushed with her arms and legs, but she could find no leverage; for all she knew, she was pushing herself further down. Cold water filled her lungs. She could feel the blood pounding behind her eyes as the darkness engulfed her mind.

"Marilyn, don't you die on me!" cried William.

She heard his voice as if from a long way off. She had the vague impression of a compressing weight on her chest, pulsing. Then a pressure on her lips, a pinch of her nose, a filling of her lungs. The pressure on her lips lifted, and she felt a magnetic pull as her energy left her body. She felt weightless, happy, and free from pain. She floated just above the tree tops where she looked down and saw her body lying on the ground. Fear was written all over William's face while the rain poured around him.

"William, I'm fine." She had never felt so light and alive in all her life.

He gave her another chest compression but she couldn't feel it any more. A tunnel spiraled around her. In the calm of the storm, she zipped toward a pinpoint of light until she reached a realm of radiant, golden-white light.

Love, joy, ecstasy and awe poured into her, through her, and engulfed her. She was swallowed up and enveloped in more love than she ever knew existed. A gentle current of electricity flowed through her being as she sensed the presence of a loving spirit. It softly caressed her face; it was a touch she had felt so many times before when she was a child.

"Mom, is that you." Marilyn wasn't speaking those words; she was merely thinking them and feeling the emotions behind them.

"Yes, dear."

"Oh, Mom, I've missed you so much."

"Marilyn, you have to go back. It's not your time."

"I don't want to go back. It's so peaceful here."

"Emily needs you."

"Emily is gone. I don't know where she is."

"Your sister needs you."

"Mom, wait—don't go." She felt the essence of her mother leaving.

"Be strong, my daughter." Her mother's spirit gently flowed through her.

"Mom, I don't know how to get back!"

"Daughter, tilt your head. Now, feel the liquid drain from your mouth. Now open your eyes and see."

She felt William pulling away from her lips. She coughed and  sputtered, struggling to get the water out of her lungs. He lifted her head to the side so she wouldn't choke while he rubbed his hand  across her back.

"I thought I lost you!" William gathered her up in his arms and held her while her eyes fluttered open.

She looked past him, through the tree branches, searching for the tunnel with the bright light but it was gone.

"Are you okay?" He wiped her hair out of her face.

Marilyn's head felt like it was about to explode when she shook her head yes.

"Listen." He gently laid her on the ground. "I've got to find shelter."

The last thing she remembered before losing consciousness was him softly kissing her on the forehead.

Marilyn moaned at the sound of water dripping while her head thumped in response to peals of thunder. She heard the sound of whispering hisses, sizzling pops, and a thick intoxicating smell of smoke and pine needles. She opened her eyes to a yellow and orange kaleidoscope as the heat washed over. In a daze she saw a silhouette sitting in front of the fire and realized it was William.

"How long have I been out?" She tried to sit up.

"A couple of hours." He got up and walked past the mouth of the cave covered with moss to her sleeping bag.

"Where are we?"

"I believe we're in a hiker's cave." He helped her up into a sitting position.

"A hiker's cave?"

"Yes, somebody must come here regularly because the cave was stocked with sleeping bags, blankets, a first aid kit, instant coffee, and even granola bars."

"I feel like I've been hit by a Mack truck." She lightly touched the bandage on her forehead and started to lean back against the wall.

"Wait." He knelt down, reached for the blanket next to her, leaned in, and placed it behind her.

"Thank you." Their eyes met.

She held in a breath as she became aware of his heartbeat. His closeness sent warmth through her body and her skin began to flush. She leaned back against the wall and he softly stroked her cheek.

"I thought I lost you." He leaned forward and softly kissed her lips.

His kiss left a trail of heat stirring something within her she hadn't felt in a long time. Just as he started to get up, she leaned forward with her eyes shining, glossing over, and softening. Her breath quickened as she placed her lips on his, allowing the kiss to linger.

"Rebecca." He whispered.

Marilyn caught her breath when she heard the name against her lips.

"I'm sorry." He searched her eyes realizing what he had done.

"So am I." The foolish kiss shrank from her lips, and she leaned back against the wall feeling a little awkward. "Did you say you had granola bars?"

"Yes, let me get you one."

"Do you have any water? I'm really thirsty." She licked her lips, still feeling the sting of his kiss.

"Sure do." He went to the cooler he had recovered from the river, pulled out a bottle of water and grabbed a granola bar.

She thought about the kiss and decided it was just a delayed emotion from him saving her life and nothing more.

"Here you go." He handed her the water and the granola of oats, nuts and honey.

"Thank you."

"Marilyn, there's something I want to show you." He slipped his hand in his front jeans pocket and pulled out a necklace.

"What is it?" She picked up the silver heart shaped locket out of the palm of his hand.

"It's the locket I gave Rebecca."

On the front, the initials R and W were engraved in an old English font, inscribed on the inside was the inscription: "I.C.U. I.C. Me."

"Why are you showing me this?"

"I found it in the cave under a pile of wood that I was gathering up to build a fire."

The benefit of a doubt Marilyn had given William about having something to do with Rebecca's disappearance began to waver.

"Are you expecting me to believe you found this in the cave?"

"Yes, so whoever kidnapped Rebecca brought her here and she  left this necklace behind, hoping someone would find it."

"How do I know you didn't have it the whole time, and you planted it there yourself?"

"That's ridiculous."

"Is it?"

"Marilyn." He took the necklace from her. "I loved Rebecca with every fiber of my being. I would've never harmed her. Did you read the inscription on the inside of the locket?"

"Yes."

"Do you know what that means?"

"No."

"It means, when I see you, I see me. When Rebecca came into  my life, I had no clue what love was. I had a father who beat up my mother, ignored my sister, and used his son as a punching bag. Love, in my family, was toxic. So when Rebecca came along, I found  something I never knew existed. For the first time in my life, I had met someone that saw my heart and I saw hers. She was the wind beneath my wings that made me want to be a better man. The day she was found missing turned my whole world upside down. So, don't tell me I'm responsible for whatever happened to her.

I would've given my life to save her." He stomped away and sat down in front of the fire.

A part of Marilyn believed he didn't have anything to do with Rebecca's disappearance. The other part didn't want to be naïve like she was with Jim. She had learned that just because someone cared about you didn't mean they wanted the best for you. Sure he had risked his own life to save her from drowning and that should count for something. But what if there was a side of him she hadn't seen yet?"

"So, when do you think we can leave?" she broke the silence.

"I don't know." He shook his head while he rubbed his hands in front of the fire. "Our cell phones were lost in the river, so we can't call anyone. The weather is too bad for us to leave. Besides, I wouldn't take the chance of moving you because of your injuries. The only option I see is to stay here for the night and re-evaluate everything in the morning."

Regardless of what she thought, he did risk his life. "William, I want to thank you for saving me from drowning."

"So does that mean you believe I had nothing to do with Rebecca's disappearance?"

"I don't know what I believe. The necklace just doesn't make sense. For all I know you could be the one responsible for what happened to her. Maybe even killed her and buried her body somewhere along the C & O Canal."

"Marilyn, I loved Rebecca and I assure you I would've never hurt her, much less kill her."

"I still don't understand why you had to change your name. It's too suspicious. To me, that's something you would do if you were guilty."

"I already explained to you why I changed my name. I knew if I wanted to move on with my life, Will Mitchell had to die."

"I don't know if I'm buying it. There has to be a better reason than that. Just because you're a successful businessman and an upright citizen in the community doesn't mean you're not capable of kidnapping and killing Rebecca. Look at the BTK killer. He was married with two children, a Boy Scout leader, served honorably in the U.S. Air Force and was employed as a local government official. He was also a member of the Christ Lutheran Church and had been elected president of the church council, and it didn't stop him."

"Marilyn, I assure you I am not a killer, and I don't know what else to say to convince you otherwise. If you're not going to believe me, I'm just wasting my time." He started to leave.

"I didn't say I didn't believe you. I just don't know if I trust you."

"You know you're starting to give me a headache with your Dr. Jekyll and Mr. Hyde personality. Once we're out of here, perhaps it would be best if we parted ways. From here on out, I'll look for Rebecca on my own terms, and you can do whatever the hell you want."

William stormed out of the cave. She knew he was pissed, but she didn't care. She couldn't afford to let her guard down any more than she already had. She slipped down into the sleeping bag, trying her best to forget the heat of his kiss that still lingered on her lips. As her eyes grew heavy she remembered him calling her Rebecca and  was reminded it hadn't been her lips at all he was kissing.

# CHAPTER 13

Kathryn woke up in the semi-dark room with her mind in a drug induced fog. Her mouth felt like it was full of cotton as she ran her tongue over her lips. She slowly sat up without the faintest idea where she was or how she got there. She was in a bed that much she could see. She scooted back against the headboard, closed her eyes and took a deep breath. David's face flashed before her and, with it, the reason for why she was here.

She remembered coming home after having dinner with her parents and finding the flowers in her bedroom she had made up for David. The cleansing ritual, the romantic interlude on the patio, the failed attempted to escape through her backyard and the handkerchief over her mouth. The moment she remembered her real name was, Rebecca Hilliard, just before she lost consciousness. Several hours later she woke up in the back seat of a car, gave him such a fit that he had handcuffed her and stuffed her in the trunk. She had made such a ruckus that he stopped the car and gave her a shot in the arm that had rendered her unconscious.

Kathryn's body stiffened at the sound of a floorboard creaking somewhere in the room. David emerged from the shadows and she realized he had been watching her the whole time.

"Rebecca, I see you're finally awake." David stepped further into the light.

She decided she wasn't going to let him know she remembered  who she was. Besides, she had no recollection of her life as Rebecca and, if it included the man in front of her, she was better off not knowing.

"How many times do I have to tell you my name isn't Rebecca?  It's Kathryn Rubin. You've got the wrong woman."

"Don't worry. I've got all your lost memories stored right up here in safe keeping." He tapped the side of his head.

It was a little scary knowing her memories shared the same space with the other voice in his head. For all she knew, they were only his delusional thoughts of what her memories should be, not what they actually were.

"I don't know whose memories you think you have, but they're  not mind. I've never met you until you came into the flower shop. If you let me go, I'll forget this ever happened and we can chalk this up to a case of mistaken identity."

"Sorry, no can do. You're here to stay, so you might as well get used to it."

"I'm thirsty." She decided to change the subject, realizing she wasn't going to be able to reason with him.

"Ask nicely and I might get you a glass of water."

"Please!" She raised her eyebrows and gave him a glassy stare.

"Rebecca, let me give you some advice." He grabbed a pillow off the bed, placed it behind her head, and slightly lifted her chin. "Keep sweet because you get a lot more with honey than you do with vinegar."

He picked up the pitcher from off the nightstand and poured her a glass of water. She decided if keeping sweet is what it took to get out of here, she would be like a bee on honey.

"Here you go." He handed her the glass.

"Thank you." She took it and leaned back on the pillow.

"I see you catch on fast."

She took a sip of water while he went over and took down the wooden plaque above the dresser with the words 'Keep Sweet' engraved in bold black letters.

"From here on out, this will be your mantra, and as long as you adhere to its meaning, we will get along fine."

"And what might that meaning be?" She raised her eyebrows and took another sip of water.

"It's simple. You will be submissive at all times and keep sweet doing it." He hung the plaque back up on the wall.

She thought about her family and the day they were ripped from her arms. If she could survive burying two children and watch her husband dwindle away to nothing, keeping sweet should just be a walk in the park, for now, but once she found a way to escape it was game on.

"Where am I?" She reached over to place the glass back on the table but missed her mark.

David quickly stepped over, grabbed the glass, placed it on the table and said, "Why, your home."

"This isn't my home." Kathryn slightly shook her head and narrowed her eyes.

"Yes, it is. This is where you grew up as Rebecca Hilliard and where I first met you eighteen years ago at a dinner party. Your mother, God rest her soul, would've done anything to get you away from your boyfriend. She invited me to the party hoping we would hit it off so she could get rid of the bum that was ruining her image and the life of her daughter. However, our relationship only lasted for six months because one day you just up and left me. I searched everywhere for you, but it was like you vanished into thin air. Now you're back and we've been given a second chance. What a shame your mother didn't live to see it."

"I have no recollection of what you're talking about. Besides, my parents are thriving and very much alive in Madison."

"I'm not talking about the impostors. I'm talking about your real parents. Unfortunately, two years ago your mother died from cancer and your father is now in an assisted-living facility. And the day he put this place up for sale, I bought it just to be close to you."

The sad news about her real parents had little impact on her because she had no memory of them. It sounded more like a sad story she had read many times in the newspaper with no emotional strings attached. Besides, as far as she was concerned, her real parents were Lillian and Garth Oates.

"I'm tired and I'd like to get some rest."

"Not until you've had your cleansing ritual."

"I'm exhausted and I'm still groggy from the drugs you gave me."

"Well, whose fault is that?" He poked his tongue lightly into his cheek, crossed his arms and tapped his foot. "If you hadn't tried to escape, we wouldn't have to start all over again. And as far as the drugs are concerned, if you would've cooperated, they wouldn't have been necessary. "

"I'm sorry." She quickly apologized realizing he was getting irritated and didn't want to take the chance of him drugging her again.

"Sorry just doesn't …"

The sentence was cut off when his eyes began to shift. She knew the other personality was about to emerge to add his own two cents worth.

*"For crying out loud you're giving me a headache. Let the woman rest,"* said the voice quickly disappearing as fast as it came.

The way David spoke from both sides of his mouth reminded her of a man named Pete. Every day he would ride his imaginary horse to The Little Inn Café where she worked while going to college in Madison. One day he showed up with aluminum foil wrapped around his head.

"Pete, what in the world do you have on your head?"

"Aw, Ms. Katie, this is a special helmet for protection so no one can read my thoughts."

Pete was special and wouldn't have harmed a flea. However, David was an egotistical psychopath who would stop at nothing to get what he wanted. She waited to see if David was going to listen to the sound of his own voice. She knew the voice of reason had won as his eyes softened and he took her hand.

"Rebecca, I will grant your request because you apologized but I want you to understand something. The only authority in this house is me and from here on out, you will do as I say, when I say it, or suffer the consequences. Do I make myself clear?" He brushed the back of her hand with his disgusting, wet lips.

"Yes." She fought the urge to spit in his face.

"Good, now get some rest."

. After David turned to leave, a puff of cool air caused the little hairs on the nape of her neck to stand on end.

"Are you cold?" David turned, rubbing his hands up and down his arms.

"Yes." She could faintly see her breath as she pulled the pink floral comforter up around her shoulders.

"I can see my breath," whispered David making his way over to the thermostat next to the door and turned it on. He waited for the sound of the oil furnace to kick on.

"Must be out of fuel," he muttered when he didn't hear the humming sound through the vent. He went to the other side of the room, opened the closet door, and pulled out several blankets.

"Here, I guess I'm out of fuel so this will have to do for the time being." He laid them on the bed.

"Thank you." She grabbed the white thermal blanket and placed it on top of the comforter.

"You're welcome, now get some rest." He left, locking the door behind him.

The puff of cool air on the back of her neck and temperature change in the room was not unfamiliar territory. Several weeks after her children were killed she had been curled up in the corner of their playroom hugging their pink and blue baby blankets, contemplating suicide. Suddenly, the temperature in the room changed and a puff of cool air brushed the back of her neck. That's when she saw the bluish and pink orbs floating just above the toy chest. She got up and the spheres had disappeared inside. She opened the lid where a quick breath of warm air radiated from the box causing her to change her mind.

Remembering her children's presence that day, Kathryn knew there must be a presence here as well.

"Who's here?" she called out.

An apparition of a woman wearing a lavender pants suit with a floral silk top emerged from the right corner of the room. Her blonde hair was swept up in a French twist giving her a sense of style and sophistication. She glided weightlessly across the floor and stopped in front of the wooden bookcase. She seemed vaguely familiar.

The woman gave a ghostly smile and slowly shrank into an orb of transparent light. It pulsated with a bluish aura causing the tension in Kathryn's body to subside. The ball of light slowly melded into the book, *The Lion, The Witch and The Wardrobe* by C.S. Lewis. Kathryn's eyelids began to flutter as she curled under the covers and fell into a peaceful dreamless sleep.

Kathryn stretched her arms over her head and thought about Janet. *'Wasn't she supposed to come over this morning for breakfast?'* She threw back the covers and started to get up to go downstairs when the reality of her situation set in. She quickly looked around the room but there was no sign of David. Her eye caught the book by C.S. Lewis on the bookshelf. She remembered the woman's apparition. After it had morphed into an orb, it exited through the book and she had fallen asleep.

She wondered why the woman's spirit was haunting the house. Did it have some unfinished business before she died? Was it lingering behind because of some loving memory that tied her to the house? Or was she there to communicate some imminent danger? Whatever it was she knew it wasn't here to harm her and in some strange way, she felt a sense of comfort knowing she wasn't alone.

Kathryn got up and went to the window. She pulled back the curtains and looked past the bars where the sky is overcast. She wondered if David was somewhere in the house or had he left. She quickly tiptoed over and pressed her ear against the door. She closed her eyes and listened. A floorboard creaked in the hallway. She quickly went back into bed and the instant she pulled up the covers the door slowly opened.

"Rebecca, are you awake?" whispered David.

She lay there shaking, holding her breath, with her heart beating like the thrumming wings of a caged bird. She prayed he didn't come any further. The door closed and she waited. She sighed with relief as his footsteps echoed across the hall and down the steps. She sat up, stared at the door and wondered how she was ever going to get out of this mess.

The sun peeked through the window, causing a prism of light to dance across Kathryn's face. She rolled over on her side, thinking she was home; safely snug in her own bed. However, the ugly truth emerged when she opened her eyes and the deadbolt slid back on the door.

"Wake up, my Sleeping Beauty." David cheerfully bounced into the room carrying a breakfast tray of eggs, bacon, toast, orange juice, and coffee.

*Sleeping Beauty?* If he thought, he was her Prince Charming, he had another thing coming; just the thought of him giving her one of those sloppy kisses on the lips, made her skin crawl.

"I hope you're hungry." He set the tray on the dresser and pulled back the curtains on the window. "The bars add a special touch, don't you think?" He turned and lifted his eyebrows.

"If you like jail." She forgot her promise to keep sweet.

"Well, get used to it." He strutted to the dresser and picked up the tray. "Until you can be trusted, the bars will be a permanent fixture."

If she hadn't been so hungry, she would've slapped the tray out of his hands as he set it across her lap.

"I see the room is nice and toasty. I checked on you during the night and you were snug as a bug in a rug." He grabbed a couple of pillows and placed them behind her back.

She picked up the glass of orange juice and took a sip. "Right after you left, the room temperature went back to normal."

"Are you insinuating I was the reason the room was cold?"

"No." She set the glass back on the tray.

"Because if you are, I can make this room pretty toasty." He gently touched her hair and let his fingers trail lightly down the side of her neck.

"Thank you for breakfast." She picked up the napkin and pulled out the fork wanting to stab him with it.

"You're welcome." Pleased she was staying sweet. "I have a few errands to run today. I shouldn't be gone too long. Once I get back, I will prepare your bath, so you can get ready for our special romantic evening together."

After he turned to leave, she picked up the glass and placed a bull's eye on the back of his head. She had been a pitcher on an  all-women's baseball team and could throw a pretty mean curveball. Deciding it wasn't worth the risk she placed the glass back on the tray.

"Oh, before I leave," he turned and touched his index finger to his chin, "I'll be using the intercom on the nightstand to communicate. So, when you hear my voice, I expect you to respond immediately." With a nod he left.

She picked up the toast, took a bite, and knew keeping sweet under these conditions wasn't going to be easy. However, if she wanted to  survive, she had to reign in her temper and control her tongue.

After she finished her breakfast, she placed the tray on the dresser, and went to the window. She looked past the bars where a forest of trees lined the border of the property. The mountains towering in the background, mocked her with a challenge she couldn't match, and knew there was a slim chance of ever escaping. Her heart fell into a trapdoor of hopelessness as she crawled back into bed, pulled the covers over  her head and wept.

Ninety minutes later her eyes started moving rapidly back and forth beneath closed lids at the distant sound of someone calling for Rebecca. When no answer was forthcoming, the voice only got louder.

*Why don't they answer so the obnoxious voice will just shut up?* She thought.

"Rebecca!" This time the voice was firm.

She slowly opened her eyes, feeling a little disoriented. The voice called a second time but she wasn't sure where it was coming from. She peeked out from under the covers and saw the red light flashing on the intercom. Immediately, she knew the voice was David's. She started to answer, but it was too late; he was already pounding up the stairs. She scooted against the headboard, hugged her knees to her chest as the deadbolt slammed back. He burst through the door and she knew she was in trouble.

"Why didn't you answer me?" He demanded as he rushed over, his hand raised in the air to strike.

"I'm sorry I didn't hear you."

"I fix you breakfast and this is how you repay me?"

"I promise it won't happen again!"

"You're damn straight it won't!" He slapped her across the face with his lips pulled back baring his teeth.

Kathryn cowered against the headboard at the guttural sound coming from the back of his throat. His neck muscles coiled with tension. The blackness of his eyes gave her a death stare and she knew this man could kill her at any moment, or at least severely harm her.

David jerked his hands through his hair, pursed his lips, and started pacing the floor like a wild man. Suddenly, he stopped in front of the mirror and stared at his reflection.

*"Calm down you imbecile and get a hold of yourself. She still thinks she's Kathryn. You've got to give her a little more time to get used to being Rebecca again."*

David acted like he never heard a word the voice said as he blindly sat down in the chair next to the bookcase. He leaned forward, placed an elbow on his knee, and supported his chin with his hand. Absorbed in thought, he was the perfect image of *The*

*Thinker.* After several minutes, he sat up and stared at Kathryn.

"I'm sorry. I didn't mean to lose my temper but, from here on out, you will answer to Rebecca. Understood?"

"Yes, I'm sorry. I just need a little more time to adjust." She lowered her eyes.

"Apology accepted." He got up and stood in front of the bookcase. "In a couple of hours I'm going to prepare your bath. Until then I suggest you read a book to occupy your time. When I'm ready, I'll call you on the intercom and I expect you to answer to Rebecca." He made his way to the door and left.

Kathryn promised herself she would do everything she could to play by his rules. So, if he wanted her to read a book, answer to Rebecca and keep sweet while doing it, she would be the sweetest bee in his honeycomb. Once she figured out his weaknesses, she would plant her stinger so deep into his jugular; he was going to regret he ever stirred up this hornet's nest.

She stepped into the white clawfoot tub and, inch by inch, lowered herself into the hot water. Her skin turned beet red and she was tempted to turn on the cold water, but she had been instructed not to. It was her punishment for ruining the first cleansing ritual and, if she disobeyed, a bucket of boiling hot water would be added to the mix.

She grabbed the bar of sage soap and rubbed it across the loofah sponge like it was a magic lamp. All she needed now was a genie to pop out and grant her three wishes. To be transported back to the morning Richard asked her to stay home so the accident would've never  happen. To grant her a long life with her family so she could love them unconditionally. And finally, to wipe this psycho off the face of the earth so he couldn't hurt another living soul.

After she made sure all the dry skin was exfoliated off her body, she grabbed the white washcloth and washed her intimate parts as he had instructed. With twenty minutes to spare, she laid back, closed her eyes, and drifted off to sleep.

Fifteen minutes later, her eyes jerked opened and she glanced over at the timer. With only five minutes left, she quickly stood up hoping she had enough time to finish before David showed up. She pushed down the stopper to drain out the water, pulled the shower curtain around her, washed her hair, and rinsed herself off. The second she turned off the water she heard footsteps outside the door.

"Rebecca."

"Yes?" She pushed back the curtain and stepped out onto the white rug.

"Time is ticking."

"I'll be out in a second."

"Do you need any help, because I can certainly oblige?"

"No, I'm almost done." She reached for the towel hanging on the silver ring next to the sink.

Kathryn wiped herself down, wrapped the towel around her hair, and tiptoed across the ceramic tile. She grabbed the black terry cloth robe off the back of the door. Engraved in gray on the right breast pocket were the initials TC. She put it on, tied the belt several times into a knot, took a deep breath, and stepped out into the hallway. David was nowhere to be found. She wondered if this was a test to see if she would try to escape. Even though it was tempting to run down the stairs, she knew it was a bad idea, so she made her way to the bedroom for further instructions.

She stepped into the room where the emerald gown was lying on the bed along with a black laced bra and matching panties. The closer she got, the more she realized they were identical to the ones Richard had bought her last year on Valentine's Day before the accident. She narrowed her eyes, took a step closer realizing he had altered the initials engraved in red on the lace underwear from KR to RH. The thought of him touching anything intimate of hers made her sick, but to alter a memory she had cherished with her husband made her down-right furious.

David quietly stepped up behind her, slipped his arms around her waist, and lightly kissed her on the back of the neck.

"Mm … You smell delightful. You're obedience has pleased me."

Kathryn began to chant the 'keep sweet' mantra in her head to keep her from turning around and nailing him right between the legs.

"I'm glad you're pleased." The words left a bitter taste in her mouth as she closed her eyes and took a deep breath.

David gently squeezed her shoulders, stepped to where the bouquet of daylilies, tulips, daises, and stargazers graced the dresser in a crystal vase.

"Unfortunately, I had to leave the original bouquet behind, so I've tried my best to duplicate the arrangement you made for me back in Madison."

"Thank you. They're lovely."

"Rebecca, I want to remind you after your little escapade through the woods, I had to take your gown to the cleaners. This dress is very important to me. It's identical to the one you wore the night we met eighteen years ago, so it has sentimental value. I assure you that if you mess it up again, this time both of you will be buried six feet under. Do I make myself clear?"

By the firm look on his face she knew he meant it. "Yes, I understand."

"Now, I took the liberty of taking some intimate belongings from your house," he picked up the black panties. "I hope you don't mind."

"Would it make any difference if I did?"

"Not really. So get dressed. I have a romantic evening prepared for us. So don't ruin it like you did the first time because you don't want to know what I'm capable of. Now, when you're ready I want you to use the intercom to let me know and I'll come and get you." He marched out of the room.

After she got dressed, she went to the nightstand, not looking forward to the evening. Sure she was hungry and could use something to eat. However, she didn't think she would be able to stomach what he had planned afterwards. Just the thought of his soft, manicured hands touching her made her skin crawl. If she had anything to do with it, that was never going to happen.

Kathryn took a deep breath, pressed the intercom button, and said, "David, I'm ready."

"The door is unlocked, so I want you to go out into the hallway and wait."

She stepped out into the hall and waited under the chandelier while David made his way up the steps dressed in a black tuxedo.

"Beautiful."

"Thank you." She forced a smile.

"Shall we?" He extended his arm.

She slipped her arm through his as they made their way to the stairs. With each step, she repeated the 'keep sweet' mantra in her head, a total of thirteen times. It was the same traditional number of steps in the old west that had led up to the gallows. She knew somewhere along the line, a hangman's noose was waiting. She just didn't know when, how, or what kind.

He led her through an archway on the right into a room dimly lit by an antique bronze-plated chandelier. He escorted her across the hardwood floor to where two matching, rose-colored, wing back chairs stood in front of a brick fireplace. The warmth and glow of the fire would've made the atmosphere romantic and cozy if the situation had been different. She thought about the flashback she had back in Madison while looking at her reflection in the mirror and realized this was the same room.

"Do you think she's beautiful?" David reached above the mantel on the fireplace and took down the portrait of a woman with bright red hair pulled back into a French twist.

"She's lovely."

"Looks are deceiving."

"Who is she?"

"Why, this is my beloved mother."

"You must care about her very much."

He gently caressed his mother's face. "Rebecca, did you know according to English folklore, redheads are expected to be hot-tempered, treacherous, and cause nothing but trouble?"

Kathryn wasn't sure where he was going with this folklore about redheads, but she decided to engage in his little sidebar.

"Well, I think most redheads get a bum rap." She raised her  eyebrows and slightly shrugged her shoulders. "I believe we are just very passionate about life."

"You may be right. However, folklore also states redheads have such bad breath that they can raise blisters on other people simply by breathing on them." He hung the picture back on the wall. "Rebecca, are you going to breathe on me just like my mother?"

"I guess that's yet to be seen," she said, realizing it was contempt he felt for his mother and not love.

"I'll take that as a challenge." He raised his eyebrows.

He escorted her back out of the room where she noticed a fully stocked bookcase with white pane glassed doors on her right. Most of the books had to do with the culinary world. However, when she spotted the book *Prophets Prey: My Seven-Year Investigation into Warren Jeffs and the Fundamentalist Church of the Latter Day Saints*, she knew where he got the 'keep sweet' mantra ideology.

They continued out of the room where she noticed a child-sized princess table with four matching chairs in the corner. It was the exact same set she had bought Rachel for her birthday. The morning before the accident, her daughter sat Pooh Bear, Panda Bear, and Pearl Bear at the table and promised she'd be home after school to have a tea party. Later that evening, Kathryn trudged up the stairs where the bears were waiting, closed the door, and left the room untouched. She glanced at David and had a notion to slap him across the face for contaminating the sacred space of her daughter. Instead, she vowed she would get even and show him just how hot this red-haired dragon's breath could get.

# CHAPTER 14

The evening sun filtered through the glass door while dust particles danced in mid-air to the soft music in the background. The candlelit table dressed in a white tablecloth covered with red rose petals set the mood for a romantic evening. However, the only thing Kathryn could think about was the princess table in the sitting room. Who did he think he was, strolling right into her life and touching everything that was sacred? She still had a notion to reach across the table and slap him across the face.

"Rebecca, let's make a toast to our perfect evening together." David lifted his wine glass.

"May I do the honors?" She picked up her glass.

"Please, by all means." She could tell he was a little caught off guard.

"Let this evening be one to remember." She slammed the top of her glass on the edge of the table, stood up, leaned forward, and drove the jagged edge into his juggler.

*Wishful thinking,* she thought, lightly tapping his glass and took a sip. No way was she going to make the same mistake twice. She would keep herself in check, stay sweet, win his trust, catch him off guard, and blindside him.

"I hope you don't mind, but I took the liberty and confiscated this song from your CD collection at your house before we left."

The song playing in the background was "Nightingale" by Yanni. There was no way she was going to let this moron contaminate the special memory of this song. Before she was tempted to follow through with slicing his jugular, her mind drifted back to the day Richard proposed to her in his one bedroom apartment.

"This song is beautiful," Kathryn had laid her head on Richard's shoulder.

"I knew you'd like it." He gently kissed the back of her hand.

"Who's the artist?" She snuggled closer to him.

"It's called "Nightingale" by Yanni, a Greek composer with a little bit of jazz, classical, and soft rock blended together."

"Well, it's lovely."

"Did you know the nightingale gets its name because it sings at night?"

"Really, I would've never have guessed, considering it's the first syllable of the bird's name." She laughed.

"You're real funny." He pulled her even closer and kissed the top of her head. "They also claim it's only the nocturnal unpaired males that sing regularly hoping to attract a mate."

"Now when did you become so smart about birds?"

"The moment I fell in love with you." He got up and knelt down in front of her. "Kathryn Irene Oates, will you be my nightingale?" He reached into his pocket and pulled out a princess cut, diamond engagement ring.

"Rebecca." David's voice brought her back to the reality of her situation.

"What?" She looked up.

"Would you like to dance?" He extended his hand across the table.

"I'm hungry. Could we please eat first?" She pressed a hand against her stomach determined not to let him taint the one song that meant everything to her.

"Certainly, but before we do, I want to remind you. That if you try to escape, like you did the last time and ruin our beautiful night together, you will live to regret it. Rebecca, one way or the other you will be mine. You can make it easy or difficult—it's up to you."

"You have nothing to worry about. I'm looking forward to our evening together," she lied.

"Very well, I hope you enjoy the dinner I've prepared."

Aphrodisiac was the first word that came into her mind when David served a dinner of cream of asparagus soup, broiled lobster tail with melted butter for dipping, and mushrooms cooked with risotto. She had to admit the food looked delicious, but if he thought his cooking was going to stimulate her brain and libido, he was sadly mistaken.

"So you're a chef." She took a bite of the soup.

"Yes."

"This is delicious." She actually meant it.

"I'm glad you like it."

"So where do you work?" Wanting to know a little bit more about him.

"I'm the sole business owner of, Temporary Chef. I started the business about ten years ago after I got out of culinary school. My job is to go into restaurants and revamp their old menu to something more adventurous. I stay for a couple of weeks to train their cooks and, when everything is running smoothly, I leave. After about a month, I go back just to be sure they've stayed on track."

"So, did you always want to be a chef?" She took a sip of her wine, remembering the initials on his robe.

"Yes, don't you remember? We talked about it the night of your parent's dinner party? How I wanted to be a chef, but my mother insisted I become a lawyer and your mother insisted you marry one?"

"I'm sorry. I don't remember."

"It doesn't matter. The important thing is we're here now. Let's eat our dinner and hopefully our time together will help regain your memory of us."

After they finished, he grabbed her plate off the table. "Would you like dessert?"

"Yes, thank you."

David left and several minutes later he was back carrying a plate of strawberries with homemade chocolate dipping sauce.

"Here you go." He set the dessert on the table and sat down.

"They look delicious." She picked up a strawberry, dipped it into the sauce, and casually popped it into her mouth to make it as non-sensual as possible.

"Rebecca, there's something I want to show you." He reached inside his jacket, pulled out a picture, and handed it to her.

The picture was of a much younger David standing in front of a fireplace wearing a black suit next to a young girl dressed in the same identical gown she was wearing now. By the way she was raising her eyebrows and tilting her head, you could tell she really didn't want to be there. She realized the picture was the merging of the two flashbacks she had in the flower shop and in her bedroom mirror back in Madison.

"Does it help bring back any memories at all?"

"Why, should it?"

"Yes, because the girl is you, eighteen years ago in this very house. Your mother took the picture in the sitting room the night of the dinner party where we first met."

While she stared at the picture the music in the background began to fade and her field of vision started to turn black. She placed her elbows on the table and rubbed her right temple. A white light flashed before her while her amnesia receded like a tsunami, creating a wave trough of memories. She stood up. A sharp pain started at the base of her skull and traveled up across her head. A memory shard of David rushed in, and she crumbled to the floor.

✄    ✄    ✄

"You're mom tells me you'll be graduating from high school this year," David stood in front of her next to the fireplace.

"Yes." Rebecca took a step back, not comfortable with him  invading her space.

"So, I guess you'll be heading off to college in the fall?"

"Not sure." She was short and straight to the point, not wanting to have this trivial conversation.

"And why's that?" David took a sip of his punch with a little vodka he added to the mix.

"Listen, I know what my mother is trying to do, so let's just quit  all the small talk."

"What are you talking about?"

"Oh, I'm sure you don't have any idea?" She clenched her jaw and crossed her arms while she tapped her foot.

"No, I don't."

"So we're playing that game." She rubbed her brow as if to ward off a headache.

"What game?"

213

"Well, let me enlighten you." She lifted her glass and took a sip of punch. "Mother invited you here tonight so I'd fall madly in love with you and hopefully dump my boyfriend, who she desperately hates, so her world will be perfect again."

"I had no idea." He stepped toward her.

"I'm sure you didn't." She took a step back knowing this boy was a sleaze ball even if her mother couldn't see it. "So, this conversation is over, and Mother's perfect plan has just backfired."

She glared at him for a second, flung her long auburn hair back over her shoulders and left. She stepped through the hallway and into the living room where the so-called high society people milled around as if their behinds didn't stink. She strode across the dining room and made her way into the kitchen where her mother was bent over the stove.

"Mother, if you think your little scheme is going to work, you got another think coming. I'm going upstairs to change. Afterwards, I'm going out in the barn to brush down Sadie."

Olivia Hilliard looked up at her daughter while she pulled the tray of chestnuts wrapped in bacon out of the oven.

"The horse can wait. I'd like you to keep David company." She closed the oven door with her knee, set the tray on top of the stove, and removed the mittens from her hands.

"I know what you're trying to do, and it won't work." She planted her hands on her hips. "I'm in love with Will and there's nothing you, David, or anybody else can do to change that."

"No daughter of mine is going to date the son of the town drunk. I won't have you disgracing the Hilliard name with the likes of him." Her mother pursed her lips and blew a strand of blonde hair off her forehead.

"Mother, I'm almost eighteen and you can't tell me what to do."

"Young lady, as long as you live in this house, you will abide by my rules, and I forbid you to see that good-for-nothing bum."

"Fine, have it your way." She crossed her arms and cocked her head to the side. "I'll abide by your rules for now, but after graduation, I'm out of here." She stomped out of the room.

❡      ❡      ❡

The memory faded as Kathryn realized the apparition in the room had been her real mother. David picked her up off the floor and it felt like her head was about ready to explode as he carried her through the kitchen, up the back stairs, and into her bedroom.

"Rebecca, tonight you will not deny me what's rightfully mine," he whispered. He laid her on the bed, slipped his finger under the strap of her dress, slipped it down over her shoulder and lightly kissed her neck.

She decided to play possum because if he was going to kiss her with those wet, pink, ugly full lips, she'd be damned if she would participate. She allowed her muscles to go limp and imagined herself walking on a white sandy beach with the wind caressing her face next to Richard.

"*Stop!*

Startled by the harsh whisper against her ear, Kathryn caught her breath and lay perfectly still to see what would happen next.

"*This is not the plan.*"

"I don't care! I've waited eighteen long years for this and nothing you say will change my mind." He turned her on her side and started to unzip her dress.

"*Go ahead.*" The voice warned. "*If you go through with this, we're finished and this time I mean it.*"

David let go of the zipper and she knew he was giving some thought to what the voice said. The instant she rolled back onto the bed, she wanted to reach up and kiss the voice square on the lips.

"Okay!" He threw up his hands and got up.

He opened the top drawer of the dresser, pulled out a red silk, knee-length gown, and stared at his refection in the mirror.

"You know sometimes you can be a kill joy and a pain in the ass."

"*Yeah, well, the feelings are mutual.*"

Without another word, David sat down on the edge of the bed, rolled Kathryn on her side, and started to unzip her dress.

"*Close your eyes!*" the voice demanded.

"What the hell for?"

"*The covenant states, until the will of the woman is broken into submission, you can't look upon her. If in three months she does not submit willingly, the covenant is void, and you can do with her whatever ever the hell you want."*

With a sigh, David unzipped her dress and gently let her roll over onto her back. He slipped the straps of the gown over her shoulders while Kathryn peeked to see if he was looking. Blindly, he took off the dress, laid it on the bottom of the bed, and put the nightgown on her.

"Happy?" David opened his eyes.

*"Ecstatic. Now let's go get a drink."*

"Sounds like a great idea." He covered her up, lightly kissed her on the cheek, got up and paused.

*"Don't even think about it!"*

"I'm not." He took a step back, strode across the floor, and left.

Several minutes later the front door opened and slammed shut. Kathryn got out of bed and made her way to the window. She slowly opened it while David crossed the graveled driveway toward his truck, having a heated conversation with himself. He got in and she heard him mumble, "You better make this worth my while," before he slammed the door shut and drove off.

She quickly stepped back when the headlights shone through the upstairs window. When she no longer heard the gravel under the tires, she pressed her cheek against the bars. On her left stood a red barn with the advertisement logo, "Chew Mail Pouch Tobacco, Treat Yourself to the Best," painted in big white letters on the side. A sudden, sharp pain shot across the top of her head like a brain freeze, but ten times worse. She grabbed a hold of the bars and, as they slipped through her fingers, she collapsed on the floor, where the rest of the memory played out.

※　　※　　※

"So there you are." David strolled into the barn.

"I guess Mother sent you out to look for me." Rebecca continued to brush the chestnut mare without looking up.

"No, I asked her where you were."

"Well, here I am. You can leave now."

"Please, don't send me back to those fuddy-duddies."

"You can stay under one condition."

"Just name it."

"You tell my mother we hit it off so she can get off my back."

"No problem."

"Great." She put down the brush and started to leave.

"Where are you going?"

"I'm going back to the house."

"Well, I'm afraid you're not going to get off that easy. If you want me to get your mother off your back, you're going to have to do better than that."

"Like what?"

"Well, for starters, you can get me something to drink and we could sit down, have a nice little conversation, and get to know one another."

"Okay, but we're going to make this short and sweet." She headed for the loft.

She started up the steps when an uneasy feeling came over her. Something told her she should turn around and go back to the house because there was something about this guy that just didn't add up. Yet, getting her mother off her back was more important than her intuition, so she made her way up into the loft.

"So what do you want to drink?" She stepped into the kitchenette on her left and opened the refrigerator.

"Do you have any beer?"

"Nope, just water and Coke."

"Powder or liquid?" he laughed.

"Don't be stupid. I don't do drugs." She grabbed a can of Coke and tossed it to him.

"It was just a joke." He raised his eyebrows while he caught the can with one hand.

"Sorry. I'm just pissed off at my mom, and I'm taking it out on you." She grabbed a bottle of water and slammed the door shut.

"No problem. Parents have a way of doing that." He opened the can and took a drink.

"So where do you go to school?" She hopped up on the counter and sat down.

"I'm in my second year of a four-year, undergraduate degree in Criminal Justice. Once that's finished, it's on to three years of law school."

"So you want to be a big time lawyer?"

"No, what I really wanted to do was go to culinary school to become a chef."

"Why didn't you?"

"My mother insisted she was going to have a lawyer in the family come hell or high water."

"Well, my mother insists I marry one, which is why I'm assuming she invited you here tonight, just to make sure that happened."

"Well, it looks like we've been setup."

"It certainly does, but her little scheme is not going to work, so she might as well give it up."

"So, what's the deal? Who's this boyfriend she wants to get rid of?"

"You know, I really didn't come up here to talk about my personal life." She hopped down off the counter.

"Where are you going?"

"I'm going back to the house."

"Come on, we just got here."

"Okay, but no more personal stuff."

"Deal. Do you have any music to go along with this Coke?"

"Sure, what do you want to listen to?"

"Do you have any Rolling Stones?"

"Duh … What's music without Mick?" She went to the cassette player on the counter.

"Don't you have a CD player?"

"Yes, but this collection of songs belongs to my dad, and he's old school." Rebecca opened a case on the counter, pulled out a Rolling Stones tape, slipped it into the player, and pressed play.

"Want some?" He pulled a joint out of the inside pocket of his jacket while the song, "I Can't Get No Satisfaction," filtered through the air.

"Nope, I told you I don't do drugs. Bad for the brain."

"Suit yourself." He pulled a lighter out of his pocket and lit it up.

"Well, I'm going to go. You can see yourself out when you're ready to leave."

"Here, it'll calm your nerves and make you feel better." David handed her the joint.

"No thanks."

"Maybe we can do this again sometime."

"I don't think so. I held up my end of the bargain and now all you have to do is tell my mother we hit it off." She headed for the door.

"You're not going anywhere, until I get what I came out here for." He grabbed her from behind.

"Let me go!" She kicked and screamed while he dragged her across the floor to a pile of hay in the corner.

"If you scream one more time I will cut you from ear to ear." He pulled out a knife and placed it across her throat.

David pushed her to the floor and, as she scrambled to the corner of the barn, he cut the rope off a bale of hay. He grabbed her, turned her over on her stomach, and tied her hands behind her back.

"Let me go and I'll forget any of this happened." She puffed a piece of straw out of her mouth.

"I don't think you're in a position to negotiate." He turned her over.

"Please don't." She begged when he straddled her.

221

"Oh, God, you're beautiful." He laid down the knife. "Shall we give your mother what she wanted?" With a grin he took off his jacket.

❆ ❆ ❆

The pain in her head subsided, leaving in its wake a sense of  numbness. An unnatural stillness came over the room when the memory of the violation faded and she got up from the floor. Heat flushed through her body, causing her nostrils to flare. She clutched the bars, stared out the window, and knew there were three things she was sure of. One, she was Rebecca Hilliard and Kathryn Rubin all wrapped up in one. Two, she was mad as hell at the man who stole her innocence. And three—hell hath no fury like a woman scorned.

# CHAPTER 15

M arilyn sat in the corner of the Blue Moon Café. It had been three days since the incident in the cave with William. True to his word she hadn't seen or heard from him. She leafed through the guide book of Ireland and thought maybe it was time for a change. What better way to do that than to go to Dublin and have a beer for her brother? After she found out he wasn't her biological brother she realized it didn't matter. He had been everything a brother should be and more. He had been her best friend, her confidant and she missed him terribly. He always had a way of calming her fears and making her see things in a different light. Perhaps honoring his memory and going to the land he loved would make her feel closer to him. Besides, she could use the change of scenery.

She took a sip of wine as Jim and Sarah came through the door. After the waiter seated them across the room, she watched while he tenderly brushed a strand of long, blonde hair away from her face. He covered her hands with his, leaned forward, gazed into her eyes, and lightly kissed her natural, full lips.

Marilyn had experienced that same touch, that same look, that same kiss. Now she was on the outside looking in. She wondered how long before the other woman would notice he no longer gazed into her eyes as he kissed her, and that she no longer felt the tender touch of his hands. She wondered when Sarah would start to notice how  he criticized every little thing she did, like a fork left in the sink or a shirt lying on the floor. When she decided not to sweat the small stuff, and made sure everything was in its rightful place just to please him? And before she knew it, he would have complete control of every aspect of their relationship. The day would come she would have his baby, and when she was no longer his trophy wife. She would be right where Marilyn was, on the outside looking in at the other woman.

She took another sip of wine while Sarah got up and went to the restroom. Jim glanced around the room and spotted her in the corner. As he stood and headed for her table she remembered the day he came into her café while William was there.  He had apologized for hurting her and blaming her for Emily's disappearance. Granted, she was still hurt by his betrayal. However, she decided to give it a rest, call it a truce, and put their differences aside to try to get through this  terrible ordeal.

"Hey." Jim stepped up to the table. "You must've had a craving for the Kimster."

The Kimster was a sandwich of breaded eggplant cutlets, fresh mozzarella cheese, and basil pesto heated and served on a ciabatta roll. When she was pregnant with Emily, there were weeks she ate the sandwich for lunch every day. After a while, she was known as 'the Kimster lady' to the employees of the Blue Moon.

"I guess some habits die hard."

"You're not working at the café tonight?"

"Yes, I'm just taking a break. After I leave here I'm going back to close up."

"Are you doing okay?"

"I'm doing fine."

Sarah returned to the table and Jim said, "I'm sorry. I didn't know you were going to be here."

She looked at him and knew her feelings for him had changed. It was more of a sadness of what they could have had, not what they lost. She knew his affair was only a symptom of a broken relationship. It had only become a scapegoat for all the other problems that had already existed in their marriage. It was time to move on and let go of the bitterness so they could spend their energy on finding their daughter, not fighting with each other.

"Jim, it's not a problem." This time she actually meant it. "I was just getting ready to leave anyway."

"Well, I better go."

"Okay, have a good evening."

"You, too," he strolled back to his table while Sarah kept an eye on him.

Marilyn finished her wine and, just when she was about to get up, William strolled through the door dressed in a pair of jeans and a black t-shirt. She quickly sat back down when he went to the bar and ordered a beer. She thought about the kiss they had shared and him calling her Rebecca. He had made it perfectly clear it wasn't her lips he was  kissing. Now she realized the cave had only been their foxhole, and the kiss was the emotional result of him saving her life.

Several minutes later he got up and headed to the restroom. Not wanting to be here when he got back, she dashed across the floor, and headed to the counter to pay her bill. She got behind a woman who was taking her good old time searching through her purse for the right change. She ran a hand through her hair while her eyes darted toward the men's room. Please stay there until I leave, she prayed. She folded her arms and started tapping her foot when the woman finally  found the thirty-five cents she needed to pay the rest of her bill.

"Sorry." The woman glanced back at her.

"No problem." Marilyn raised her eyebrows and stepped up to the counter. She handed the cashier the bill along with a twenty, told her  to keep the change, and quickly headed for the door.

"Marilyn," said William.

Her body stiffened and she closed her eyes at the sound of his voice. She knew she couldn't ignore him, so she took a deep breath, turned, and confronted him.

"William." She slowly exhaled hoping he didn't notice.

"Do you have a minute?"

She thought about the last conversation they had in the cave after he had rescued her from drowning.

After he had showed her the necklace and she accused him of having something to do with Rebecca's disappearance, he dramatically left the cave. He had returned some time later, got into his sleeping bag and gave her the silent treatment. It had been one long night. The next morning, when the hikers showed up to rescue them, she had never been so relieved.

"So you're talking to me now?" She slightly cocked her head.

"Please, I promise I won't keep you long."

"Just for a few minutes because I've got to get back to the café." She decided it wouldn't hurt to hear him out.

They stepped out onto the patio where a spring-fed stream ran through the outdoor seating area, and sat under a canopy of trees. The rushing water always had a way of relaxing and soothing her spirit, but this time it did nothing to calm the nerves she felt in the pit of her stomach.

"Do you want something to drink?"

"No, just say what you have to say so I can go."

"Well, the truth is I was on my way to your café tonight, but I chickened out and ended up here. I thought if I had a couple of drinks it might help me get up the nerve to come and talk to you."

"I don't understand. After we left the cave you made it perfectly clear you had no intention of seeing or talking to me again."

"I know. I was wrong. I shouldn't have flown off the handle like I did, and I'm sorry."

"Why the change of heart?"

"I've had time to think about it and you had every right not to trust me, especially after I showed you the necklace. Marilyn, I swear I didn't have anything to do with Rebecca's disappearance, and I don't know what to say to convince you otherwise."

"You're right. I had every right not to trust you. However, I shouldn't have jumped to conclusions. Besides, the more I thought about how you risked your own life to save me from drowning, I knew there was no way you were responsible for Rebecca's disappearance or harming her."

"So, all is forgiven and we can call this a truce?"

"Yes, I guess so."

"Good, because I really didn't want to have to get down on my hands and knees and beg."

"Well, on second thought," she cocked her head and raised her eyebrows, "I might enjoy seeing you beg."

"If you want, I can do it right now." He started to get down on one knee.

"No, that won't be necessary." She looked around and saw several people staring.

"Are you sure? Because I'm not beneath eating some humble pie." He laughed.

"I'm sure."

"Good, now that I've got that out of the way, I could use a drink. How about you?"

"Okay, why not."

After the server brought them their drinks, William took a sip of his beer and leaned back in his chair. "Marilyn, there's something I want to ask you."

"What's that?" She took a sip of her wine.

"I'm thinking about going back to the cave and doing some exploring to see if Rebecca left any more clues. Are you interested in coming along? This time instead of taking the river, we can drive to the site and hike down to the cave."

"What? You don't want to take the canoe?"

"No, I'm not willing to take the risk of losing you again. Besides, I'm still having nightmares from the last trip. Only this time I'm bent over your body giving you a chest compression when all of a sudden you take a deep breath, open your eyes, and for a brief moment blankly stare at me. You exhale, close your eyes, and you're gone."

"Well, I'm afraid that wasn't a nightmare."

"What do you mean?"

She told him about her near death experience. How she floated above the trees and watched him trying to save her and begging her not to die. The next thing she knew, she was traveling through a tunnel toward a bright light where she enters the presence of her mother. Her mother told her it wasn't her time because Emily needed her and so did her sister. Told her to be strong. The next thing she knew, she was back in her body.

"Why didn't you tell me about it while we were in the cave?"

"Well, if I remember correctly, you were pretty upset with me after you showed me the necklace and I accused you of having something to do with Rebecca's disappearance. Afterwards you gave me the silent treatment, so I guess I never got the opportunity to tell you."

"Ah, yes, I remember now," he nodded his head. "So, will you go with me to the cave? I promise this time I won't give you the silent treatment."

"Sure, why not. When do you want to go?"

"I've got to go see my sister in Savannah. The authorities told her they may have a lead in finding her ex-husband Seth. I'll give you a call when I get back and we can make plans."

Marilyn looked down at her watch. "Listen, I've got to get back to the café and help Carmen close up."

"Let me walk you out."

They walked outside where William realized she didn't have her car.

"Do you want a ride back to the café?" he offered.

"No, it's not that far. Besides, the walk will do me good."

"I'll give you a call in a couple of days."

"Okay." She started to leave.

"Marilyn." He touched her arm.

She looked into his eyes as her heart quickened. It was the look her father had given her mother while they glided across the dance floor. It was the look that passed between Charlie and Violet on the patio the night of the dinner party. It was the look she had never experienced until now.

"Marilyn, make no mistake this kiss is for you." He placed his lips gently on hers and let them linger for several seconds. As he pulled away, the sparks in his eyes left her speechless.

"I'll call you in a couple of days." He gently lifted her chin and kissed her a second time leaving her breathless.

"Okay," she whispered.

She started back to the café after he went back inside the Blue Moon. Mesmerized by the kiss still lingering on her lips, she didn't notice the gray truck approaching until it pulled up alongside her.

"Excuse me. Can you help me?"

"What?" Marilyn glanced into the truck where a man with light hair was leaning across the seat.

"Can you tell me how to get to the Bistro 112 restaurant?"

"Yes, all you have to do is turn around, go to the end of the road, make a right onto German Street, and it'll be on your left."

"Hey, Ms. J.," Kyle yelled while he ran across the street. "Everything alright?"

"Yes, just giving some directions to the Bistro."

"Oh really." He looked inside the truck, sizing up the occupant. "I think it's time for you to move on."

"Kyle, don't be so rude."

"Ms. J., I don't like the way this 'bozo' is looking at you."

"Don't be ridiculous." She looked at the man. "I'm sorry. He gets a little over protective."

"I can see that. Before I leave, can you recommend something on the Bistro menu?"

"Try the L'entreote au poivre. It's the French-style grilled steak with peppercorn sauce served with pommes frites."

"Sounds delicious. Thank you Ms …"

"Marilyn and you're welcome."

After the truck drove away, Kyle said, "Ms. J. don't you know you shouldn't talk to strangers? You never know what they're up to."

"Kyle, as long as I have you around, I don't think I'll have anything to worry about."

"I'm going to walk you back to the café just in case that pervert comes back to bother you."

"Okay, if it makes you feel better."

Once he safely escorted her back to the café, and she'd closed up shop, she decided to stay there for the night instead of going home. She made herself a cup of Chamomile tea, headed to the sitting room, and sat in front of the fireplace. She stared into the flames and thought about her evening at the Blue Moon. It was there where her past, present, and future collided all in one place. Jim was her past, the present belonged to her, and her future rested, perhaps, in a kiss.

She finished her tea and decided to go upstairs and lay down. She grabbed the remote off the nightstand and turned the channel to *WHAG-TV* evening news. Exhausted, several minutes later the remote slipped from her fingers and she nodded off to sleep. About an hour later something jolted her awake. She laid there for a second and listened. It sounded like someone was downstairs, so she got up to investigate. She reached the top of the steps where she could hear somebody walking around in the café. She quietly stepped back, closed and locked the door, ran to the night stand, grabbed her cell phone, dialed 911, and turned off the light.

"911. What is your emergency?"

"Someone has just broken into my café," she whispered.

"Marilyn?"

"Yes."

"This is Libby."

"Libby, somebody has just broken into the café."

"Where are you?"

"I've locked myself in the upstairs apartment."

"Good, the police are on their way."

"I hear them coming up the steps."

"Just stay calm."

"They're pounding on the door. Can you hear them?"

"Yes, just stay on the line. Help is coming."

"Marilyn, I know you're in there, so let me in or I'm going to knock down this door." The voice was deep and drawn out.

"Libby," she whispered.

"Do you have another room you can go to and lock yourself in?"

"Yes, the bathroom."

"Go, just stay on the phone."

Marilyn ran into the bathroom and just as she closed and locked the door the intruder kicked the apartment door in.

"I know you're in here."

Marilyn quickly locked the door and looked around the room for something to protect herself. Her dad always told her she had everything she needed around her if she had to protect herself in the spur of the moment. She spotted the comb with the long slim handle on the sink, grabbed it, and hid in the shower. She slipped it between her fingers, wrapped her hand around the fine tooth comb, ready to jab the point into his juggler. At the sound of the sirens blaring in the background, the intruder hit the bathroom door, promised he'd be back, and ran out of the room.

"Libby, he's gone and the police are here."

"Okay, they'll take over from here."

"Thank you."

"You're welcome."

Marilyn stepped into the bedroom where the red and blue lights were flashing brightly. She looked out the window facing German Street where she saw Officer Tom getting out of the cruiser.

"Tom, I'm up here," she called, throwing open the window and leaning out.

"Marilyn, you okay?" he called back.

"Yes, whoever it was left the minute you pulled up."

"You stay put and we'll check things out."

Marilyn leaned against the window, grateful to have such a good relationship with the local law enforcement. When she'd first opened the shop, every morning for several weeks, she would always forget to turn off the alarm. After a while, she became known as the woman who cried wolf in the police department. Afraid they wouldn't heed her cry if it was really an emergency, she offered them a free coffee and donuts. Eventually, it graduated to a breakfast sandwich, to a full-fledged meal. Even after she stopped forgetting, the officers still came in and ate for free. She knew it was a small price to pay for her peace of mind. Besides, in the process she had forged a relationship with a great group of men and women.

"Marilyn, you can come down now." Officer Tom hollered up at the window.

She made her way downstairs to find Officer Tom and Officer Allen standing in front of the counter.

"Well, did you see anybody?"

"No," said Officer Tom.

"How did they get in?"

"Looks like a window was broken and they came through your patio door. Do you have any idea who it could've been?"

"No."

"Has there been anyone in the café acting strange lately?"

"Not really."

"What about in the neighborhood?"

"No not that I can think of. Kyle was suspicious of a man asking me for directions earlier, but the guy didn't do anything strange. I pointed him to the Bistro, he asked me what was good, I recommended the steak, and he thanked me and left."

"Marilyn, did you set your alarm?" asked Officer Allen.

"I must've forgotten because it didn't go off."

"Marilyn, if you forget to turn on the alarm, we can't get our free meals."

She looked up at Officer Allen wondering if he was serious but, when she saw him grinning, she knew he was only pulling her chain.

"Sorry, I'll make sure it won't happen again." She laughed. "But the intruder threatened me. He called me by name, and said he'd be back later."

"Well, the only thing we can do now is to file a report," said Officer Tom. "If you find anything missing, report it to your insurance company along with the damages to your door. For now, I suggest you go home and come back in the morning. Better yet, stay with a friend. I'm sure whoever it was won't be back tonight because we'll be patrolling the area."

"Alright, I'll give Dana a call to see if I can stay at her place."

"Good. I'll wait until you gather your stuff and on your way before we leave."

"Thanks guys. I guess I'm going to owe you big time for this."

"Don't worry about it. It's about time we earned all those free meals." said Officer Allen.

Marilyn smiled, thanked them for coming and made her way to the sitting room. She called Dana and told her what had happened. When Dana insisted she and Jason pick her up she didn't refuse.

She pulled back the curtain where a cruiser was parked across the street. Whoever had broken into the café could very well still be out there waiting for her to leave. She thought about the man's deep voice, and how it sent chills up her spine. It made her feel a lot safer knowing the police were close. If they hadn't shown up when they did, it's hard to tell what would've happened. With all the negative press law enforcement had been getting lately in the news, maybe it was time the world started focusing on the good officers. Without them, neighborhoods would be a lot more dangerous.

Dana's jeep pulled up out front, so she grabbed her overnight bag and went out into the café.

"Marilyn, are you okay?" Dana came running through the front door.

"Yes, I'm fine."

"Are you sure?"

"Yes."

"Let's get out of here."

"Dana, I really appreciate you letting me stay the night."

"No problem. That's what best friends are for. I'm just glad you're all right."

Marilyn started to get in the back seat of Dana's jeep and paused when she felt like someone was watching her. She looked around the empty streets with a gut feeling that what happened tonight was far from over.

# CHAPTER 16

Kathryn's stomach started to growl and it reminded her that the only thing she'd eaten for the last twenty-four hours were her returning memories, fully exposed like a six course meal. After she remembered David violating her in the barn, little by little her amnesia began to lose its grip. She knew now she was Rebecca, the daughter of Olivia and Frank Hilliard. This house is where she grew up, and the bedroom where she was being kept prisoner had once been a sanctuary from an overbearing and controlling mother. Her father had been a kind and gentle man, always trying to smooth things out. Most of the time, his tactics worked. Until, that is, the day her mother found out about Will Mitchell.

❋　　❋　　❋

"Rebecca Lynn! Get out here right this minute!" Her mother yelled outside the barn door.

"Well, Sadie, looks like I'm in trouble again. I'll be back once I'm finished getting my ass chewed." She put down the brush, kissed her horse on the cheek, and left.

"What now, Mother?" She came out of the barn wearing a pair of dirty overalls.

"What's that God-awful smell?" Olivia stood there with her blonde hair swept back into a French twist, dressed in a pair of designer jeans, and red silk blouse.

"Well, Mother, if you must know. I just finished shoveling a crap load of manure out of Sadie's stall." She pulled the gloves off her hands.

"I'll never understand why you want to mess around with that animal."

"Mother, did you want something? If not, I'm going to finish grooming Sadie."

"Well, I just got off the phone with Margaret."

"Oh, what did she want?"

If you wanted to know anything about anybody, all you had to do was call Margaret the busy-body. Rebecca was just wondering how she got on the town gossip's radar.

"I heard you've been hanging out with that good-for-nothing, son-of-a-drunk, Will Mitchell."

"Oh really? And where might I ask did Miss Busy Body get her information?"

"Her daughter Anne said she saw you two sitting at a corner table looking pretty cozy at Millie's."

"Well maybe little Miss Anne should mind her own business."

"So, it's true."

"Yes, I was sitting with Will during one of his breaks. So what? He's a nice guy. A lot nicer than the guys you want me to hang out with. At least Will treats me like a lady and not some piece of meat he wants to eat."

"Well, I forbid you to see him." Her mother crossed her arms and tapped her foot.

"Mother, I'm almost eighteen and you can no longer tell me who I can or cannot hang out with, much less tell me who I'm allowed to love."

"Oh, so you're in love with him now?" her mother yelled.

"Yes, and there's not a thing you can do about it?"

"Well, as long as you're under my roof you will abide by my rules and you will not see that … Well, for a lack of a better word, parasite. Do I make myself clear?"

Her mother did an about face like a drill sergeant and went back into the house. The screen door slammed shut behind her and Rebecca knew the discussion about Will was off the table.

Kathryn stepped to the window where the sun was slipping behind the mountains and remembered the day she had broken up with Will. Several weeks after David had brutally deflowered her in the barn, he had called asking why she was avoiding him. That's when she told him she didn't want to see him again.

"What do you mean you don't want to see me again?" asked Will. "I don't understand. Everything was fine a couple of weeks ago. What happened?"

"I'll be going off to college soon, and I don't have time for a boyfriend. It's better this way."

"Better for whom?"

"It's just the way it is. So don't call me anymore."

"Rebecca, I know there's something you're not telling me. Is it your parents?"

"No, it's my decision." She remembered David's promise to kill Will if she told anyone about the rape, and she knew without a doubt he would follow through with his threat.

"Come on Rebecca, we can work this out."

"Will, let me make it very simple." She took a deep breath. "I don't love you." The painful words cut deep into her heart.

"Rebecca, it's not that simple."

"Yes it is." She hung up the phone with tears streaming down her face.

"Rebecca, you did the right thing." Her mother appeared in the doorway of the kitchen.

"Mother, you don't know what you're talking about."

"He would have never fit in with this family."

"No, Mother, you would have never fit into his."

"Well, either way it's time to move on."

"Move on to what?"

"I was talking to Mrs. Sawyer the other day. She said you and David really hit it off at the party. Maybe you can give him a call."

"Oh, Mother. You're like an ostrich with its head in the ground and only see what you want to see as long as it serves your purpose. Just go back to your perfect little world and leave me the hell alone."

She left her mother standing in the doorway and headed outside. She strolled into the barn where the smell of cigarette smoke lingered in the air. Several seconds later her dad walked out of one of the stalls. If her mother knew he was out here smoking she would have a hissy fit.

"Hey honey."

"Hi Daddy." She rubbed the back of her neck as she headed toward Sadie.

"What's the matter?"

"Nothing."

"Have a fight with your mother again." He followed her into the stall.

"Why does it show?"

"I know your mother can be difficult sometimes but she's worried about you. Besides, she only wants the best for you."

"Daddy, I tired of her meddling in my business. Thinking she knows what's best for me. I can't wait until I'm eighteen so I can get out of this house."

"Honey, she's not the only one that's worried. I've noticed lately you're not eating or socializing with your friends, and with the dark circles around your eyes, I guess you're not sleeping."

"I'm fine, so stop worrying." She grabbed the saddle and put it on Sadie.

"I know when something is wrong with my little girl."

"Daddy, just give me some time and I'll be back to my old self." She buckled the cinch snuggly around the horse.

"Honey, if you ever want to talk I'm here."

"I know." She placed her foot in the stirrup and mounted Sadie.

"Don't be gone too long. Supper will be ready soon."

Rebecca headed out of the barn and galloped across the open field where the sky burst into a beautiful shade of orange and purple. All she wanted to do was to keep going until she faded into the sunset so she could start over and act like none of this ever happened. Finally, she got to the river where she tied Sadie to a tree and sat along the bank. She thought about Will and the way she had hurt him. She still loved him but what happened to her in the barn had changed everything. She was wondering what she was going to do about her situation when she heard a noise behind her. She glanced over her shoulder and there was David. She leapt to her feet and dashed towards Sadie.

"Going somewhere?" He stepped in front of her.

"Get out of my way."

"Make me."

She darted around him and headed for her horse. She grabbed the horn of the seat, placed her foot onto the stirrup, and was about to pull herself up when David's arms wrapped around her waist.

"Oh, no you don't." He pulled her back.

"Get off of me!"

Sadie's soft brown eyes gapped open. Her neck and flanks stiffened at the struggle that was going on around her. David planted both feet on the ground, tightened his grip, and pulled one more time. Her hands slipped from the saddle and she landed right on top of him. She quickly reached back, grabbed a hand full of his hair, and pulled hard.

"You little …" He lifted his legs, wrapped hers in a deadlock, and tried to pry her fingers from his hair.

"Let me go!" She lifted her head and slammed him in the nose with the back of her head.

"Damn you! You're going to pay dearly for that one." He touched his bloody nose.

"I don't think so!" She lifted her head again, but before she could give him another blow, he blindsided her with a rock to the side of the head and darkness overtook her.

She woke up to David lifting her off of Sadie's back and slinging her across his shoulder. She started kicking and screaming, desperate to escape or attract attention. He hit the animal on the rump, making the poor horse startle and gallop away. He dumped Rebecca into a dirty, white, fiber glass boat. If her hands hadn't been tied behind her back, she would've strangled his little chicken neck, and dumped his body overboard.

"If looks could kill, I'd be dead." He got in the boat.

"Then consider yourself dead." She gritted her teeth. "Where am I?"

"If I tell you, I'm going to have to kill you." He laughed.

"What do you want from me?"

"Everything." He grabbed her and plopped her on the seat.

"Don't you think you've already taken that?"

"Rebecca." He sat across from her, scooted forward and touched the side of her cheek. "I want you every moment of every day."

"Don't touch me!" She turned her face away.

"Oh, I'm going to do more than touch you." He grabbed her chin and planted a kiss on her mouth and when he pulled away, she bit him on the lower lip.

"Oh, so we like to play it rough. Well, I'm sure I can accommodate you."

"Why are you doing this?"

"Because I can." He lightly caressed her lips with his thumb.

Kathryn stepped from the window as the memory faded. She paused. There was something else. Something about this room. A faint memory, still mostly lost to the amnesia, tickled the edge of her mind. She was eight years old and her dad was grinning ear to ear, asking her if she was ready… Ready for what?

She went to the bookshelf pulled the book, *The Lion, the Witch, and the Wardrobe,* off the shelf. The memory of her father reading the book to her about the adventures of the four Pevensie children, who had disappeared through the back of a large wardrobe into a magical, snow-covered land filled with weird and beautiful creatures, resurfaced. She leisurely flipped through the pages and wondered  why her mother's orb chose to exit through this particular book.

"Mother, what are you trying to tell me?" she whispered as she closed the book and slipped it back on the shelf.

She turned to walk away when she remembered why she had been so excited that day. She took a deep breath, closed her eyes, grabbed the edge of the bookcase, and pulled. Butterflies fluttered in the pit of her stomach as she unlocked the door to the secret passage way of her forgotten childhood memories.

The moonlight filtered through the window and played on the windowsill, leaching color from all it touched. It cast a silver veil over the secret room, shimmering, dancing in a quietness all of its own. She watched her younger self laugh and twirl in the middle of the room the day her father revealed her own secret Narnia, where she was transported back to a time of innocence and magical kingdoms. Imagining she was Rapunzel, she let down her golden auburn tresses to be rescued by a handsome prince.

She stepped to the wall on her right where her father had painted a mural of a pink castle surrounded by fluffy white clouds. Under the painting stood the same green hammock where she would swing for hours reading about far off lands enchanted with fairies and unicorns.

On the opposite wall was a picture of her in a field of wildflowers standing next to Sadie, her trusted mare, under a clear blue sky. Her father had her facing the castle to remind her one day she would ride upon her trusted steed and become the princess of her own kingdom. And she had, but the big bad wolf had come along and blew it down. He stole her memory, her children, crippled her husband, and brought her back to where it all started.

She spotted the white toy box in the corner where she had played for hours. She opened it and pulled out her favorite doll, She-Ra. It was still dressed in a red leotard with long white sleeves, gauntlets, matching boots, and a black belt. She looked back in the box and pulled out Swift Wind, her trusted winged and talking unicorn.

She-Ra was the twin sister of He-Man, who had been kidnapped by Hordak, leader of the Evil Horde, and taken to a planet called Etheria. There she was brainwashed and raised as the Force Captain of The Horde. One day, a sorceress sent her brother with a magical sword to break the spell and rescue her. With her new-found powers, and riding upon Swift Wind, she led the rebellion against Hordak to free the people from his evil rule.

*Where's She-Ra when you need her?* She thought, putting the doll and unicorn back in the box. Just as she moved toward the desk in the corner the moon withdrew its light leaving the room in total darkness. Her heart began to race as she heard a noise coming from the bedroom. She glanced toward the bookcase and waited for her own version of Hordak to enter the room. The noise moved above her, and she realized it was just a squirrel scurrying around in the attic.

If David found her here she knew there would be hell to pay. So, she made her way to the bookcase where a loose floorboard creaked beneath her bare feet. She stopped, pushed against it a second time, smiled at the memory, and dropped to her knees. Let it still be there, she pleaded. She slipped her fingers under the end of the loose board and just as she pulled it up, a moon-beam shone through the window revealing the yellow rope ladder she had placed there years ago.

She had bought the ladder with the money she made working part time at the Humane Society. On weekends, after her parents went to bed, she would use it to meet Will in the barn. Several times, they almost got caught when her dad had come outside to sneak a smoke. If her mother knew her husband was smoking behind her back and her daughter was still seeing that 'parasite,' well, she would've been like a bull in a china shop.

She pulled out the ladder and underneath was an envelope addressed to Rebecca. She lifted it out from under the floor and remembered it was the letter Will had written to her after they started dating. She light-ly pressed it to her chest and stepped to the window where dust particles danced like little fairies under the moonlight. She stared out into the night sky where the wind gently caressed the top of the trees, took out the letter, and began to read:

*Dear Rebecca*

*In all of my life, I never thought I could love someone as I love you. I thought this kind of love was just in fairy tales. You fill my heart with so much love and passion without asking anything in return. When I see you or hear you, my heart strings begin to play a melody I've never heard before. There is not a time of day or night that I am not thinking of you.*

*You are that special person I can talk with openly or just sit in silence without a word and feel at home. You have given my stale life a breath of fresh air. Your voice is like a warm spring breeze, lifting my spirit to the tallest mountain. At your touch, I get this warm, soft, comfortable feeling. I sense your acceptance of who I am, which makes me want to be a better man. Then reality hits me that you are just a dream and soon I will wake up to my empty life.*

*I know the odds are against us, but I'm not giving up. For the first time in my life, I have met someone that sees my heart and I see hers. You are the fire that burns in my soul, the wind that carries me onward, and the rain that quenches my thirst. I hope someday I will get a chance to show the world that when I.C.U., I.C. Me.*

*Love, Will*

Kathryn gently pressed the letter against her heart at the remembrance of young love. It was magical, with a sense of freedom; no apprehensions, just living in the moment. And yet it was the love her mother hated with a passion and would walk through fire to destroy, even if it meant forcing her into the arms of a psychopath.

She glanced to her right where the moonlight had cast the barn into a ghoulish glow. The place had once been her sanctuary from a controlling mother, and it held the fond memories of her trusted mare Sadie. Now it stood as a reminder of how quickly evil could step into your life and destroy everything that was innocent. A cloud captured the moon withdrawing its light as if it agreed with her sentiments. Seconds later a window in the barn lit up. Had she gotten too busy with her forgotten memories that she didn't realize David had returned?

Just as she readied herself to go back where she belonged, Kathryn looked out the window again and was shocked at what she saw. In the window of the barn, a little girl stepped forward and pressed her face against the glass.

# Chapter 17

The silent engine was betrayed by the chatter of gravel under the tires as the truck prowled up the driveway. Just when the headlights hit the side of the barn, the window went dark and the little girl disappeared. Kathryn grabbed the ladder and put it back under the floorboard, along with the letter. She ran to the bedroom, closed the bookcase, and jumped into bed at the sound of footsteps coming up the stairs. She pulled the covers up to her chin and turned her back toward the door. With her heart racing she waited for him to come in, but instead David started having a full-fledged argument with himself out in the hallway.

"All I wanted to do was to go out and have a beer to unwind. Was that too much to ask? I hate it when you do something stupid without telling me. What were you thinking, breaking into that café? What if they find some evidence you were there implicating that I was involved?

*"I got bored and decided I needed an adrenaline rush. I thought what better way to do that than to get up close and personal to the woman that will take Rebecca's place."*

"What do you mean take her place?"

*"What if I said you can keep your beloved Rebecca, while still offering sacrifice for our Mother's sins?"*

"Oh, really, why don't you enlighten me?"

*"Let the other woman be the substitute and take Rebecca's place. She can be the sacrifice and your beloved doesn't have to die. You can have the family you always wanted. You and Rebecca can live happily ever after and raise the little girl as your own daughter."*

Kathryn knew David was giving some deep thought to what the voice was saying after he went deadly quiet. She wondered who the woman was that they were talking about. Who were *they* talking about … ? She was actually starting to think as if there were two men in the hallway instead of one. This whole situation was getting too bizarre, and if she didn't find a way to escape soon, she would end up just as crazy as he was.

"That just might work." David finally broke the silence.

The thought of someone dying in her place so she could live made her sick to the stomach. There was no way she would allow that to happen if she had anything to do with it.

Out of the darkness two bright orbs appeared and hovered in the room. They streaked across the floor and exited through the bookcase as the light from the hallway filtered through the doorway. David stepped inside and she wondered who had joined her mother.

Whoever it was, she sure hoped it was reinforcements because right now she could use all the help she could get, even if it did come from the outer limits of the twilight zone.

David sat down next to her on the bed and whispered, "Rebecca. I'm so sorry how I treated you earlier after you fainted at the dinner table. I didn't realize how exhausted you were. Darling, everything is going to be okay, you just wait and see. Soon we will be a family and live happily ever after."

He got up to leave and as his shoes lightly tapped across the floor she slowly turned over.

"Where were you?" The three words bounced off the silence in the room.

"I didn't mean to wake you." He calmly turned around.

"David, I have low blood sugar and if I don't get something to eat soon, I could go into a coma." She lied.

"I'm sorry, I got sidetracked and I didn't mean to neglect you. Would you like something to eat?"

"Yes, please."

"What would you like?"

"Breakfast would be nice."

"Breakfast it is. Would you like to go downstairs and eat in the kitchen?"

"Could I?" She slowly sat up. "I could cook for you if you like."

"That would be great. Let me change and I'll be back to get you."

After he left, Kathryn knew she had to buy herself some time in order to find out who the girl was in the barn. In order to do that, she would have to play the 'Keep Sweet' card to her advantage. She had to be harmless as a dove but wise as a serpent because now, three lives hung in the balance. She was going to do everything in her power to make sure no one was a part of David's sick sacrificial plan.

Kathryn sat across from David at the kitchen table. She could almost sense her mother's presence in the room. She realized if her mother had known David was going to harm her, he would never have stepped foot in this house. Her mother was not responsible for David's actions. So, she gave herself permission to let go of the hatred she had felt for her mother eighteen years ago.

*Mother, I forgive you.* She silently spoke those words. In response, a light glow formed inside the oven, and slowly disappeared. Her heart felt a sense of lightness when she realized her mother's unfinished business was taken care of and now she had the forgiveness she needed to crossover.

"You have outdone yourself. This Eggs Benedict is delicious. Are you sure you're a florist and not a chef?"

"No, I just like to cook in my spare time." She hugged the white coffee cup with the TC logo engraved on the side.

"So, do you have any memory of this farmhouse at all?"

"It seems slightly familiar," she lied, looking around the room.

"You don't remember your mother introducing us at a dinner party right here in this house?"

"Sorry, I'm afraid not."

"The instant I laid eyes on you I thought my heart was going to pound out of my chest. I knew I would do anything to have you. Later that evening, when we were alone in the barn, I realized you felt the same way. What a shame you don't have the slightest recollection of us making love in the loft that night. It was one of the most fulfilling moments in my life, and I hope, in time, you'll remember what we had together."

She glanced at the knife set on the counter and was tempted to let him know just how much she remembered. If she didn't get some fresh air soon, she was going to show him just how delusional his concept of love was.

"David, do you think it would be possible if we could go outside and get some fresh air?"

"I don't see why not, but only for a few minutes because I've got to leave." He picked up their plates from the table.

"What happened?" She lightly touched his hand.

"It's just a cut, nothing serious."

"Why don't I take those?" Kathryn stood and waited for him to hand them over.

"Thank you Rebecca." He gave her the plates.

"You're welcome." She stepped over and put them in the sink.

Afterwards, they went outside on the back porch and sat down. One by one, small points of light popped up in the sky while a wispy cloud briefly eclipsed the full moon and cast a halo around its edges. Somewhere in the night, a nightingale sang a love song, hoping to win a mate. According to Richard, if he didn't get lucky he would be back the next night and the next until his lady love showed up. She thought about the conversation she had with Janet at the hospital about taking Richard off a life support. If she got a second chance, she was going to do everything in her power to bring back the man who meant the world to her.

"Do you know why I bought this place after your father put it up for sale?"

"No," a little annoyed that he had the audacity to interrupt the birds mating call and her thoughts about Richard.

"It was the only way I could be near you. Do you know how many times I've slept in that old barn just to feel you next to me?"

She didn't say a word for fear the anger in her voice would give away that she remembered the night he had brutally taken her.

"God, you were so beautiful that night." He closed his eyes. "Hopefully something will spark your memory and you'll remember how much I loved you."

"David, perhaps if you let me explore the barn maybe it will help me remember that night."

"That's a good idea, but not tonight."

"What about tomorrow?"

"Will see," he said as he stood up. "I've got to go inside for a second. Can I trust you to stay put, or do I need to lock you back in your room?"

"I'm not going anywhere." She looked toward the barn thinking about the little girl.

"I'll be right back."

After David left, she wondered if it was a test to see if she would try to escape. Well, he would be waiting a long time because at this point she had no intention of leaving. Not until she found out, who the girl was in the barn, and why she was there.

Kathryn got up and stepped to the edge of the porch to get a glimpse of the backyard. She placed her hands on the railing when she started feeling a little light-headed. The sides of her head started to throb like a low-playing bass drum while blind spots clouded her vision. With a flash of light, the rest of the memory after David put her in the boat, played itself out.

❊    ❊    ❊

They had coasted downstream for about three miles. He seemed to be looking for a landmark and, spotting it, he paddled to the river-bank. They covered the boat with brush and entered a cave several yards away; where David had been hiding out for several weeks to spy on her. Before he forced her to help gather up his things, she remembered taking off the silver heart-shaped locket Will had given her and left it behind just in case someone came looking for her. Afterwards they stumbled through the woods where he made her get inside a truck parked on a dirt road.

"I demand you take me home right now!" Rebecca screamed while he got into the driver's seat.

"Scream all you want because no one is going to hear you." He put the key in the ignition.

"You know people are going to be looking for me."

"Yeah, by the time they start looking, you will be long gone."

"I want to go home!" She took the bottom of her foot and repeatedly banged it against the glove compartment.

"Well, your home is with me now." He put the truck in gear.

"Somebody help!" she screamed shaking her head back and forth.

"Shut up!" He drew back his fist and hit her on the side of the head. "Now, if you keep acting like a child, I'll do worse than that." His nose flared while his face turned red.

He reached back behind the seat, pulled out a bottle of water from the cooler, and handed it to her. "Here put that on your face to keep it from swelling."

"Where are you taking me?" She grabbed the bottle.

"Not another word, or so help me God …"

Rebecca stared out the window, twisted the lid off the bottle, took a drink, and didn't say another word. After she had finished the water, she started feeling a little light-headed.

"What's in the water?" She squinted at him.

"It's something to make you sleep. We have a long night ahead of us. Besides, it's better if you don't know where I'm taking you."

She passed out and, the next thing she knew, he was carrying her from the truck into an old barn in the middle of nowhere.

"Where are we?" She slurred her words.

"That's for me to know and you to find out." He laughed.

David had managed to build a room in the corner loft of an old, rundown barn, where he kept her locked up. In the beginning, he was patient and gentle until she continued to defy him. That's when he began beating her into submission and started violating her on a daily basis. She became like the walking dead and lost any hope of ever escaping. One day, the inevitable happened. He had gone for a walk, and forgotten to lock the door behind him.

She remembered running through the woods while the shadow of a night owl flapped across her path. She followed the moon with her eyes, allowing it to guide her past the scattered beech and conifer trees. She could hear branches snapping behind her, and she knew he was gaining on her. A cloud captured the moon, and she blindly tripped over a tree root and fell to the ground. With no time to waste, she scrambled to her feet. Just as she was about to take off running again, the cloud released the moon and illuminated a cliff several feet in front of her. From far below she could hear the rushing of water. Every muscle in her body tensed when she heard his voice coming from behind her.

"Poor, Rebecca. Trapped, like a caged animal."

She whirled around to face him as the moonlight spilled over into the woods just enough to see his silhouette.

"There's no place to run." David moved toward her with a rope in his hands.

She knew she would rather die than go back to her living hell. With no reservations, she turned and jumped. The powerful sensation of fear soared through her. She hit the cold, murky water and everything turned black. Miles downstream, her body washed up on the bank of the river, but the memories of her first eighteen years of life were left behind in a watery grave.

❈   ❈   ❈

"Penny for your thoughts." David stepped out on the porch.

"What?" Kathryn glanced over her shoulder and shook her head.

"I said I'll give you a penny for your thoughts."

"I've got a slight headache. Do you mind if we go back inside?"

"Sure, I have to be going anyway." He reached for her hand. "You're trembling. Are you okay?"

"Yes, I'm just tired and the air is getting a little chilly."

"Well, let's get you inside so you can get some rest."

"David." She looked into his eyes. "Thank you for breakfast and allowing me to get some fresh air."

"You're welcome."

She could tell he was pleased with her gratitude and realized the only way to defeat David was the 'Keep Sweet' rock in his own sling shot.

After she could no longer hear his truck she got out of bed and went to the secret room, careful to close the hidden door behind her. She hung the ladder out of the window and glanced back at the bookcase wondering if she was making a mistake. What if he knew about the room and this was just a part of his sick game of letting his victim escape just for the thrill of the hunt? It didn't matter; she had to find out who the girl was in the barn, and why she was there. She hurriedly climbed out the window and dropped to the ground. She heard a noise behind her. Afraid David had caught her in the act, she slowly turned around. She sighed with relief when she saw a mother raccoon along with her babies crossing the yard. She zipped up her jacket, flipped up her hood, and made a bee-line toward the barn while the moon cast her moving shadow upon the ground.

She stepped inside the barn and went straight to the stall where she used to keep Sadie. Her father had bought her the mare on her thirteenth birthday, despite her mother's protests, which had shocked the hell out of her. She inhaled, hoping the scent of her faithful companion still lingered. At the pitter-patter of little feet overhead she made her way to the stairs. She reached the bottom of the steps, froze, the memory of the assault locking her feet in place. Screwing up her determination, she forced her feet to take the next step. She knew she could never change what had happened to her in the loft, just like she couldn't rewind the high speed chase that had killed her children. But she'd be damned if she was going to be a coward and leave this little girl's fate in the hands of a madman. She plowed through her fears, went up the steps, and slid back the lock.

She stepped into the loft, lit only by the moonlight casting a silver organza veil over the room. The girl was nowhere in sight and she wondered if the girl in the window had been her imagination or a flashback of a childhood memory. She made her way to the kitchen-ette. Her dad's cassette player was still on the counter, and she wondered if the Rolling Stones tape was still inside. She glanced over to the corner and she saw the top of the girl's strawberry-blonde hair behind a bale of hay.

"Hello." She slowly moved toward her.

Kathryn gasped as the little girl popped up with these big blue eyes and wearing princess pajamas. The resemblance was unbelievable. If it hadn't been for the hair, she would've been the splitting image of her daughter Rachel.

"Mommy, is that you?" asked the girl.

Her heart quickened at the sound of her voice be-cause it sounded so much like Rachel's. The girl ran, wrapped her arms around her legs, and started to cry. Kathryn gently picked her up and as the girl blindly hugged her neck, a picture of her sweet little Rachel lying in the morgue, flashed before her. So still, so life-less, and so alone. She vowed right there she would do everything in her power to rescue this little one from the madman who took her.

"Honey, it's okay." Kathryn tenderly hugged her.

The girl lifted her head, searched Kathryn's face, and touched the mole just above the right corner of her mouth.

"You're not my mommy." She sobbed and gasped between words. "My mommy doesn't have a brown spot like you and me."

The girl laid her head on her shoulder and cried some more. Kathryn carried her to a bale of hay, sat down, and held her until she quieted down.

"Honey, what's your name?"

"Emily Jantzen. What's your name?"

"Kathryn Rubin, but you can call me Kat. Emily, can you tell me why you're here?"

"I was in the big mall, sitting on a bench eating ice cream with my mommy. She saw daddy holding hands with another woman, so she got up and yelled at him. Then this man showed me a picture of this cute little puppy. He said if I came with him I could have it. When we got to his car, he made me get in and there was no puppy. I cried because I wanted to go back to my mommy, but he wouldn't let me."

"Emily, can you tell me how long you've been here?"

"Do you want to see?" She jumped down, grabbed her hand, and led her across the room.

On the wall behind her bed were groups of four lines slashed  together by a fifth. Kathryn counted the groups; fifty-four. Two-hundred and seventy days.

"Honey, you've been here for nine months."

"I don't know. I can only count up to two-hundred, but my mommy said that was good for a five-year-old."

"Your mother was right, but how did you get so smart to count your days by putting marks on the wall?"

"Sometimes, my daddy would go on his business trips, and he told me to put a mark on my chalk board every time the sun woke up and on the fifth mark he would be home. But this time he didn't come." She pouted.

"Honey, does David always leave you out here in the barn alone?"

"Who's David?"

"He's the man who took you."

"Oh, his name isn't David."

"What is it?"

"Foxy Loxy."

"Foxy Loxy?"

"Yes, just like the name of the fox in the *Chicken Little* story."

The childhood memory of her dad reading the same story to her right here in this barn resurfaced. Foxy Loxy was the last character Chicken Little, Henny Penny, Ducky Lucky, Goosey Loosey, and Turkey Lurkey had met along the way to tell the King the sky was falling. However, the fox took them straight to his den, and they were never seen again.

"So does Foxy Loxy make you stay out here all alone?"

"No, most of the time I stay in the house, but this time he said I had to stay in the barn because he had a guest. But sometimes Daniel watches me when Foxy

Loxy has to leave and we have a Chicken Little barn-yard party."

"Who's Daniel?"

"He's a funny guy that makes me laugh."

Kathryn wondered how many personalities David had. "What does Daniel look like?"

"Like Foxy Loxy, but he's nice and likes to play."

"Does anyone else visit you?"

"Sometimes my grandma visits me."

"Your grandma?"

"Yes, she's my guardian angel and stays with me until I fall asleep."

"So your grandma is in heaven?"

"Yes, when she's not here."

Now Kathryn knew who the other orb was in her bedroom. Somehow, someway, two matriarchs had found a way to cross the veil of time to bring hope and comfort to a dire situation.

"Emily, you remember when Foxy Loxy outsmarted Chicken Little and all her friends by taking them to his den?"

"Yes."

"Well this time, we're going to outsmart the fox and escape from his den."

"Right now?" Her eyes widened.

"Yes, do you have other clothes besides pajamas to wear and a pair of shoes?"

"Yes." She ran to the table next to her bed and opened the drawer.

Kathryn glanced out the window and caught her breath at the sight of the headlights coming down the driveway. She knew there was no way they could leave now. So, she calmly went over to Emily where she was pulling out a pair of jeans and getting ready to put them on.

"Honey, were not going to be able to leave tonight."

"Why not?" She cried.

" I've got to make sure it's safe for us to leave first."

"Can you stay with me?"

"I wish I could but I can't. If Foxy Loxy finds me in his den he's  not going to like it very much. I promise I will come back for you."

Kathryn could hear the engine getting louder and if she didn't get out of here soon she would fail to keep that promise.

"Now before I leave. You've got to promise me you won't tell anyone that's I've been here or I won't be able to come back and get you."

"I won't." She put the jeans back in the drawer. "I promise."

After Kathryn tucked her in and was getting ready to leave Emily said," Wait! Do you know how to sign, good night, sleep tight?"

"Yes." She thought of Rachel signing those very words.

"After my mommy tucked me in at night she would sign good night, sleep tight, and blow me a kiss before she left. Could you do that  before you leave?"

"Sure." She bent down, lightly kissed Emily on the cheek and  hurried to the door.

Just before she headed down the stairs she turned to Emily with a smile, she raised her hands, signed, good night, sleep tight, blew her a kiss, and went down the steps. With the promise nothing would stop her from getting this little girl out of the foxes den and safely back to her family.

After Kathryn reached the bottom step she ran to the window where she saw David grab something off the front seat of his truck and headed for the barn. She dashed to the stall where she used to keep Sadie and hid, hoping he wouldn't notice the ladder hanging outside the window. Just as he stepped inside, her foot slipped making a brushing sound. She quickly pulled back her leg, held her breath and waited. She slowly exhaled as his shoes tapped across the floor and up the stairs. At the sound of the loft door opening and closing she darted outside and sprinted across the yard to the rope. She climbed up the ladder hoping David didn't catch her in the process. Once inside she pulled the ladder out of the window, closed it, stepped back and shook like a leaf.

She stared across the great divide and wondered how she was ever going to rescue this little girl who looked so much like Rachel? 'Keep sweet' David's mantra entered her thoughts. With that in mind she signed, good night, sleep tight, blew a kiss to Emily with the promise; she would do everything in her power to rescue her.

# CHAPTER 18

The main street of Shepherdstown was quiet as David sat in his car across from The Natural Springs Café. It had almost been a week since he had saw Marilyn outside the Blue Moon and thought for sure it was Rebecca. The resemblance between the two was remarkable. If it hadn't been for the fact that she didn't have a mole on her face, they would've been identical. He almost rode back to the house to be sure Rebecca was still there. Instead, he decided to stop and ask for directions to the Bistro 112, though he knew exactly where it was. He would've stayed and chatted a little longer just to find out more about her if the little twerp hadn't showed up acting like her bodyguard.

After he left, he went to the Bistro; a small restaurant, but with a very warm and friendly atmosphere. The décor was in the soft colors of Southern France, accented with eclectic art. He ordered the French-style, grilled steak as suggested and, he had to admit, it was quite tasty. He had asked one of the waiters about Marilyn, and was told she owned the café. After he had a few drinks, paid his bill, and left, the next thing he remembered was running down a dark alley with sirens blaring in the background and no clue what he was doing and why he was there. He got back to his truck that's when he noticed a cut on his hand. He demanded to know what happened and after the voice told him he had broken into the café, he lost it. Until he suggested that the woman who looked like Rebecca was the answer to keeping his beloved.

David gripped the steering wheel when he saw Marilyn step out onto the porch wearing a Shepherd College t-shirt and a pair of fitted jeans. *What a shame I can't keep both of them*, he thought. A tingling sensation cascaded over his brain and, by the time it reached his toes, the college chatter in the streets began to amplify. It was a sign that the voice was trying to take control. David glanced at his reflection in the rearview mirror where his eyes looked like a deer's caught in the headlights. Little by little, he could see himself disappearing into the dark abyss and knew if he didn't intervene, the voice would end up doing something really stupid.

"Not this time!" He glared at the reflection. "This time I'm in charge!"

David quickly looked toward the café where Marilyn was stepping back inside. He let go of the steering wheel, rolled up his window, and got out of the truck before the voice had a chance to speak. He glanced across the hood where an elderly, black woman was sweeping the sidewalk. He greeted her with a nod while the brushing sound swept through his mind like a street sweeper. He took a breath just to make sure he was in charge, fed the parking meter and made his way across the street. Each footstep was like a sledge-hammer pounding against the asphalt. By the time he reached the café, the sound of his heartbeat was thudding through his brain. He quickly stepped inside when he saw the twerp who called him 'bozo' riding towards him on his skateboard.

On his left, a couple of college kids were playing chess at one of the game top pedestal tables. One of them moved his rook and it sounded like a piece of furniture moving across the room. He could still feel the voice trying to take over, but he wouldn't let him. He walked past the tables on his right where a child in a highchair screamed like a banshee. It made him cringe as he headed to the front and sat down at the counter.

"What can I get you?" Carmen smiled at David when she handed the woman sitting next to him her change.

The sweet voice of the young girl caused the tingling sensation to exit through his toes while the chatter around him reduced to a normal volume.

"What do you recommend?" he asked

"Reuben on Rye is my favorite." She wiped off the counter in front of him.

"That sounds great."

"Do you want a cup of soup, salad, or French fries with that?"

"What kind of soup do you have?" He was glad the voice in his head had disappeared and he could carry on a normal conversation.

"We have roasted tomato soup and barley vegetable."

"I'll have the barley."

"What do you want to drink?"

"I'll have a beer, whatever is on tap."

"Okay, I'll be right back with your beer."

David got a glimpse of Marilyn in the kitchen causing his heart to flutter. With her hair pulled back, she was wearing a green bib apron with the name of her café written across the pocket. He couldn't believe how much she looked like Rebecca. And she could cook. Maybe there was a way to keep them both, one to share his kitchen and the other his bed.

"Here you go." Carmen set the chilled mug of beer in front of him.

"Thanks …" He looked for a name tag, but didn't see one.

"Carmen, and you're welcome."

"Carmen, do you think I could have a word with Marilyn if it's not too much trouble?"

"Sure, I'll go get her."

Several minutes later, Marilyn came out of the kitchen wiping her hands on her apron.

"Carmen said you wanted to speak with me?" She looked up and recognized him as the man she saw the other night in front of the Blue Moon.

"Yes, I just wanted to apologize. I hope I didn't give the wrong  impression the other night when I asked for directions. You're little friend was rather protective, and I don't blame him with the way the world is these days."

"Don't worry about it. Kyle, is like the neighbor-hood watchdog. He's suspicious of anybody who's a stranger to the streets."

"Good. I also wanted to thank you for recom-mending the L'entreote au poivre at the Bistro. It was delicious."

"I'm glad you enjoyed it, Mr ..."

"Sawyer, but you can call me David."

"You're the owner of The Temporary Chef?"

"Yes, I am."

"I have several friends who used your service and they were very pleased with the results."

"Well, that's good to know."

"Anyway, I've got to get back to the kitchen."

"Marilyn, I know I'm being a little forward, but would you be interested in going out for a cup of cof-fee sometime?"

"Sorry, but I'm not really into the dating scene at the moment. If there's nothing else I can do for you, I hope you enjoy your meal, and have a great day."

"But you're the first woman I've asked out in three years. Please, won't you reconsider just this once?"

"It's nothing personal, but I'm just not interested in dating, period."

"Well, I guess you can't blame a man for trying."

"No, I guess not." Marilyn slightly tilted her head and went back into the kitchen.

"Here you go. Enjoy." Carmen set down the soup and sandwich in front of him.

"Thanks."

"You're welcome."

David started to eat his soup when the woman with a bumblebee waist, around forty-five, with short, brown hair sitting next to him decided to strike up a conversation.

"Hi, my name is Selma. I have a friend who used your service."

"Oh, really, and who's that?" David was a little annoyed that she had the audacity to talk to him while he was eating. Food was his passion, and he didn't like being interrupted because it distracted from the taste.

"Veronica Small. She's the owner of The Cutting Edge Steak House in Winchester, Virginia."

"Yes, I remember her."

"Ever since you came in and revamped her menu, her business has been skyrocketing. People travel for miles just to try her food."

"That's great. I guess I'm going to have to stop in and pay her a visit."

"Do you know the reason why she won't go out with you?"

"Excuse me?"

"Marilyn, do you want to know why she won't go out with you?"

"Sure."

"It's because nine months ago some man kidnapped her daughter from the mall in Tysons Corner. The scoop is she was distracted because she caught her husband cheating. She went to confront him and left Emily sitting all alone on a bench. Afterward she turned around to go back and her daughter was gone. And on top of that, the scumbag husband divorced her. So, she's telling you the truth when she says she's not in the dating scene."

The face of the little girl who was in the barn flashed before him. The resemblance was definitely there, but he could be wrong. Was it possible Marilyn was the girl's mother? If so, it had to be fate. It only made sense he would raise the daughter of the woman who would be the sacrificial lamb for his own mother. It was perfect. Perhaps the voice knew what he was doing after all.

"I'd give her a little more time."

"What?" David squinted his eyes and looked at Selma.

"I said if I were you, I'd give Marilyn a little more time to go through the grieving process and then ask her out."

"Maybe I'll do that."

"Well, I've got to go. David, it was a pleasure."

"I assure you, the pleasure was all mine."

After David finished his meal, Carmen stepped up to the counter. "So how was it?"

"Great. Where do I pay the bill?"

"I'll take it."

"Hey, Carmen," yelled a boy at one of the game tables.

"What Jeff?" She raised her eyebrows at the guy dressed in jeans and a white Nike t-shirt.

"I spilled my drink. You have something I can wipe it up with?"

"Sure, I'll be there in a second." She took the fifty out of David's hand. "I swear a girl's work around here is never done."

"Keep the change." He got up from the counter.

"Why thanks! I think that's the biggest tip I've gotten since I started working here."

"You're welcome. I'm sure you'll earn every cent of it before the day is done." He looked at the boy sitting at the table and laughed.

David was turning to leave when he noticed the door on his left with a warning stenciled on a half-moon window about the oath of silence.

"Carmen, what's behind the door?"

"It's a place where people can get away from the crowd, unwind, and relax."

"Is it okay if I take a look?"

"Sure, that's what it's there for."

He loved the bronze finished décor inside the small foyer because it gave it a sense of masculinity. He read the script above the archway that stated peace and quiet could be contagious. *What I wouldn't do for a little peace and quiet,* he thought as he ambled into the room.

The tiffany chandelier cast a warm glow on the mahogany finished tables where several college students were studying. To his right, several professors sat in burgundy wingback chairs, reading and sipping glasses of wine. In front of the large hearth, where a picture of the library on the old market square hung above the mantel, were a man and a woman playing chess. Behind him, to the right of the archway, were shelves of books from all different genres. Self-help books, how-to-books, fiction and non-fiction. He spotted the title, *Dearie: The Remarkable Life of Julia Child*, by Bob Spits, and reached to pull it off the shelf. A sudden burst of cool air sent a chill across the back of his neck as a book from the top shelf fell to the floor, almost hitting him on the head.

"I see you've found the best place in the café," said Marilyn.

"You have quite a book collection." He grabbed the book off the floor, slowly stood up and took in every inch of her.

"Do you like to read?"

"Yes, when I get a chance." He slipped the book *Ireland for Dummies* back on the shelf, and wondered if the place was haunted.

Several people looked up to see where the voices were coming from and when they saw Marilyn, they just smiled and went back to what they were doing.

"Mr. Sawyer, I'm afraid I'm going to have to abide by my own rules of peace and quiet so do you mind if we step out into the foyer?"

"Not at all." He was glad to have an excuse to leave; the room had taken on a sudden hostile feel.

"Carmen said you were here, so I thought I'd come back and check up on you. So what do you think about the sitting room?"

"Nice." He rubbed his arms. "It's just a bit chilly."

"Well, that's the nature of these old buildings."

"So how long have you been in business?"

"Almost three years."

"Well, I must say. The Rueben on Rye was delicious, and I assure you I will be back to check out the rest of the menu."

"David, I wanted to ask you something about the other night when you asked for directions outside the Blue Moon."

"Sure." He glanced down at the cut on his hand and slipped it inside his front pants pocket, hoping it had gone unnoticed.

"That same night my café was broken into. Do you recall seeing anyone suspicious around the neighborhood?"

"I'm sorry to hear that. No, after I left you, I went straight to the Bistro, tried out your recommendation, and went directly home." He was feeling a little perturbed that the voice put him in this predicament.

"Okay, I just thought I'd ask. Well, I best get back to the kitchen."

"You wouldn't reconsider that cup of coffee?"

"No, I appreciate the offer but like I said, I'm just not interested."

"Well, let me know if you have a change of heart."

"Mr. Sawyer, enjoy the rest of your day." Marilyn headed back into the cafe.

David started to go back into the sitting room but something in the air shifted and he felt again the hostile coldness of the room. He quickly turned and left.

✄   ✄   ✄

Marilyn walked out of the café wearing a black leather jacket and matching chaps. She slipped on her helmet and thought about David. The night her café had been broken into, she thought perhaps he had something to do with it. However, once she found out he was the owner of the Temporary Chef, her suspicions subsided. Everyone she knew who had used his services in the tri-state area spoke highly of him. However, she still hoped he might've seen something that would point to the identity of the intruder. That's when she noticed the cut on his hand as he slipped it into his pocket. It was probably just a coincidence. Being a chef, he may have just cut himself. Still she couldn't shake the feeling that he had seemed a little nervous.

"Hey, Ms. J.," Kyle skateboarded up to her. "I saw that guy who asked for directions a couple of nights ago go inside the café earlier. I was about ready to go in and throw his behind out, but I didn't want to make a scene."

"Kyle, it's fine. He just wanted to let me know he didn't mean any harm, so you don't have anything to worry about. But thank you for looking after me."

"Well, I don't trust his beady blue eyes. Let me know if he gives you any trouble because I'll be on him like a flea on a dog."

"Thanks, Kyle, I will." She got on her bike.

"Ms. J., when are you going to take me for a ride on your bike?"

"When you get rid of those wheels and dry out behind the ears."

"Oh, come on Ms. J., don't be like that. You know I have a big crush on you."

"Yeah, well I wouldn't look now if I was you, but your little friend with the dark hair and blonde streak is sitting on the stone wall, glaring at you."

"Are you serious?"

"I'm serious as a heart attack."

"Ms. J., you have a good evening." He said it loud enough for Candy to hear.

"You, too, Kyle." She started up the engine. Kyle turned and, acting surprised to see Candy there, strode over to her.

Marilyn pulled away and passed the couple now sitting on the stone wall. Kyle nonchalantly nodded his head while he slipped his arm around the girl's waist. She reached the four-way stop sign and decided to take the back way home so she made a right. She thought about William and he still hadn't called her about going back to the cave. Perhaps he had a change of heart and decided not to waste his time. Well, at least she didn't have to come up with an excuse why she couldn't go. After she had given it some thought she decided it would only complicate her life. Besides, she didn't need any distractions while her daughter was still missing. A slight flutter stirred in her stomach when she remembered the look that passed between them and the soft touch of his lips. *Damn it! Why, did he have to ruin everything with that kiss,* she thought.

The cool air penetrated her jacket when she entered the canopy of trees. She drove through a puddle of leaves and as they swirled up around her, she thought about her dream. When the oak tree and the woodpecker didn't materialize, she sighed with relief. About a half mile down the road, she glanced in her rearview mirror and saw a silver truck. As it got closer, she realized it was David in the driver's seat. The vision she had along the river flashed before her, but with one difference. This time she could see the man's face and David's blue eyes stared back at her.

Marilyn opened up the throttle when he started tailgating her. Within minutes, she flew out from under the trees and into the clearing. She leaned hard into the curve and the bike scraped against the road. She knew she was in trouble when the ground pushed the pegs upward, squeezing her feet against the engine. She quickly removed her feet and lightly squeezed the brakes, but it was too late because she was already in the curve. Her limbs began to shake when the bike began to pivot and the rear tire lost traction. A silent scream ran through her head while a pitiful puff of air escaped her lips, and she skidded across the road landing in a nearby field.

She lay there, hurt and confused at the sound of somebody running toward her. Suddenly, she left her body. Gone was the pain. Peacefully, she gazed across the field into the horizon while a figure of light moved toward her. Its relaxed and easy-going attitude seemed familiar as it got closer.

'Mare, why did the chicken cross the road? So it could get to the other side.' The words weren't spoken but merely thought, and she felt the humor behind them.

Out of the light the face of her father appeared and her soul filled with laughter. 'It's not your time to cross to the other side. You have to go back.'

"Marilyn, are you okay?" asked David as he knelt down beside her.

The instant he touched her arm, she was sucked back into her body and her father's face disappeared.

David took off her helmet and, when he placed his fingers on the side of her neck to make sure she was still alive, her eyes fluttered open.

"Marilyn, I'm sorry, but you shouldn't have tried to outrun me."

She stared into his blue eyes when she remembered the words of the snake in her dream after it sank its teeth into her jugular. 'I told you, you couldn't outrun me.'

"So … you're the snake." She lost consciousness.

# CHAPTER 19

Marilyn stood on the edge of the woods while an eerie glow of lights passed through the dense fog. A low rumble echoed through the night sky as a cold drizzle of rain began to fall. Small animals scurried in the dark when she moved toward the partially obscured farmhouse. Seconds later, a moonbeam slipped out from behind a cloud and penetrated the ghostly mist, revealing a barn on her left. Perched on top of the roof was an owl, its eyes fixed in its white heart shaped face. It twitched its head toward her, let out a blood-curdling scream, sending chills up her spine as the barn door slowly creaked open.

Inside, a dimly lit rustic oil lantern hung on a wooden post while shadows danced on the rough hewn walls. The warmth of it made her feel oddly at peace, yet she knew things weren't always as they seemed, so she proceeded inside with caution.

The rain on the tin roof drummed a steady beat while the earthly smell of compost filled the air. She snapped her head to the right where she heard the hypnotic sound of a rattle. She felt a flush of heat as her heart rate began to race. She willed her legs to stop, but the rattle amplified to fifty times per second, inducing her into a trance-like state. She peeked around the corner of the stall where Emily was sitting on a bale of hay, guarded by a snake.

Her heart began to beat in her ears, blocking out all other sound except for the pounding in her chest. The snake snapped its head toward her while its nose and eye caps began to scale back where a man's face pressed against a layer of loose skin. The snake's tail slithered toward Emily, wrapped around her tiny hand, and squeezed.

"She's mine." David hissed while his face broke through the barrier and lunged toward Marilyn.

"Emily …"

The last remnants of her daughter's name faded, leaving her mind in a fog. She cautiously opened her eyes, allowing her brain to focus, unsure of where she was. She cringed when she tried to sit up. It hurt. She grits her teeth and pulled through it. She pushed back against the metal headboard and glanced around the dimly lit room where David emerged from the shadows.

"I see you're finally awake."

Marilyn pinched her arm to be sure she wasn't still dreaming. He sat down beside her as the image of

Emily in the barn flashed before her. She grabbed him around the neck and squeezed.

"Where's my daughter?" She growled through clenched teeth.

David pried off her hands, stood up, and grabbed her by the legs. He jerked her down in the bed, straddled her, and pinned her hands above her head.

"Feisty, just the way I like them."

She wiggled back and forth without batting an eye, letting him know she wasn't backing down. His whole countenance began to change when his pupils pushed back the blue until all she could see were the blacks of his eyes. He started having a two-way conversation with himself and she knew this man was insane.

*"Tame her!"* The words spilled out from the right side of his mouth.

"It's the same old broken record. I get to tame the wild horse and you get to ride her." David let go of her right wrist and opened the drawer of the nightstand.

*"That's right. You're the brawn and I'm the brains."*

"Yeah, yeah, yeah …" He pulled out the handcuffs, and attached one end to the bedpost.

"You're crazy!" Marilyn lifted her head and spat in his face.

"It's going to get a lot crazier than this." He started to cuff her wrist.

"Let me go!" She jerked her hand, surprised it slipped from his grip.

"Oh, so you like to play it rough." He reached for her wrist again.

She wondered how she was going to get this two-headed snake off her when she found her target. She grabbed him between the legs, squeezed, and didn't let go until he doubled over. She pushed him off the bed and as he tumbled to the floor with a moan she ran out the door. Once her eyes adjusted to the dimly lit hallway, she flew down the stairs on her right and into the foyer. She went out the front door wearing only her t-shirt and black, cotton underwear. She blindly sprinted across the porch into the front yard, not knowing where in the hell she was going.

She ran to the left side of the house and started to head for the barn. She stopped dead in her tracks realizing it would only be a death trap. So she ran down the graveled driveway instead, hoping it would lead out onto the main road. Several minutes later she glanced over her shoulder at the sound of an engine humming. The headlights of the truck were barreling down on her so she darted into the apple orchard on her right. Her body was hurting like hell from the injuries she had sustained from the bike wreck. She wasn't sure how much further she could go without collapsing. She urged herself forward at the sound of a door slamming and her name echoing through the night air.

"Marilyn." David slowly pronounced her name in three syllables. "You can run but you can't hide."

She stumbled forward, grazing her hands across the ground and tearing the skin from her palms with a painful sting. She lay there trying to catch her breath. Several seconds later he yelled her name again this time it sounded closer. She started to get up when he slithered on top of her like a snake, grabbed her hair, and jerked back her head.

"Get off of me!"

"I'll get off on one condition." He whispered in her ear. "You be a good little girl and do as I say."

"Not on your life!" She wiggled her body from side to side while he pulled her arms behind her back, handcuffed her, and jerked her off the ground.

"Let me go!" She turned and spat in his face for the second time.

"If you spit on me one more time, you will live to regret it."

"The only thing I regret is not having enough sense to listen to Kyle. He knew exactly what kind of, bozo, you were."

"Yeah, well if you don't start listening, I'm going to pay your little twerp a visit and show him just how much of a bozo I really am. Now move!" He pushed her forward almost making her stumble back on the ground.

After they got into the truck and drove back that's when she noticed the large maple tree with the branches sheltering the walkway in front of the farmhouse. It was the same image she saw in her dream, when her bike glided through the mirror and turned into a snake. After they got back to the house, David got out of the truck, went around to the passenger side and opened the door.

"Get out!"

Marilyn got out with her t-shirt pushed up over her stomach, revealing a visual map of contusions, along with abrasions highlighted in red and purple. A sharp pain shot behind her eyes as she looked up at David and staggered against him. As she lost consciousness, she knew what the road hadn't finished, the man in front of her would.

With a moan Marilyn rolled onto her back, wondering how long she had been out. Her eyes darted back and forth in the room waiting for David to emerge. She waited several minutes, took a deep breath, slowly sat up, and scooted back against the headboard. She lightly rubbed her wrist where the cuffs had left their mark and took in her surroundings. At the bottom of the bed, a rustic foot bench sat across from a fireplace encased in an antique oak mantel with great leaf and vine carvings. To the right stood a nineteenth-century, free-standing pie safe. The original decoratively pierced tin panels used for ventilation had been removed and replaced with mirrors. Once used for pastries, it now served as extra storage space.

She inched her legs over the side of the bed and staggered barefoot across the wood floor still dressed in her t-shirt and underwear. She pulled back the ivory lace curtains from the window, opened the blinds and squinted against the morning sun filtering through the room. She shielded her eyes with her hand and looked past the bars to the barn which stood on her right. She thought about her dream, and wondered if it was a premonition letting her know Emily was there. She knew it seemed far-fetched but, the way her life was going lately, anything was possible. She quickly glanced toward the door at the sound of the deadbolt sliding back. The door creaked open, and in walked David, carrying a tray of food.

"You shouldn't be out of bed. You're going to catch a death of cold dressed like that." He set the tray on the dresser.

She inhaled through her nose and exhaled slowly through her mouth, determined not to show him how vulnerable she felt standing there half-naked.

"How are you feeling?" He made his way to the window.

"I'm fine." She slowly turned around.

"Well, you don't look fine. Let's get you back into bed." He gently placed his hand on her elbow.

He helped her back into bed and placed several pillows behind her back. Gently he pulled the peach comforter up over her while his fingers trailed lightly up her thigh.

"Where am I?" She jerked her leg away.

"I hope you're hungry," he said, ignoring her question as he grabbed the tray from the dresser.

"You didn't answer my question." She stared at him when he placed it across her lap.

"If I wanted you to know where you were, I would've told you."

"What do you want from me?"

"I want you to behave." He touched the marks around his neck. "Don't you ever pull another stunt like you did last night, or I swear … Well, let's just say you will live to regret it. Do I make myself clear?"

"Yes." She clenched her jaw, wanting to give him a piece of her mind but thought better of it.

"Good, I'm glad we understand each other. Now, after you finish eating, you might want to put something else on or I might think you're trying to seduce me."

*'Seduce him'* he was the one that took off her clothes while she was unconscious not the other way around.

"Unfortunately, the jeans I was wearing have mysteriously disappeared and all I'm left with is this dirty red t-shirt. So, unless you have something else for me to wear, I'd say I'm sh …"

"First, it's not my fault you ran your bike off the road and ripped your pants to shreds. If you had slowed down, the accident would've never happened. Plus, if I hadn't been there, you could've died."

The memory of lying there in the field after the accident where she briefly left her body resurfaced. She slightly chuckled when she thought about seeing her father and hearing his silly joke.

"Do you find all this amusing?" asked David.

What she found amusing was that she had cheated death twice; once on the river and now on the road. Only now she was the prisoner of a madman who spoke out of both sides of his mouth. *Three strikes, you're out,* she thought.

"Answer my question."

"What I find amusing is that you think you're going to get away with this. Once someone realizes I'm missing, they are going to come looking for me. So, if you know what's good for you, you'll let me go."

"I'll tell you what's good for me. You, shutting that hole in your face and apologizing for smart-mouthing me." He knocked the tray off her lap and sent it flying across the room. "See what you made me do. Now clean that up!"

"Make me!" As soon as the words left her mouth, she regretted it.

"Well, I'd be glad to oblige." He grabbed her by the arm and dragged her off the bed to where the oatmeal was splattered on the floor.

"What are you waiting for?"

"I don't have anything to clean it up with."

"Well, you have two choices. You either eat it off the floor or take off your shirt and clean it up. You decide."

Marilyn knew if she struggled against him, she would be fighting a losing battle. Until she recovered from her injuries and regained her strength, she had no choice but to obey. She bent down and lapped the oatmeal off the floor like a dog because there was no way she was going to take her shirt off and leave herself more vulnerable than she already was.

"And don't get up until its spic and span."

She lapped up the oatmeal until the floor was tasteless. She started to get up, but he placed his foot in the middle of her back, and pushed her down.

"Now, I want you to apologize for your arrogance and being disrespectful."

"I'm sorry." The words flew out of her.

"I'm sorry. That's it?"

"What else do you want me to say?"

"What about showing some gratitude for saving your life and taking care of you?"

She decided to swallow her pride and lay it on thick, or pay the consequences. "David, please forgive me. I didn't mean any disrespect, and I really do appreciate all you've done. It's just that I'm tired, my body hurts, and I really don't feel well. The accident has really drained me, and if I could get some rest, I would be so grateful."

"Apology accepted. Now I've got to go. In the mean time, to let you know I'm not totally unreasonable or insensitive, you will find extra clothes in the pie safe."

After he left, she went to the safe determined to beat him at his own game. If he thought she was going willingly to his whipping post, he was sadly mistaken. Her parents had always taught her and Dillon the rules against bullies were simple and finite. You told them to stop and if they didn't, you told an adult. If they didn't do anything about it, you had the right to walk away or defend yourself. She told David to stop, but he didn't listen. Since she was the adult and couldn't walk away, the only thing left to do was defend herself. And the only way to do that was to be smart, stay calm, be nice, and feed his ego until she came up with a plan. In the mean time she had to find a way to tame down her Irish temper.

She glanced in the mirror and saw that her hair looked like a rat's nest. She was so glad she decided to wear her full face helmet because, if she hadn't, she'd have more than dark circles under her eyes. She opened the safe where David had stocked it with jeans, t-shirts, pajamas, underwear, socks, and a pair of Nikes. She grabbed the jeans off the shelf and remembered the injuries on her stomach. So she opts for the red cotton pajamas instead. After she dressed she got back into bed with an excruciating headache. The pain became so unbearable that she covered her head, curled up into a fetal position, and fell asleep.

Marilyn awoke with an unpleasant awareness of her own heartbeat. She started to hyperventilate at the sensation of her heart pounding in her chest, throat, and neck. She got out of bed and started pacing the floor. Blindly, she bumped up against the wall and placed her palms against the cold, hard surface, dropped her head, and started gasping for air. Her anxiety finally started to subside as she pressed her back against the wall and slid to the floor. An aura of grey surrounded her like a mist that wouldn't rise. She thought about what her life had been reduced to, and wondered what it was about her that God detested so much.

She tried to rise above the gloom, but she was just too mentally, physically, and emotionally strained. She lay down on the floor and curled up in a fetal position as the room yielded gracefully to the moonlight. Though it cast her defeated silhouette in a pale shade of grey, it was just enough light to cause her to get up and make her way over to the window. She turned her face to the moon as a shooting star streaked across the sky, carrying with it a special childhood memory.

It was early spring and her parents, along with her brother, were lying on the ground in the cool crisp air wrapped up in a blanket under the night sky. The slight curve of the moon made it a perfect stage for seeing the Big and Little Dipper. Shots of light followed by orange and white mist cascaded into the earth's atmosphere about every fifteen to thirty seconds. Her visible breath carried the oohs and ahhs of the meteor shower and she had never been happier. After nature finally made its final bow to the greatest light show on earth, she knew she had been a part of something special.

She pressed her forehead against the glass and briefly closed her eyes, wishing she could experience the magic of that moment one more time. But it was too late for wishes. Life had stripped her of the one thing that mattered most—her family.

Marilyn was starting to step away from the window when a shadow moved across the yard. She waited, and David stepped into the moonlight. At the same time, she thought she heard a noise coming from the hallway. Thinking it was only her mind playing treats on her, she ignored it. She heard it again, but this time it was louder. She tiptoed over, and pressed her ear against the door.

"Hello, is anyone there?" a woman's voice cried out.

Marilyn wasn't sure if she should answer. What if there was someone else playing along with his sick game and this was all a setup.

"Please, if you're there, say something."

She couldn't ignore the urgency in the woman's voice. "Yes, I'm here."

"What's your name?"

"Marilyn Jantzen. What's yours?"

"Kathryn Rubin."

"Wait, I hear something."

Marilyn rushed to the window where David was coming toward the house, and darted back to the door.

"We've got to be quiet, he's coming back inside."

She jumped into bed, pulled the covers up to her chin and turned her back to the door. She took a deep breath, trying to stay calm at the sound of footsteps prowling up the stairs. She waited for her door to open, but instead he stepped into the room across the hall. She quickly got out of bed, pressed her ear against the door, and listened. All she could hear was mumbling, and didn't understand a word they were saying. Maybe she had made a mistake when she called out earlier.

The door across the hall opened, she jumped back into bed, hoping and praying he wouldn't come into her room. Just like clockwork her prayers were left unanswered when he stepped inside, made his way to the other side of the bed and faced her. He stood over her without a word. She held her breath, wishing he'd say or do something just to break the silence.

"Marilyn, I'm sorry it has to be this way."

*"Don't even think about changing your plans."*

"Just give me a minute." David whispered crossing his arms.

*"Your minute's up. She needs her rest."*

David huffed and she could tell he was getting sick and tired of being bossed around by the other guy inside of him.

"I said I need a minute, and if you don't like it, leave!"

Though she knew no one else was in the room, she could almost sense the other presence leaving when

David sat down next to her on the bed. She held her breath and lay perfectly still as he gently caressed her hair.

"Perhaps, if we had met on different terms, things could've been different," he whispered. "However, I do feel something for you because you are my little lamb. Your sacrifice will make it possible for me to have the life I always wanted and, for that, I am grateful."

She cringed inside when he smoothed back her hair, lightly kissed her cheek, and quietly got up.

"Sweet dreams, my little lamb." He paused for a few seconds and left.

Marilyn slowly sat up, inched back against the headboard, and thought about what he said. 'You are my little lamb. Your sacrifice … ' Hadn't she sacrificed enough? The sacrifice of her parents and brother because one man refused to get some shut eye? The sacrifice of her daughter because one man thought he had the right to take her? The sacrifice of her marriage because the two people who were supposed to love each other failed to communicate? The more she thought about it, the angrier she became. If David thought he was going to sacrifice her without a fight, he was in for a rude awakening. No matter how broken and messed up her life was, she refused to let one more person take what didn't belong to them.

# CHAPTER 20

Marilyn's eyes fluttered to the rain lightly tapping on the tin roof and the hint of fresh flowers. She slowly scooted back against the headboard where she noticed the bouquet in a crystal vase on the mantle above the fireplace. In the midst of daylilies, tulips, daises, and stargazers, was a single black rose. She knew the rose meant one of two things—death or rebirth. She had the suspicion it wasn't the latter.

She got out of bed and proceeded to the window where beads of water pitter-pattered against the glass. Large gray clouds moved across the sky while a gentle wind rustled through the oak tree, causing droplets of rain to drip off the leaves. Suddenly, a wall of rain moved over the oak and drummed against the canopy. She thought about what David had said, 'Your sacrifice will make it possible for me to have the life I always wanted and, for that, I am grateful.' Did he mean; that he was actually going to kill her? If so, did her sacrifice have something to do with the woman across the hall? Had David kidnapped her too or was she just part of his sick plan. Whatever it was she didn't want to stick around to find out.

She thought about Carmen and Dana. Before leaving the café Friday evening, she had reminded Carmen she wouldn't be in on Saturday. She needed a mental health day and would be back on Sunday to meet up with Dana for breakfast. Afterwards, they were going on a bike ride, something she had been promising her for months. She wondered if her bike was still in the field after David had forced her off the road, or had he taken it with him to cover his tracks. Either way it probably didn't matter. Even if by some miracle they figured out where she was; most likely she would already be dead.

Dead; isn't that what she had wanted. So many times after Emily was taken, she just wanted to curl up and die. Now she realized, all she ever really wanted, was to find a way to ride the pain that kept coming in wave after wave, so she could feel again, live again, and love again. It's ironic; now that death was staring her in the face, she had a change of heart. All because she had found her 'somewhere over the rainbow' that made her want to live again; and all it took was a simple kiss.

She flinched when the door opened and David stepped inside. She took a slow breath to regain her composure and prayed she could stay sweet as he strolled across the floor to the fireplace.

"Aren't they lovely?" He lightly touched the black rose. "I had them arranged especially for you." He pulled the flower out of the vase and wandered over to the window.

"Yes, they're lovely." She stayed sweet not wanting another episode like the one with the oatmeal and hoping to buy herself some time.

He lightly trailed the flower across her cheek, down the side of her neck, paused, gently lifted her chin and gazed into her eyes.

"You are my black rose. My unexpected surprise. Because of you I'll have a new beginning and the family I always wanted."

Again his words, 'Your sacrifice will make it possible for me to have the life I always wanted' ran through her mind. She was convinced her death had something to do with the rebirth of the woman across the hall? Was she the atonement for her indiscretions? To cleanse her white as snow so she could be pure and without blemish so they could be a family. If David insists she be part of his sick ritual, she was determined not to go quietly into the night.

"But, first things first," said David as he placed the rose back in the vase. "My little lamb has to be without blemish. Therefore, I'm going to go prepare for you, your cleansing ritual."

"Could I please have something to eat first?" she asked.

"Sorry, it's too late for that. Besides, it's not my fault you slept through breakfast and lunch."

"Even criminals get a last meal before they're executed." Her 'stay sweet' attitude was slipping.

"Marilyn, if you had followed the rules perhaps things would've turned out differently."

"How did you expect me to follow the rules when you nearly killed me on the road? Besides, your rules aren't going to change a damn thing. You already have your mind made up that I'm going to die, regardless."

"The accident wasn't my fault." He took a step toward her. "However, you're right about one thing. Nothing is going to change my mind and I'm looking forward to breaking you."

"Breaking me?" She sneered. "That's impossible."

"Now, why's that?"

"Because, I'm already broken and there's nothing you can do to me that hasn't already been done." She stared him in the eyes, daring the other guy to show his face.

"Well, we'll just have to see about that." He started to unbutton her top.

*"What are you doing?"* The voice shouted.

Marilyn jumped back when a spray of spit splattered across her face as his calm demeanor slowly changed into an all-consuming anger. His nostrils flared, his eyes flashed and closed into slits as he stepped into the middle of the room with his mouth quivering.

*"Are you trying to ruin everything?"* He ran around in tight little circles.

"No!" David jerked his hand through his hair.

*"Then get hold of yourself."* He balled up his fist and crouched forward. *"The covenant states, 'The sacrifice is not*

*to be defiled. She has to remain untarnished. So keep your filthy
hands off of her or you're going to ruin everything!"*

Marilyn knew she had to do something to defuse
the situation or it was only going to get worse. She
glanced around the room and spotted the 'Keep Sweet'
plague hanging above the dresser.

"David, I'm sorry."

"What?" He stopped and stared at her with his eyebrows scrunched in the middle of his forehead, looking
confused.

"I didn't mean to upset you. I'll stay sweet. I
promise."

"All right then." Her words instantly switched off
his anger. "I'll go prepare your bath." He left as if nothing had ever happened.

Thirty minutes later, David came in and led her
out of the room. She glanced at the door across the
hall where Kathryn Rubin was being held prisoner. She
hoped she was her ally and not her enemy. He guided
her toward the bathroom at the end of the hallway on
her left. The candles lit around the room gave the atmosphere a sense of warmth and intimacy. However,
when she stepped up to the clawfoot tub, the black rose
petals floating in the water told a different story.

"I've prepared for you a bath of lavender oil along
with rosemary lavender scented soap. This will relax
you and help in the healing process of your injuries."
David picked a black rose petal out of the water and
stared at it for several seconds. "Did you know it's believed Mary used lavender to anoint Jesus' feet with her
hair? They say the house was filled with the fragrance

of the perfume. I imagine this room smells exactly the same way."

Marilyn thought about the story she heard so many times in Sunday School and Judas Iscariot's response to the woman's actions. Judas said he wanted the perfume to be sold and the profit given to the poor, even though it was really his own pocketbook he was concerned about. In response, Jesus told him to leave her alone because she did it for the preparation of his burial. Now, David was using it for hers.

"Anyway, I've also provided you with a loofah sponge to exfoliate any dry skin and a wash cloth for your most intimate parts. This cleansing will assure all the impurities are washed from your body to prepare you for the next stage, which is in the representation of the black rose petals—death and rebirth."

David picked up the wooden egg timer from the white pedestal sink. "You have thirty minutes to bathe, wash your hair, and rinse yourself off in the shower." He twisted the top of the timer and placed it back on the sink. "After you're finished, dry off with the towel hanging next to the sink, and put on the robe hanging on the back of the door. Go back to the bedroom, there you will find everything thing you need to do your hair and makeup inside the pie safe. Once you're finished put on the dress that I've laid out for you and go to the nightstand. Tap the bell three times and walk to the center of the room with your back facing the door and wait. Now, do you have any questions?"

"No." She shook her head.

"Remember, you only have thirty minutes."

Once he left, Marilyn locked the door behind him, knowing very well if he wanted to get back in, it wouldn't stop him. It just made her feel better knowing there was a small barrier between them when she started to undress.

She inched her bruised body into the tub and under the black petals. She had to admit, even though the water was a little hot, it felt wonderful just to get the dirt and grime off her. She grabbed the sponge out of the water, brushed the soap across its rough surface, and carefully washed her tired, aching body. After she washed her most intimate parts, she leaned back and rested her head against the bath pillow. With the combination of fatigue, lavender, and rain tapping on the tin roof she gently closed her eyes and relaxed.

Fifteen minutes later she glanced over at the timer and flipped down the lever. She stood, pulled the curtain around her and washed her hair. She turned off the water and paused when a noise came from inside of the room. Slowly, she pulled back the curtain hoping David wasn't playing tricks on her. Her jaw dropped as she saw her name written across the smooth, wet surface of the bathroom mirror. Cautiously, she stepped out onto the rug, grabbed the towel next to the sink, and wrapped it around her. She rubbed her eyes to be sure she wasn't seeing things. A puff of cool air kissed her neck.

"Mom, is that you?" Marilyn recognized her handwriting.

"Did you say something?" said David out in the hallway.

"I'll be out shortly." She glanced toward the door.

She wiped herself off and wrapped the towel around her head, grabbed the white robe off the back of the door, put it on, and looked back at the mirror. When she got a whiff of her mother's favorite perfume, Tabu, she felt better knowing she wasn't alone.

Dressed in a bias cut, backless emerald silk gown with her hair cascading over her shoulders, she tapped the bell three times. She went to the center of the room with her back to the door as David instructed and waited. Several seconds later the door opened. She glanced at the 'Keep Sweet' plaque hanging on the wall. The scent of her mother's perfume filled her senses. She knew her mother was telling her if she stayed sweet she would live.

David strolled up behind her wearing a tuxedo, gently caressed her bare shoulders, and turned her around. He traced his fingers lightly over her arms, grabbed her hands, and stepped back.

"Amazing! I swear if I didn't know better ..." He paused while his eyes roamed over her from head to toe.

"Didn't know better ... ?" She didn't like the way he was looking at her.

"Never mind," He gently kissed her on the forehead. "I don't want to ruin the surprise."

She looked at the plaque and thought about her mother's warning to stay sweet. She knew no amount of sweet-talking was going to change a damn thing. Besides, listening wasn't her best attribute when she felt threatened.

"I don't like surprises. They make me nervous."

"Well, you'll love this one." He extended his elbow. "Shall we?"

"I'm not going anywhere with you until you tell me what you have planned." She crossed her arms with defiance.

"I'm warning you." He grabbed her arm. "Watch your attitude, follow the rules, and keep sweet while doing it." He started to escort her to the door.

"Rules! Well, I have a few rules of my own." She stared at him and jerked back her arm.

"Really, now what would that be?" He acted like he was enjoying the challenge.

"One, I'm not going to walk on egg shells around you. Two, I will not go down without a fight. And three, I will find a way to escape your sorry ass." After the last two words came out of her mouth, he was sent over the edge.

"Don't ever undermine my authority again!" He raised his hand and slapped her hard across the face.

Marilyn lightly touched her cheek and glared at him to let him know she wasn't backing down.

"So that's the way it's going to be!" He grabbed her by the hair, dragged her across the room, and threw her on the bed. "Well, we'll see who's ass is about to be sorry!"

*"What are you doing?"*

"Letting her know who's in charge," he huffed.

*"This is not part of the plan. Get yourself under control!"*

"I'm sick and tired of her mouth." He got on the bed and straddled her. "David, do this!" he shrieked, his voice imitating the higher voice of an older woman. He slapped Marilyn hard across the face. "David, you are so stupid!" He slapped her again. "David, you are one sorry ass!" He grabbed the front of her dress.

*"She's not your mother! You fool!"*

"No, well she sure sounds like her."

"Get off of me!" Marilyn rocked back and forth.

"You will show me some respect! I'm tired of you bossing me around and telling me what I can and cannot do. You better start listening or so help me God, I'll kill you." David let go of her dress and grabbed her around the throat.

Bang! Bang! Bang! The pounding sound echoed in the room.

"What the hell!" He quickly glanced at the door realizing the noise was coming from the room across the hall. "Don't you dare move a muscle." He pointed his finger in her face, crawled off the bed, and left, slamming the door behind him.

❋   ❋   ❋

Kathryn was lying in bed when the argument in the room across the hall had escalated. Marilyn was putting up one hell of a fight, which only fueled his rage. And when she called him a sorry ass, Kathryn knew Marilyn was in big trouble. The one thing David couldn't tolerate was any form of criticism, especially from a woman. Women were to be seen and not heard. Speak only when spoken to. He treated them like second-class citizens, stripping away their dignity by raping their body, soul, and spirit. She had suffered brutally at his hand eighteen years ago for six months, day in and day out, until she finally escaped and lost any memory of it ever happening. Now she considered it a blessing that she had lived so long without knowing the torment he had put her through.

The door slammed across the hall and she knew he was furious because she had broken the number one rule in the house—the code of silence; which she had did by pounding on the door. She didn't care. She refused to let this woman go through the same hell she suffered, even if it was at her own detriment.

David stormed through the door blinded by anger and stomped to the corner of the room where she was sitting.

"Rebecca, I hope you have a good explanation for breaking the rules." He planted his hands on his hips.

The phrase 'You can catch more flies with honey than vinegar' popped into her head.

"Please." She stood and lowered her eyes in submission. "I didn't mean it as a sign of disrespect. It's just that I didn't want you to do something you would regret later. I was just trying to help."

David blankly stared at her while a tug of war was going on inside of him. She knew the voice wanted to speak, but David detained the words inside his throat.

"Maybe you're right." He slightly cocked his head to the side. "Perhaps, I was a little harsh."

The veins alongside his neck began to bulge and the voice pushed the words right out of his mouth.

*"Harsh!"* The voice chimed in. *"It was plain stupid! Don't you realize what you could've done? If you had tainted the*

*little lamb, you would have ruined any chance of keeping your beloved Rebecca alive."*

"Okay, let's just all settle down and let me think." David started pacing the floor.

*"Think! Since when did you ever think for yourself?"*

"Shut up!" He squinted his eyes and grabbed his head. "Just get out of my head and leave me alone. You're starting to sound like my mother."

Kathryn gently placed her hand on his shoulder, knowing very well he could lash out at her. Yet, if she didn't try to defuse the situation, it's hard to tell what he would end up doing next.

"David," she whispered. "I bet you could use a drink."

He gazed lovingly into Kathryn's eyes and said, "I guess I could use a drink or two. Rebecca, thank you for being so concerned."

"You're welcome." She softly returned the gaze knowing honey had won the battle.

"Well, I guess we better go and have that drink." He softly kissed her on the cheek and left.

Kathryn looked out the window where a smorgasbord of red, orange, yellow, and pink painted the sky while the sun settled down for the night. The motion detector light on the side of the house came on so she stepped back from the window. David walked across the gravel driveway dressed in a pair of jeans and a black t-shirt. He got in his truck and sped down the road, sending rocks scattering behind him like little meteors. With no time to waste she ran into the secret room, got the ladder, and went out the window. Her

307

Saint Jude necklace got hung up on a nail. She stepped up, unhooked the chain, and silently prayed. "Patron of Desperation and Hopeless Causes, I need your help." She sealed it with a kiss and climbed down.

She dropped to the wet ground, grateful it had stopped raining. She checked the back and front doors but they were equipped with electronic door locks and needed a personal code to enter. She checked the windows and they were also locked. She proceeded back to the south side of the house where the cellar door was located. The padlock on the door gave her pause. She spotted a rock next to the house, ran over, grabbed it, and gave the lock a couple of hard whacks until it came undone.

"Bingo!" She threw the rock on the ground.

She took the padlock out of the handles and raised the right side of the door. The wet, metal handle slipped from her hand and the door banged against the ground. She glanced around the yard where a black cat, paused, gave her the evil eye, and nonchalantly prowled toward the barn. She headed down the stairs into the damp, partially covered dirt cellar. She automatically flipped the switch to the single light bulb hanging from the ceiling and remembered a moment from her past.

After the October harvest, her dad would place a pile of apples in the corner of the cold cellar. She closed her eyes and remembered her mom's famous apple pie that won first place every year at the county fair. The aroma of the cinnamon with the apple, the sound of the crisp, flakey crust as the fork cuts into it. The moment it touched her lips brought the taste of heaven. She felt a sense of sadness knowing their relationship never got a chance to grow from child to mother, woman to woman, and then mother to mother. After growing up and having children of her own, she understood why she had been so protective.

She made her way across the room where cobwebs reached from the corners like thin gray fingers as if they wanted to slip around her neck to keep her from going any further. She passed the oil furnace that had been converted from coal and thought about the times she helped her dad stoke it in the middle of the night just before the fire went out. She swore if she made it out of here alive, the assisted living facility would have one last patient to look after.

She started to go up the stairs when she noticed her father's workshop on the other side of the room. He had spent many a night working late to escape the constant nagging of her mother. She thought about going over and taking a look, but decided there would be time for that later. She continued up the steps.

She made a right into the hallway, ran toward the front of the house, and up the steps leading to the second floor. She paused in front of the door on her left, took a deep breath and quietly slid back the lock.

# CHAPTER 21

The light from the hallway filtered into the room as the door creaked open. Kathryn stepped inside at the sound of someone catching their breath. Her face goes limp and her mouth slightly opens as she stared wide-eyed at the woman emerging from the shadows. They had the same almond shaped emerald-green eyes, surrounded by high-arching brows, and long auburn lashes. A widow's peak that pointed down like a one way sign to a straight nose and reached out to high cheek bones framed in a heart shaped face. They had the same long auburn hair and the same build.

Kathryn let out a sudden sigh and opened her mouth to speak. "Either I'm looking at my twin. The double that everyone talks about, or worse yet, David cloned me while I was asleep."

"I can't believe it," whispered Marilyn as she carved her hand through her hair, held it back for several seconds and released it.

"Neither can I?" said Kathryn. "If I didn't know better I'd swear I was looking at my twin."

"We're not exactly identical." Marilyn gently touched the spot just above the right corner of her mouth. "I don't have the beauty mark."

"So you're saying we're twins?" Kathryn stepped further into the room.

"Yes, but your real name isn't Kathryn Rubin. It's Rebecca Hilliard."

"How did you know that?"

"William VanWyc."

"William who?" She narrowed her eyes.

"You know him as Will Mitchell?"

"Will ..." She touched the base of her neck. "How do you know Will?"

"It's a long story and I don't have time to explain." She kicked off the black high heel slippers, unzipped the dress, and let it fall to the floor.

"What did David do, drag you through the streets?" asked Kathryn when she saw the bruises along with the lacerations on her stomach.

"You could say that." She looked passed her into the hallway. "Where is the two-headed snake?"

"He left after I convinced him he needed a drink to calm down."

"Thanks for the distraction." She dashed to the pie safe. "You probably saved my life."

"Are you okay?" asked Kathryn. "It sounded like he worked you over pretty good."

"I'm fine. I just need to get out of here before he comes back." Marilyn pulled out a pair of jeans, a red t-shirt and put them on.

"At least tell me how you know Will," said Kathryn.

"In a nutshell, I met him at a dinner party, one thing led to another, the next thing I know David kidnaps me and I end up here." Marilyn grabbed a pair of socks along with the Nikes, sat down on the foot bench and put them on.

"What do you mean one thing led to another?"

"Like I said it's a long story and the only thing I'm worried about right now is getting out of here."

"This is unbelievable." Kathryn shook her head. "This kind of thing only happens in movies."

"Well, in that case. I'm leaving this scene before the psycho comes back and kills me."

"You can't leave."

"Watch me!" She stood up.

"Listen, just because I suggested he go for a drink doesn't mean he will. That two-headed snake also has another voice. If it convinces David to change his mind and he comes back. We might as well kiss any chance of ever escaping good-bye."

"Are you suffering from, Stockholm syndrome, because nobody in their right mind would stay here, unless you're in love with him?"

"Hell no, I'm not in love with him!"

"Then what is it? Obviously, you're not a prisoner or you wouldn't be standing in front of me, unless he brainwashed you with that 'Keep Sweet' mantra crap."

"Like I said David is too unpredictable. I'm not sure leaving right now would be a good idea."

"Suit yourself. I refuse to submit to some schizophrenic psycho who talks out of the both sides of his mouth like an idiot. I'm leaving." She ran out the door.

"Marilyn Jantzen!"

"What?" She turned around.

"There's something I have to tell you."

"What is it?" She narrowed her eyes with a heavy sigh.

"Don't you have a daughter named Emily?"

"Yes, how do you know that?" Marilyn headed back into the room.

"Emily told me."

"What do you mean? Where is she?"

"David is the one who took her in the mall that day you were yelling at your husband. He's keeping her in the barn."

"So, you've seen her?"

"Yes."

"Why in the hell haven't you both escaped?" Marilyn took several steps away, ran her hand through her hair and came back.

"I tried but I almost got caught."

"I'm going to go get my daughter!" She headed back out the door and toward the steps.

"Wait! Not that way." Kathryn ran and grabbed her by the hand. "The front and back doors of the house are locked from the outside."

"Where are we going?"

"You'll see. David doesn't know all the secrets of this house."

Kathryn led her across the hall into her bedroom, opened the bookcase, and stepped into the secret room. The pitter patter of rain started tapping on the roof as they made their way to where the ladder hung out the window.

"That's where David is keeping her." Kathryn pointed toward the barn.

"How is she?" Marilyn cleared her throat with a sob remembering the dream she had where Emily was being held prisoner by a snake in the barn.

"Actually, she's fine."

"We've got to get out of here before he comes back or we may never have another chance," said Marilyn.

"I agree, but what if he's lurking outside just waiting for us to do something stupid? Besides, we're several miles away from civilization without any transportation and the way the sky looks it's going to downpour any minute. If it were just us, I wouldn't care, but we have Emily to think about."

"I've been thinking about Emily for the past nine months. All I could see was my baby girl lying in some ravine with her throat cut like some slaughtered animal. Now that she's in my reach, not you, David, or even God himself, is going to keep me from going out this window."

Kathryn thought about her own children whose lives had been cut short. They were deprived of the opportunity to grow up. To experience their first kiss, their first date, getting married, and perhaps having children of their own. Grandchildren that she had been denied and would never know. She knew if it was Rachel and Ricky being held prisoner only yards away she wouldn't hesitate for one second to rescue them.

"Let's do this." She stared into Marilyn's eyes, gave her a curt nod and ran toward the bedroom.

"Where are you going?"

"I can't go dressed like this." She grabbed the top of her red silk pajamas and looked down at her bare feet."

"You've got to hurry because time is wasting!"

Several minutes later Kathryn came back into the room and handed Marilyn a jacket. "Here you might need this."

"Thanks." Marilyn grabbed it and put it on.

Kathryn inhaled deeply through her nose and exhaled through her mouth. "Okay, are you ready?"

"Yes, but one more thing before we go. You know David is planning on sacrificing me for the sins of his mother. So you and Emily can be a part of the family he always wanted. If we get caught and he follows through with his sick plan you have to promise me. You will do everything in your power to escape. I don't want my daughter being raised by a madman with his 'Keep Sweet' mantra crap."

"Marilyn, I know what it's like, for someone to come into your life and steal everything you've ever cared about. Eighteen years ago, David kidnapped me. He stole my innocence, my life and my memory. However, in the process I met my husband Richard and had two great children. We had a beautiful life together until a year ago. I lost my five-year-old twins in a car accident by a drunk driver which left Richard in a coma. I promise you. I will do everything in my power to keep your daughter safe—as if she were my own."

Marilyn gazed into her sister's eyes and saw the reflection of her own pain. In the stillness of the waiting room of thirty-six years, they stepped into each other's arms and wept. They cried for lost time and the pain they had endured while apart, but found comfort in knowing they had found each other in the dark abyss of their lives.

Several minutes later, Marilyn stepped back and cried, "I'm so sorry for your loss and the pain you had to endure."

"I know and I don't want you to go through what I went through. So, let's go get your daughter."

They climbed out the window and headed straight for the barn without looking back. All they were focused on was getting Emily and getting out of there. Once inside they dashed across the room and up the stairs to the loft. Kathryn slid back the lock, quietly opened the door, stepped inside and allowed Marilyn to go in first.

❋　　❋　　❋

Marilyn trembled at the thought of seeing her daughter for the first time. Her heart beat with the pounding of the thunder as it rolled across the sky. Her lips quivered at the sight of Emily dressed in jeans and a pink t-shirt playing in the corner with a doll house.

A pearl shaped tear slid down from her eyes, followed by another one, and another one, until soon, a steady stream of salty tears flowed its way down her pale cheek, releasing the sadness and sorrow that she had held inside.

"Emily." The sound of her daughter's name coming from her lips made her heart quiver with joy.

"Mommy?" Emily's eyes widened as she slowly stood up

"Yes honey, it's me." The quiver rushed up and spread across her face.

"Oh, Mommy, it's really you." Emily sprinted across the floor, jumped into her mother's arms and wept.

In her daughter's embrace the world stopped still on its axis. There was no time, no wind and no rain. Her little body pressed in, soft and warm as she wrapped her arms around her neck. With Emily safe in her arms, Marilyn's worries disappeared like rain on summer earth. In that embrace she cocooned her daughter with all the love she had stored in her heart for the past nine months. She inwardly thanked God and hugged all the tighter.

Kathryn stepped up and lightly placed her hand on Marilyn's shoulder and whispered. "We've got to go."

"Honey, you ready to go home?" cried Marilyn.

"Yes." Emily shook her head with a sniffle, glanced over at Kathryn and said, "Kat, I told you, you looked like my mommy."

"Yes, you did," she smiled. "Now go put your shoes and jacket on. It's time to outsmart the fox and leave his den."

"Are you going with us?"

"I sure am."

"Mommy, is it okay if Kat comes and lives with us?"

"Yes," She put her down and glanced up at Kathryn.

Marilyn didn't take her eyes off of Emily for a second as she ran to the nightstand. For fear a boogey man would appear out of nowhere and take her.

"Marilyn, I think our best route of escape is to go through the woods behind the barn. If I remember correctly there use to be a farm about two miles away."

"Okay, whatever you think is best. I just want to get out of here before David comes back."

"Can I take Twinkie?" Emily grabbed the pink bear off the bed.

"Yes, honey," said Marilyn. "Now let's go."

Marilyn picked up Emily, held her tight and followed Kathryn down the steps. They ran across the floor and just about the time they reached the barn door it swung open.

"Well, well, well …" David stepped inside waving a gun. "What do we have here?"

Marilyn and Kathryn backed away in quick, jerky steps while a look of 'what do we do now' passed between them. Realizing they were trapped Marilyn put Emily down and protectively placed her behind her.

"So it was you that took my daughter!" Marilyn's eyes flashed and closed in slits while her nostrils flared.

"Yes. However, I didn't realize Emily was your daughter until after the fact." David strutted into the room.

"Why?" Marilyn's mouth quivered, slurring the one question she had asked for the past nine months.

"Well ..." He raised his eyebrows.

*"David had nothing to do with it."* The voice interrupted. *"It was all my doing. Your daughter was sitting there all alone on that bench and I knew it was fate. David always wanted a child of his own, but he was afraid he would end up like his mother and treat her badly. Besides, she looked so much like his beloved Rebecca, I couldn't help myself. Children are so trusting; especially when it comes to puppies."*

Marilyn balled up her fist and was about to charge him until she felt the tiny arms slip around her legs with a whimper. So, instead she planted her feet, crossed her arms, and stared him down like her brother had taught her to when she was confronted with a bully. 'Always stare them down, Mare. There's nobody so damn tough they won't back up if you stare them down.'

The voice's dark eyes were small and spaced evenly apart, sitting below trim eyebrows that seemed to curve as a natural extension of his slender nose. He kept his mouth closed in a thin straight line. His face held forward in a steady gaze and had an air of authority that was palpable. Seconds later his eyes turned to a soft blue and as David emerged he turned his attention to Kathryn.

"Rebecca, you disappoint me. I thought I could trust you."

"It wasn't her idea." Marilyn interjected.

"I didn't say you could open that hole in your face. You know I should just put a bullet in your head and be done with it."

"David, please," Kathryn begged.

He looked at Kathryn and back at Marilyn. "God, it's amazing how you two look alike. If I didn't know better, I'd swear you were twins."

"I know it's unbelievable." Kathryn cautiously moved toward David. "The only difference is I have a beauty mark and she doesn't."

"It's my beauty mark." David softly touched her face.

The gentleness in which David caressed Kathryn's face convinced Marilyn he truly cared about her in his own way.

"Come to think of it, you're just the moonlight exposure of the real thing." His eyes darted toward Marilyn.

Marilyn knew David meant she was just a cheap imitation of the real thing. Just like the moon was the reflection of the sun, she was just a reflection of his precious Rebecca. They were like the same red rose, one basking under a clear blue sky vibrant, beautiful, and full of grace. The other one under the moonlight, though brightly lit, its petals faded to a shade of gray paling in comparison.

"However, you do have your purpose," he continued. "Because of you I will be able to keep my beloved and have the family I always wanted."

"David." Kathryn lightly rested the palm of her hand against his cheek.

"What." He lovingly gazed into her eyes while he reached behind him and placed the gun in the waist-band of his pants.

"I love you." Kathryn blurted out the three words, leaving a sour taste in her mouth. "Why don't we just leave? We'll start where we left off eighteen years ago and have a family of our own. We don't need Marilyn and Emily because we'll have each other."

While Kathryn was distracting David, Marilyn cautiously turned to Emily and whispered, "Honey, I want you to quietly go back up into the loft and wait for me."

"But Mommy…"

"Shh …" Marilyn placed her finger over her lips. "Please, do as I say."

"My sweet Rebecca." Marilyn heard David say as Emily made her way upstairs. "I love you too, but in order for us to be together I can't let Marilyn go. Without her; there is no us."

Marilyn knew she had to do something if she wanted to stay alive. She looked around the barn and spotted a shovel leaning against the wall several feet away. While David and Kathryn were engaged in conversation she slowly reached over and grabbed it. She inhaled and without another thought she charged forward.

"Kathryn!" she yelled.

Just as Kathryn stepped aside the shovel hit David square in the face. He stumbled backward, tripped over his feet, and fell to the floor. She raised the shovel to give him another blow. He grabbed hold of her ankle and gave it a yank, causing her feet to slip out from under her. He scrambled to his feet and pulled the gun from his waistband as she hit the floor. She started to get up and David pressed his foot against her chest and pushed her back down.

"You know I'm really getting tired of you." He pointed the gun at her.

"David, please don't do this," Kathryn pleaded.

"Rebecca, shut up!" He looked at her with eyes like daggers. "I don't what to hear another word. Now, go get that rope hanging on the wall and tie her up or so help me God I'll kill you both."

After Kathryn tied Marilyn's hands behind her back David said, "Rebecca, upstairs!"

"But David …"

"Move!" He pushed her toward the steps.

"Where's the girl?" David looked around the barn.

"She's up in the loft," said Marilyn.

"Call for her." Marilyn hesitated and David said, "Now. . . " He gritted his teeth.

"Emily!" She gave him one of Dillon's stare me downs. "Come here baby."

Overhead you could hear the pitter patter of feet and several seconds later Emily emerged hugging Twinkie.

"Stand where you are and don't you dare move." He gave Marilyn a warning. "Go!" He pushed Kathryn toward the steps following close behind.

A feeling of hopelessness came over Marilyn at the sound of the door closing behind them with a thud. The lock clicked into place as desolate tears ran from her blinking eyes. Once again she had failed to keep her daughter safe as she slipped through her fingers for the second time. The only consolation, Emily was with someone she trusted and knew she would do everything in her power to escape.

"Save the tears." David pushed Marilyn out the barn door. "You're going to need them later."

Marilyn stumbled across the yard while a child's voice emerged behind her and filtered through the night air.

*"Dave, you promised."*

"Tommy, she's no good for you." said David.

*"Please, you said you wouldn't hurt her."*

Marilyn glanced over her shoulder where David's face had softened. His blue eyes were that of a child, so innocent, so pure. She waited for David to speak, but when he remained silent, she slowly turned around.

"Tommy," Marilyn softly whispered hoping the little boy was still present.

*"Yes."* He giggled.

"My name is Marilyn."

*"I already know that silly."* David softly looked at Marilyn and bit on his lower lip.

David's right arm hung alongside his body with the gun dangling from his finger tips. Marilyn didn't know how long the boy personality would be out so she had to act fast.

"Tommy, you know little boys shouldn't play with guns."

"*Oh.*" He lifted his hand and stared at the gun. "*Dave is going to be mad because I got his gun. He said little boys should never play with guns.*"

"Why don't you give the gun to me?"

"*Okay.*"

"First you have to untie me." Marilyn slowly turned around holding her breath.

He placed the gun on the ground and started to untie her. The rope slipped off her hands and just as she made a dash for the gun David firmly gripped her wrist.

"Tommy! What the hell are you doing?"

"*Don't be mad, Dave. She's nice. She wasn't going to hurt us.*"

"You fool! You almost got us killed." He grabbed the gun off the ground.

"*I'm sorry Dave. Please don't be mad.*" The boy whimpered.

"She's just like mother." He pointed the gun at Marilyn. "Acting all nice and the next thing you know, you're being whipped like a dog and locked up in the basement. Is that what you want?""

"*Dave, I'm …*"

The childlike voice faded and the menacing eyes of grey and blue threatened floods of fury. "Move!"

David pushed her toward the house almost causing her to fall to the ground. She glanced toward the barn where Kathryn was standing in front of the window. A look passed between them with the understanding she may not come out alive. With a nod of her head she reminded her sister to follow through with her promise to escape. Marilyn's heart skipped a beat at the sight of her daughter running to the window.

"Mommy ..." Emily sobbed pounding the palm of her hands against the pane.

Marilyn was trembling, almost shaking, as the muffled sound of her daughter's voice repeated her name over and over again. *'Oh God.'* Her stomach twisted. *'Oh, God, God.'* She couldn't seem to breathe. She stared at the window for several seconds before she realized that she was trying to sob, but could make no sound. There was a roaring in her ears, and something was cutting her hands. Her nails—they'd bitten into her palms, and blood had started to well out under her fingertips. She barely felt the pain when her knees buckled to the ground and Kathryn disappeared from the window with Emily.

# CHAPTER 22

"Get up!" David grabbed her by the arm and pulled her off the ground.

Marilyn's face swelled up with anger as her brows furrowed into a line across her forehead. Heat stretched from her arms down into her chest carrying with it all the pain and suffering he had caused her for the past nine months.

"Let go of me you imbecile." Marilyn jerked her arm away and took a step back. "Who do you think you are kidnapping my daughter? Who gave you the right to step into my world and turn it upside down?"

"Who do I think I am?" He raised the gun in his hand. "I'm the one in control and once I get rid of you, Emily will be my daughter."

The words, my daughter, sent Marilyn over the edge. "She'll never be your daughter if I have anything to do with it. Besides, you're not fit to be a father. A real father wouldn't take someone else's child. Keep them locked up in a barn like a prisoner. A real parent's duty is to love and protect."

David slipped behind her, grabbed her by the shoulders and squeezed.

*"Not fit to be a father,"* whispered the voice in her ear. *"Well isn't that the pot calling the kettle black. If I remember correctly, you're the one who left Emily all alone in the mall that day. So what does that make you?"*

"You were asked a question." David interrupted. "So, I suggest you answer it."

"I'm her mother and nothing you say or do can change that." She drew in a slow steady breath. "Besides, just because I was only gone for a few seconds didn't give you the right to take her. She wasn't yours to take. In the law's eyes, that's considered kidnapping."

*"The moment you gave up your seconds."* His arm slipped around her waist and squeezed her body against him. *"We took them. Emily is now ours. Rebecca will be her mother and we will become a family. Unfortunately, you won't be around to see it. Now move."* He pushed her toward the house.

"You better do what he says because you don't want to make him angry." David interrupted again. "If you think I have a temper, just wait until you see his. Besides, sometimes he has a tendency to cause me to blackout. Just like the time he broke into your café without my knowledge. You were lucky—if he had gotten a hold of you, it's hard to tell what he would've done."

Marilyn decided not to press her luck, so she did what he asked, hoping she'd get another chance to escape.

The cool damp air penetrated Marilyn's jacket as they descended into the cellar. Just before she reached the bottom step, David grabbed her from behind and pressed her body against him.

"You know someone once said that if you want trouble, find yourself a redhead." He gently lifted a strand of her hair and took a whiff. "My mother was a living testament to that statement. Even after her death, I can still feel the clutches of her hell fire. However, because of you, all that is about to change. You will be the sacrifice that will atone for her sins and I will be free once and for all." He planted his foot in the middle of her back and gave her a shove.

Her already bruised body belly flopped onto the dirt floor, knocking the breath out of her. She gasped for air while David grabbed her by the hair, jerked back her head, and stared into her eyes. His pupils weren't dilated so she knew it was David who was filled with rage.

"Tell me mother, what was it this time that caused your temper to flare?" David didn't bat an eye. "Was it the way I held my mouth while I was eating supper or was it because I got a C+ on my math test instead of an A? Or, was it the way Daniel's soft blue eyes slanted at you when he smiled?"

The whites of David's eyes formed into unnerving slits as he directed his lethal stare at her. Inside his eyes were tiny flames which sparked every time he blinked. She grabbed a handful of dirt as he pulled her up off the floor and pushed her against the wall.

*"David! Get yourself under control!"* The voice didn't look in her eyes, but he stared at a spot on the wall just above her head. *"You're going to ruin everything."*

"Why should I? This one is like mother." He slipped his hand around her throat. "She can't be trusted and deserves to die!"

He tightened his grip, cutting off her airway. She was about ready to pass out when she remembered the hand full of dirt. She reached up and smeared it into his eyes as hard as she could, digging her fingers into his eyeballs. Screaming, he released his grip on her throat. She ran toward the steps that lead upstairs into the house, taking them two at a time. She could hear him cursing and stumbling up the steps after her. She reached the front door and remembered Kathryn telling her it was locked from the outside. With no time to waste, she bolted into the semi-dark room on her right, hid behind the floral Victorian couch in front of the window and listened to the three-way conversation in the hallway.

*"Well, looks like the redhead dragon won again."* The voice taunted.

"What are you talking about? You're the one that let her go." David paced up and down the hallway.

*"True, but you're the one who didn't see her grab the handful of dirt. So, technically it's your fault. The way I see it, you're the one that's been outwitted."*

"I've got it all under control!"

*"Really, then why are you standing here with your thumb up your ass? You should be out there looking for her. If she escapes, then what are you going to do?"*

*Dave, you're not going to hurt her are you?"* The childlike voice infiltrated the conversation.

"Tommy, she left her little girl all alone. You don't want another mother that's going to do the same thing to you?"

*"No, Dave. I just thought …"*

"Be quiet and go to sleep!"

*"Why are you still standing here? Go find her!"* The voice demanded.

"Quiet! Everyone just shut up! You're giving me a headache!" David leaned against the wall, holding his head in his hands.

Silence hung in the air like the suspended moment before a falling glass shatters on the ground. Marilyn tensed against the shaking of her limbs but it was useless. Hurried footsteps brought her heart racing as David made his way into the room.

"I know you're in …" His words were interrupted by a crash coming from somewhere else in the house and he darted out of the room.

His footsteps retreated back into the hallway. She waited to see if there was any indication he would change his mind and come back.

"I see you tripped over the trash can. A little clumsy aren't we?" David laughed as he picked it up off the floor. "Come out; come out, wherever you are."

Marilyn thought about the writing on the bathroom mirror, her mother tapping the lid of her trash can in her kitchen. Was it possible she was here and had overturned the trash can to distract David? She glanced around the room at the sound of his footsteps moving further and further away. That's when she spotted the skeleton key hanging from the door leading outside. She tiptoed over and noticed the portrait of a woman hanging above the fireplace. Her bright red hair was pulled back into a French twist revealing greenish blue eyes set in a triangle-shaped face. The eyes seemed soft, but the firmness of the broad and slightly square jaw, gave hardness to her countenance. The resemblance was evident, and she knew it was David's mother whom he so desperately hated.

She slowly turned the key and as the door screeched open her heart skipped a beat. She waited for several seconds, took a deep breath and quietly slipped outside. She spotted the barn on her right and made a run for it. She caught movement from the right corner of her eye as a gunshot echoed through the night sky. Fear rose in her throat, sucking away the air around her as David gave chase.

"Stop!" He commanded with a second bang.

Marilyn heard the sharp intake of her own breath as she ignored his warning. Raindrops bounced on her face like little beads as she ran passed the barn. The wind whooshed through the branches of the oak tree and it started to pour. It washed through her hair, swept over her shoulders, and down over her jacket. She could barely see as it coursed over her lips and mouth. She darted into the woods at the sound of David cursing her name. She ran faster, hoping to put some distance between them. Suddenly, her entire body was suspended in thin air and she freefell over an embankment, until she comes to a complete stop. She lay there for several seconds to catch her breath before springing to her feet and starting to run—until David stepped out in front of her.

"Going somewhere?" He pointed the gun at her.

Marilyn stopped dead in her tracks with a long, low sigh. Her shoulders hunched over in defeat as her body weaved back and forth exhausted. The dream she had weeks before had finally became her reality. The only difference, there was no moonlight, no cliff, and no raging river. It had denied her a way to escape. The snake had his fangs in her and she knew he wouldn't let go until she was dead with his venom.

"Put these on and don't you say a word." David threw the cuffs at her.

After she put on the cuffs he pushed her through the woods until they reached the edge of the forest. The lights glared in the farmhouse as the moon set itself free from the heavy gray mass that held it prisoner. The landscape was the exact replica of the dream she had after David had kidnapped her. The moonlight illuminated the barn on her left where she saw her sister standing in front of the window. A look of hopelessness passed between them because they knew, unless a miracle happened; Marilyn would be dead before morning.

The rain had reduced to a drizzle as he pushed her toward the south side of the house where they entered the basement through the cellar door. He shoved her past the steps that led upstairs and over to a door across the room. David grabbed the key off the ledge, unlocked it, and pushed her inside.

The rectangular room was a little damp but it wasn't totally unpleasant. The walls were painted an off-white trimmed in a floral border. The only furniture in the room was a double bed, a nightstand, a dresser and a tan couch. Across from the couch was an outdated box television. To the right, stood a small refrigerator and a two tier cart with a microwave.

David started to take off the handcuffs and paused at the sound of heavy footsteps stomping down the cellar stairs.

"Davie, are you down here?" A man dressed in a pair of jeans and an orange polo shirt stepped into the doorway.

"Daniel what are you doing here? You're not supposed to be here until next weekend?"

"I know but we're having a party at the group home. I wanted my Michael Jackson Thriller CD. So I asked Clyde to bring me here so I could get it. I wanted to show everybody how I could moon dance."

"Is Clyde still here?"

"No, I told him you would bring me back."

Marilyn remembered what David said when he thought she was his mother, *'Or, was it the way Daniel's soft blue eyes slanted at you when he smiled.'* She looked at Daniel and back at David. They had the same blond hair and blue eyes, though his was slightly slanted. David had an athletic body while Daniel had the body of the Pillsbury dough boy. The urge came over her to poke his tummy just to see if he would giggle.

"Looks like I'm not the only one with a double," whispered Marilyn.

"He's not my double." David turned and faced her. "We're fraternal twins. Daniel is the slow one and I'm the smart one."

Daniel skipped up behind David, gave her a smile from ear to ear, waved like a child and said, "Hi! My names Danny. What's yours?"

"Marilyn." Before she could say another word David interrupted.

"Danny boy, this one is mean like mother, so we have to be careful."

"Okay, Davie." Daniel gave her a frown.

"Danny, go find your CD so I can take you back to the group home."

"I think I left it in mother's nightstand the last time I was here." Daniel stepped passed him and headed toward the table next to the bed.

"Danny, I need to go upstairs and change my wet clothes. Do you think you can keep an eye on Marilyn until I get back?"

"Yep," said Daniel as he rummaged through the drawer.

"If you give my brother any trouble," whispered David, "there'll be hell to pay when I get back." He left locking the door behind him.

After Daniel found his CD he sat down on the edge of the bed and stared at Marilyn. "Are you mean like Mother?"

"I don't think so."

"Good, cause I don't want Davie to hurt you."

"What do you mean?"

"I don't want to talk about it." He placed the disc in the CD player, pressed play and started to sing. "Beat it. Beat it …"

"So, you like Michael Jackson?" She slowly moved toward him.

"Yes, do you want to see me dance like Michael?"

"Sure." She glanced around the room hoping to find another way out.

With a big smile on his face, he moon walked across the floor, bent his leg, gave it a shake, and spun around. Marilyn realized Daniel was just a child in a man's body, pure of heart, and wouldn't hurt a fly.

"Do you want to dance with me?"

"I would love to, but I can't." She turned and showed him the cuffs on her wrist.

He grinned, skipped to the wood stove in the corner, reached into a copper woodbin, and pulled out a key.

"You can't tell Davie." He placed his chubby finger against his lips. "He'll get mad."

"I promise, I won't tell him."

"Cross your heart, hope to die, stick a needle in your eye, pinky promise?"

"Yes, I promise."

"Good, but you have to put them back on after we're done." He unlocked the cuffs and hung them on the edge of the woodbin along with the key.

With a giggle, he grabbed her hand and they moon walked across the floor. Together, they stopped in front of the door, lifted their legs, shook them, and spun around. They started back across the floor where she heard him sing the lyrics *"strong is your fight."* Those four words hit her like a ton of bricks. How strong was her fight? Was she going to give up now? She was hard pressed on every side, but not crushed. She was beaten down, but not destroyed. She had been through too much—to hell with giving up. She was going to fight to the finish, no matter what.

After the song ended, Daniel headed to the refrigerator. "That made me thirsty. You want something to drink?"

"Do you have water?" She licked her dry lips.

"Yessiree bob!" He opened the door, grabbed two bottles, and handed one to her.

"Thanks." She took a sip and asked, "Daniel did this use to be your mother's room?"

"Yes, but she died." A veil of sadness fell softly over his round face where beads of sweat lingered from dancing.

She took another sip of water and sat down next to him on the couch. "Do you miss your mother?"

"Sometimes, but now I don't have to be locked up anymore."

"What do you mean?"

"I don't want to talk about it." He frowned and shook his head.

"It's okay." She lightly touched his hand.

Marilyn glanced around the room and on a bulletin board hanging on the wall she spotted a picture of Emily sitting on a tire swing. Daniel was standing behind her with this big grin on his face.

"Daniel, can you tell me where this picture was taken?" She got up and took it off the board.

"Oh, that's my little friend, Emmy. Davie took it in the backyard with my new camera I got for my birthday. She's so cute. I could just squeeze her little cheeks."

"Does Emmy live here?"

"Yes, sometimes I come over and watch her when Davie is gone. If it's on the weekend we have a Chicken Little barnyard sleepover in the barn. We play games, do the chicken dance, eat pizza, and watch movies. We have lots of fun but sometimes she cries because she misses her mommy. It makes me sad when she cries because sometimes I miss my mommy even though she was mean. Everybody should have a mommy."

"So Davie is nice to Emmy?"

"Yes, but I don't think she likes him much because he took her away from her family. Davie said he was going to get her a new mommy because her real mommy was mean and left her all alone. And mommies shouldn't be mean to their children. That's bad and they need to get a time out."

Marilyn quickly placed the picture back on the board at the sound of footsteps approaching outside the door. Daniel started pacing around in circles twirling his hands at a loss of what to do. She ran to the woodbin and just as she grabbed the handcuffs to put them back on, David stepped through the door.

"What's going on in here?" He placed his hand on his hips. "Daniel, why are those handcuffs off her wrist?"

"I'm sorry, Davie." He pouted like a child who just got their hand caught in the cookie jar.

"It's not his fault. I picked the lock. He had nothing to do with it." She stared into Daniel's eyes hoping he would agree."

"Daniel is that true?"

"Yes." He puckered his lips and looked down.

"You know, I can't wait to get rid of you." He grabbed the cuffs and snapped them on her wrist.

"Davie, she's nice, please don't hurt her!"

"I'm not, but I'm going to give her time out for being disobedient, just like I do when you don't listen."

"So you're going to make her sit in the corner for fifteen minutes and give her ice cream?"

"Yes. Now get your CD so I can take you back to the group home."

"Okay." He skipped across the floor.

Marilyn knew by time out David meant her time had run out, period. There would be no temporary corner to sit in, no ice cream to make her feel better. There would be no mercy as she became the sacrifice he need-ed to keep his beloved Rebecca and raise her daughter as his own.

"Let's go," said David. "It's getting late."

Daniel popped the disc out of the player and moon walked across the floor. He paused at the door and gave Marilyn a great big smile.

"Enjoy your ice cream." He waved good-bye as David closed and locked the door.

It was then Marilyn realized; David was just a moonlight exposure of Daniel.

# CHAPTER 23

William pulled up in front of the Natural Springs Café. He had just got back from Savannah and the lead in finding Abby's ex-husband Seth ended up being a case of mistaken identity. So he decided to come home and make plans to go back to the cave with Marilyn. Where they had shared their first kiss; a kiss that was short lived because he had called her Rebecca. However, the second kiss they shared at the Blue Moon had made up for it. He trembled faintly at the taste of her soft full lips. It had left him with the desire to have her lying by his side, holding him close at night and kissing him awake in the morning.

He got out of the car and headed for the café. Just as he stepped up on the porch, Dana rushed out the door

"Dana, what's wrong?" asked William.

"Marilyn is missing."

"What?"

"She was supposed to meet me here this morning for breakfast about an hour ago."

"Maybe she's late?"

"She's never late. Besides, she would've called me if she was going to be late or couldn't make it."

"Did you call her house?"

"Yes, but she didn't answer. I'm headed there now to check up on her. I'm just hoping this has nothing to do with the break-in."

"There was a break-in?"

"Yes, and if she hadn't locked herself in the upstairs apartment it's hard to tell what would've happened."

"Have you called anyone else that might know where she is?"

"I tried her ex-husband Jim and Charlie but I got no answer.

"Do you want me to go with you to Marilyn's?"

"No, Jason is meeting me there."

"Is there anything I can do?"

"Would you mind trying to get a hold of Jim and Charlie?"

"Not at all. Just give me their numbers." He pulled out his cell phone.

After he programmed the numbers in his cell he said, "Call me as soon as you find out anything."

"I will." Dana ran across the street, got on her bike and drove away.

About an hour later Dana called. "William, I checked all the rooms in the house and Marilyn's not home. I also checked the doors and windows and there doesn't seem to be any sign of a break-in. Her car is in the garage but her bike is missing. I hope nothing happened to her when she was on her way to the café this morning."

"I still haven't got a hold of Jim and Charlie."

"So what do we do?"

William could hear the panic in her voice and said, "Dana, why don't you just meet me back at the café and hopefully by that time I'll get a hold of Jim and Charlie?"

"Okay, I'll be there shortly."

William, Dana, Charlie and Carmen were waiting at the café for Jim to show up. After about ten minutes William decided to start without him.

"Since everyone's here except for Jim, let's go ahead and get started," He glanced across the counter. "Carmen, when Marilyn left Friday evening did she say where she was going?"

"No, she just reminded me she was taking Saturday off and would be back on Sunday. When she didn't show up this morning, I called her house and cell phone but she didn't answer."

"Did she tell you what her plans were on Saturday?" He wondered if she had gone to the cave without him and maybe something had happened to her.

"She just said she needed a mental health day and would be back this morning."

"Dana, are you sure she was to meet you here this morning?" William took a sip of his coffee. "Maybe you got your dates mixed up."

"No, we made plans to meet this morning, have breakfast, and then go on a bike ride. When I showed up and Marilyn wasn't here I was a little worried because of the break-in a couple of nights ago."

"There was a break-in?" asked Charlie.

"Yes, it happened Wednesday night. After Marilyn closed the café she stayed here instead of going home. She does that sometimes when she doesn't want to be alone in her big house. Anyway, she dialed 911 and by the time the police got here they were gone. She called me, asked if she could spend the night and I came over and picked her up."

"Did the police find anything?" asked William.

"The only thing they found was the broken glass from the patio door where they came in. There was nothing missing, so it was definitely Marilyn they were after."

William realized the break-in was the same night he had seen her at the Blue Moon. The night they had shared a kiss—a kiss that had been more about his future than his past. He thought about how he had fallen in love with Rebecca and months later she disappeared. What were the odds the same thing would happen twice? However, this time there was one difference; he wasn't going to run away like he did eighteen years ago. This time, he was going to stay, fight to the finish and would leave no stone unturned, no matter how long it took.

"Charlie, when was the last time you spoke to Marilyn?" asked William.

"I've been out of town, so I haven't spoken to her since the dinner party."

Everyone turned their heads when the door of the café opened. "Sorry I'm late." Jim stepped inside. "There was a wreck on Shepherd Grade Road."

The atmosphere in the room shifted the moment Jim sat down next to Dana. Without a word, she rolled her eyes, got up, and moved to the end of the counter.

"Dana, I don't bite."

"Yeah, well I have it on good authority you do. So I'm not taking any chances."

"I think I need some caffeine." Jim quipped, looking expectantly at Dana.

"I'm sure there's some around somewhere, go look for it," Dana retorted, not glancing his way.

Jim got up and went behind the counter to the coffee pot. William could tell there was definitely some animosity between them and it probably stemmed from Jim cheating on her best friend.

"Carmen, do you remember anyone coming into the café on Friday who had never been here before?"

"I don't think so." She paused. "Wait. There was this one guy who stopped in for lunch and asked to speak to Marilyn."

"Do you remember what he looked like?"

"He was dressed in jeans and a navy blue t-shirt, probably in his late thirties. He had an athletic build, was around six feet, had sandy blond hair, and these beautiful blue eyes. Plus, he gave me a big tip before he left."

When Jim sauntered past Dana with his cup of coffee she slightly turned her head and said, "Jim, that sounds like you."

Jim didn't say a word until he sat down and took a sip of his coffee. "Yeah, for all I know, it could've been you dressed in drag."

"Carmen, do you recall him saying anything?" William interrupted, not wanting to be a part of their game.

"Well, he did ask her out."

"Well, I don't blame him. Marilyn is looking quite hot these days. Wouldn't you say so, Jim?" Dana took a drink of her cappuccino.

"Okay, let's just get rid of the elephant in the room," said William. "Obviously you two have some animosity toward one another and perhaps with good reason but now is not the time. So can we just focus on finding Marilyn?" He slightly cocked his head and raised his eyebrows.

"Carmen, do you remember what Marilyn said?" asked William.

"Yes, she said she wasn't interested, told him to enjoy his meal, and have a nice day."

William looked at Dana and no matter how she felt he couldn't exclude Jim from the conversation.

"Jim, when was the last time you saw or spoke to Marilyn?"

"It was Wednesday night at the Blue Moon Café, but I only spoke to her briefly just to see how she was doing."

"You know, I don't understand," said Dana. "You weren't worried about how she was doing before you broke her heart with another woman. So why now?"

"Dana, I don't care what you think of me. I never have. Besides, Marilyn and I have managed to call it a truce for our daughter's sake. And if you don't like it, I'm sorry."

"Jim …"

"That's enough you two!" William interrupted. "If you can't be civil to one another than take it outside." He redirected his attention back to Carmen.

"Carmen, can you think of anyone else who should be added to this conversation?"

"Kyle, I saw him talking to Marilyn in front of the café when she was getting ready to leave Friday."

"Kyle?"

"Yeah, he's one of the college kids at the university who has a big crush on her."

"Do you know where I can find him?" asked William.

"There he is, on his skateboard." Carmen pointed to the window, got up, and stuck her head out the door. "Hey, Kyle, you got a minute?"

"Sure." Kyle flipped up his skateboard, grabbed it, and strutted toward Carmen. "What's up?" He lifted his chin.

"Do you have time to come in and talk for a sec?"

"Just don't make it too long. I'm meeting up with Candy in about twenty minutes." He flipped his black hair out of his dark brown eyes and followed her into the café.

"Hi, Kyle, I'm William Van ..."

"I know who you are." He leaned against one of the game tables dressed in a pair of black skinny jeans with a studded belt and a Pennywise, skull-and-bones, black t-shirt.

"Is that right?"

"Yeah, and I've got my eye on you."

"Oh, really, and why's that?"

"I saw you kissing Ms. J. Wednesday night outside the Blue Moon. You better do right by her or you'll have me to deal with. So what do you want? I've got things to do." He set his board on the floor.

"Kyle, it's about Marilyn." Dana raised her eyebrows and gave William an approving look. She reached across and picked up his coffee cup.

"Can I get you a refill? How do you like it?"

Jim rolled his eyes, acknowledging the snub.

"What's up Ms. K.?" Kyle lifted his chin. Dana responded as she walked over to the coffee pot to get a fresh cup for William.

"Kyle, Carmen said you spoke to Marilyn Friday evening before she left the cafe?"

"Yeah, what about it?"

"Did she tell you where she was going?"

"Nope. I figure she was going home. Why?"

"No one's heard from her since she left the café Friday and we're a little concerned."

"I hope it has nothing to do with the weirdo that was bothering her the other night outside the Blue Moon. It's a good thing I showed up when I did because I didn't like the way he was looking at Ms. J."

"What did he want?" Dana set the cup in front of William and sat down.

"He said he wanted directions to the Bistro but, when I looked into the creep's eyes, I knew he wanted more than directions. So I told the scumbag he best move on and escorted Ms. J. back to the café."

"When you saw Marilyn leave Friday evening, did you notice anything out of the ordinary?"

"No, not really, but did you check the back roads?" He flipped his hair out of his face again. "Sometimes she takes that route to go home. Those curves can be a little dangerous. I wrecked my dirt bike on that road once."

"No, we haven't," said Dana.

"Why don't I go and check it out?" Jim started to get up from the counter.

"The hell you are!" Kyle stared at him. "You've hurt Ms. J. enough, you two-timing snake."

"Pennywise?" Jim looked at the word engraved on his t-shirt. "Is that what you pay for a college education these days?"

"FYI, Pennywise is a punk rock band formed in 1988 that took their name from the Stephen King novel *It*. But if you had a brain and could read you would probably already know that."

"Kyle, this man may be a cheater but I don't think he's a killer."

"Well, Ms. Kowalski, that's the nicest thing you've ever said to me."

"And that will be my last. Kyle, would you mind going along with him and showing him the back roads for Ms. J.?"

"Sure, I'd do anything for Ms. J.," Kyle looked at Jim. "Give me about ten minutes and I'll meet you in front of the café."

"Okay, bro," Jim shrugged his shoulders.

"I'm not your bro." He picked up his skateboard and started to walk out the door. "Ms. K., let me know if you need anything else."

"Thanks Kyle," said Dana.

Kyle paused, looked back at William and said, "You know, come to think of it, I saw a silver truck pull out behind Ms. J. after she left. I wonder if it was that scumbag because he had the same type of truck. Do you think he could've done something to her?"

"I don't know Kyle. I guess it's possible. Anyway, thanks for the info."

"You know Ms. J is one special woman." He made a fist and tapped his chest twice. "And if anyone has harmed her, he'll have hell to pay." He looked at Jim and left.

William couldn't agree more, and if someone did take her and harmed one hair on her head, they would have two hells to pay.

"Well, if you guys don't have anything else, I guess we're done here."

"Dana, do you think I should keep the café closed until tomorrow?" asked Carmen.

"Yes, why don't you go ahead and go. I'll lock up before I leave."

"Are you sure?"

"Yes, there's no reason for you to stay."

Carmen grabbed her backpack off the floor. "If I think of anything else I'll let you know."

After she left, Charlie stood up and said, "William, I'm going to head out to the police station. I know there's nothing they can do at the moment, but I think they would want to know, especially since her café was broken into. It sounds like to me, this was more than a break-in, and whoever it was may have come back to finish the job."

"Thanks, that's a great idea."

"William, it was great seeing you again." Charlie shook his hand. "After I talk to the police, I'll let you know what they said."

"Okay."

"Jim." Charlie nodded realizing he still cared about Marilyn regardless of what happened between them.

"Charlie." Jim nodded back.

After Charlie left, Kyle tapped on the window and glared at Jim. "Let's go man. Daylight is wasting."

"Guess I better go. Pennywise is calling."

"The boy is probably wiser than you on any given day," Dana smirked.

"Dana, regardless what you think of me, I still care about Marilyn."

"Well, if that's the case. Maybe you can redeem yourself by doing all you can to find her."

"William," said Jim ignoring Dana's remark. "I'll let you know if we find anything."

"Thanks, Jim."

After he left, Dana said, "Sorry, but that man has a way of getting under my skin."

"I noticed," William stood up. "And I'm sorry, if I came across a little too strong, but finding Marilyn was more important than the little feud that was going on between you two."

"I know, no apology necessary." she shook her head. "Well, I guess I better lock up and get back to my shop."

"Do you mind if I stay a little longer?"

"No, not at all. Just let me know when you're ready to leave, and I'll come over and lock up."

"Thanks, Dana."

"No problem. I'll talk to you later." She started to leave. "Oh, by the way, if Marilyn let you kiss her, I wouldn't take it for granted. Jim really broke her heart that day at the mall when Emily was taken. If she's just one of your 'two ships that pass in the night' thing, just keep sailing. If not, tread lightly; she has been through too much for her heart to be broken again."

"Understood," he shook his head.

After Dana left, William picked up his coffee and decided to go into the sitting room to think about what to do next. He dimly turned up the chandelier and sat down at the table with the picture of the little house on Princess Street. He wondered if he was ever going to see Marilyn again, to let her know how much he loved her. She wasn't just a ship passing in the night. This time he wanted to dock and put down roots with a woman he had fallen in love with. He would always cherish the young love he shared with Rebecca, but it was only a memory of a young man's heart. The love he felt for Marilyn was fresh and something he wanted to build his future on. With a sigh, he leaned forward, propped his elbows on his knees, hung his head, and did something he hadn't done in a very long time—he prayed.

"I'm not much of a praying man, but if you're listening I could sure use your help right now. Just give me some kind of sign to let me know where Marilyn ..."

William stopped when he realized how stupid he sounded. Here he was praying to a God that didn't exist, and even if he did, he wasn't listening. It was no different than the nights he prayed and cried himself to sleep at the age of five while his old man beat up his mom. The times he dumpster-dived for food so his sister wouldn't starve to death. He leaned back in his chair and reached for his cup, realizing he was on his own and was just wasting his time. He started to take a sip of his coffee when he caught something move out of the corner of his eye. Seconds later, a man about six-two with dark hair emerged from the shadows and edged toward the table.

"Top o' the morning' to ya," said the man with an Irish accent.

William's body went rigid as he stood up. "How did you get in here?"

"Don't worry. I don't mean you any harm." The man lifted his hands and took a step back. "I was just leaving and thought you might want to read this." He placed a newspaper on the table and without another word walked out of the room.

William ran out into the café to see if the man was still there, but he was gone. He rubbed the back of his neck, took a deep breath, and wondered if he was losing his mind. He stepped back inside the room where he saw the newspaper on the table and knew the man hadn't been a figment of his imagination. Maybe he was here the whole time when they closed up the café to have the meeting and he just didn't realize it. He sat down, picked up the paper and noticed it was the, *Wisconsin State Journal*, newspaper. He glanced over the front page and read the headlines, "Prominent Doctor's Wife, Mrs. Kathryn Rubin, Kidnapped from Home."

William jerked back his head and slightly lowered the paper. Instantly, he knew the picture of the woman next to the article was Rebecca; so he continued to read.

Mrs. Rubin just won a one million dollar settlement with the state police due to a high speed pursuit that had left Dr. Richard Rubin in a coma and her twins, Rachel and Ricky, dead. After Dr. Rubin woke up from the coma the authorities agreed to make public the riddle that was left in an egg carton at the scene of the crime. It read, "Two are planted in the ground, one is sleeping in la-la town. One is left to grieve all three, and soon to be in the Raid Hill loft with me."

Anyone with information regarding the riddle or Mrs. Rubin's whereabouts should contact the Madison, Wisconsin local authorities.

William puzzled the riddle. *Two are planted in the ground.* That had to be a reference to Rebecca's children. *One is sleeping in la-la town* would then be her husband, who had been in a coma. *One is left to grieve all three* was definitely talking about Rebecca mourning the loss of her family. But *Raid Hill loft ... Raid Hill loft ...* he repeated the phrase over and over. The letters began to unscramble in his head like a jigsaw puzzle.

"Oh my God! Rebecca is at the Hilliard's farm in the loft."

William got up to leave when the picture he saw in Marilyn's sunroom the day she found out she was adopted flashed before him. The man that had given him the newspaper was her brother, Dillon. Somehow, he had managed to step through the veil of time as an answer to his prayer. So, with an Irish accent, he ran out the door, shouting his response.

"And the rest of the day to you my friend!"

# CHAPTER 24

Kathryn stepped to the window where the lights were still on in the farm house. After she had walked away, leaving Marilyn in the hands of a madman, Emily had cried herself to sleep. She had failed to keep her sister's promise; a sister she didn't know she had until now. A sister she would never get to know. Like a thief in the night, David had stolen her life for the second time with no way to escape. The windows in the loft had been sealed and the door was unbreakable. They were now sitting ducks just waiting for him to make his next move.

It started to rain and she wondered if Marilyn was still alive or had David . . . Kathryn jumped at the sound of a gunshot blasting through the night sky. Her pulse began to beat in her ears when she watched Marilyn sprint across the yard with David not too far behind. *Run, Marilyn, run,* her heart pounded with each step as if they were her own. *Please, she silently prayed. Please, let her get away.*

Another gunshot pierced the air as David commanded her to stop. Marilyn ignored it and kept going. The rain started to pour as she ran passed the barn and headed for the woods. When she entered the grove of trees at the end of the property it reminded her of her own escape eighteen years ago. Where she had jumped off a cliff as Rebecca Hilliard and emerged on the other side as Kathryn Rubin. However, she had a feeling her sisters fate would turn out differently. With her injuries and the unpredictable nature of the woods, it would only be a matter of time before David caught up with her.

She waited and as she predicted, Marilyn emerged from the woods handcuffed at gun point. The moon quivered through the clouds and lit up a portion of the yard as David pushed her toward the house. Marilyn glanced up at the window wavering with exhaustion; the fight no longer in her eyes. A look of hopelessness passed between them and they knew unless a miracle happened; Marilyn wouldn't see daylight.

Several hours later Kathryn sat at the kitchen table cradling Emily in her arms. Again she had cried herself to sleep wanting her mommy. She wondered if Marilyn was already dead when she heard footsteps coming up the stairs. *David,* she thought. She quickly got up and stepped over to the kitchen counter.

"Emily, wake up!" she whispered, opening the cabinet under the sink.

"What?" Emily moaned and blankly stared at Kathryn.

"Honey, I need you to get in under the sink?"

"Why?"

"Please, just do as I say."

"Kat, you're scaring me." Her little mouth quivered.

"Please, Emily, be a brave little girl, and do as I say."

"Okay." She crawled in hugging Twinkie.

"Now, be quiet as a mouse and no matter what, you stay here until I come and get you. Understood?"

"Yes." She puckered her lower lip and shook her head.

"Honey, I'll be right back." Kathryn promised and closed the door.

She opened the junk drawer under the counter. Please, let it still be there, she prayed. Finally her fingers ran over the brown leather sheath. She grabbed it and pulled out the five inch blade that had belonged to her dad. She hid behind several bales of hay, waited, and prayed she had guts enough to use it.

The door opened, framing the silhouette of a man. Kathryn tensed with her fingers sweaty on the handle of the blade. The man hesitated, confused by the empty room in front of him. He took a step forward. Kathryn willed herself to stop breathing so loudly. A flash of lighting lit up the room. She screamed, clamped her hand over her mouth, horrified that she'd just given herself away. The man was coming towards her. She braced herself, ready to jump out and fight for all she was worth. He was feet away, fumbling in the dark. Another flash of lighting illuminated the room.

"Will?" Kathryn gasped. She couldn't believe it. This face, older now, but still as handsome as she remembered. How could he be here? How could he know where to find her? She had prayed so many times during her six months of captivity eighteen years ago that he would somehow, miraculously find her; prayed until she gave up on prayer. But it was him, without a doubt.

William couldn't believe it. It was really her, beautiful as ever. He gazed into her green eyes and felt a sense of lightness—like a weight had been lifted off his shoulders.

"Rebecca," he whispered her name and stepped toward her.

"Will, is it really you?" The knife fell to the floor.

She ran toward him, closing the gap that had separated them for eighteen years. She collapsed in his arms with disbelief letting out an uncontrollable sob. In the embrace of his strong arms, a sense of weightlessness came over her and she knew she was safe. Several minutes later, she stepped back and softly touched his cheek.

She raised her eyebrows and offered a questioning gaze. "I don't understand. How did you know I was here?"

"It's a long story and it'll have to wait. Right now I need to know if Marilyn is with you."

"Yes, she's in the house with David Sawyer."

"Who's David Sawyer?"

"He's the one mother invited to the dinner party so she could break us up. Two weeks later he kidnapped me and held me prisoner in a barn for six months. One day I escaped and ended up with amnesia. For the past eighteen years I've been living in Madison, Wisconsin. David accidentally found me, kidnapped me again and brought me here where my memories are now fully intact.

"Kat, can I come out now?" The little head peeked out from under the sink.

"Emily?" William did a double take.

"Come here, baby." Kathryn knelt down stretched out her arms.

Emily narrowed her eyes at William, pressed her lips flat, and ran to Kathryn.

"Honey, it's okay." She bent down and picked her up. "He's here to help."

"Is he the King that's going to keep the sky from falling?" Emily shyly bit the inside of her lip.

"No, this time it's Prince William."

"Hi, Emily."

"How do you know my name?" She lifted her thumb and put it in her mouth.

"I'm a friend of your moms."

"Are you going to save my mom from Foxy Loxy?"

"I'm going to try." He gave her a wink.

"Emily, I need you to go and play with your toys while I talk to Prince William."

"You're not going to leave me again are you?"

"No, honey." She kissed her cheek and let her down. "Now go on."

After Emily left, William said, "How did Emily get here?"

"David, he's the one who took her from the mall."

"This is crazy. How is it possible all three of you were kidnapped by the same man and end up at the same place?"

"I don't know. Call it a miracle, fate, the mastermind of spirits, who knows. I guess it's no different than you showing up here to save us."

"Listen, I've got to go find Marilyn."

"Will, you have to hurry. David is planning on sacrificing her for the sins of his mother. He thinks if he does that he'll be able to keep me and Emily and have the family he always wanted. Will, he is a very dangerous man, so you have to be careful."

"Do you know where he's keeping her?"

"Marilyn tried to escape earlier, but David caught her. They went back into the house through the cellar door."

"How did you end up in the barn?"

"I climbed out the window of the secret room."

"*Our* secret room?"

"Yes. I found the ladder still hidden under the floor board along with one of the love letters you gave me. That's how Marilyn and I escaped from the house earlier. We came to the barn to get Emily and David showed up."

"Is the ladder still hanging out the window?"

"I don't know. It was earlier." They went to the window and looked out.

"No, looks like he's already taken it out." She rubbed the back of her neck.

"Okay, I'll check the cellar."

"Please, be careful." Kathryn followed him to the door.

"Come here." He opened his arms.

Kathryn stepped into the arms of the boy that had grown up to be a man. The love she felt for him at the age of eighteen was still there and fondly remembered. However, her true love lay in a hospital bed and, if she ever got out of here alive, she was going to play him their special love song, "Nightingale," and fight like hell, so she could hear his mating call.

"Rebecca," William gently placed his hand on the back of her head. "I'm so sorry it's taken me so long to find you."

"It's doesn't matter, you're here now." She stepped out of his arms. "The important thing is that you rescue my sister,I just hope it's not too late."

"Listen, I've already called the cops, so I want you to run and hide out in the woods, but close enough so you can keep an eye on things. Don't come out until the police get here."

"Just be careful."

"I will." He started to leave. "Oh, one more thing before I go. Richard's awake." He disappeared down the steps.

When it dawned on her what he had said, she clasped her hands in prayer, pressed them against her lips and staggered back against the wall. With a sob she slid to the floor, closed her eyes, and wept.

"Kat, it'll be okay." Emily lightly placed her hand against her cheek.

Kathryn looked up into her niece's eyes that looked so much like Rachel's. She folded her into her arms and touched the Saint Jude pendant around her neck. She knew William needed more than a saint of desperate causes. He needed a warrior. So she closed her eyes and simply prayed.

"Saint Michael the Archangel. Please, protect William, and bring my sister safely home."

⚜ ⚜ ⚜

Marilyn stepped into the secret room behind the bookcase dressed in a white gown of pure silk tulle over silk satin. The deep V-neck fitted bodice and high waistline accented her small waist as the shirred skirt flowed down to the floor. The cap sleeves cupped her shoulders and several strands of small pearl beads draped across her back. The top of her hair was done up in a bouffant while the rest of her mane was swept to the right draping over her shoulder.

She made her way past the murals on the wall with David close behind dressed in a black suit. They marched in sync toward an altar draped in a white lace cloth covered in a bed of black and red rose petals. A pair of metal candelabra's stood in attention at each end of the altar

"That's far enough." David placed his hand lightly on her shoulder.

David stepped behind the altar and reverently put on a black hooded cloak. His blue eyes peered out from under the hood. The glow from the candles gave them a sinister look as they started to dilate. Just like

362

the changing of the guards at the Buckingham Palace, David disappeared and the voice emerged.

*"Woman, look at me."* The voice commanded. *This is your first and only warning. You are like a dumb lamb, brought to slaughter. You will not speak unless it is to answer a question. You will not cry or plead. If at any time you do not heed this warning, your daughter will take your place, and you will watch as she takes her last breath. Do I make myself clear?"*

She thought about seeing Kathryn in the window after she tried to escape and knew they were trapped with no way out. So to disobey would only fuel the fire and her daughter would suffer the consequences. With obedience, she stared into his dark, lifeless eyes.

"Yes." She spoke barely above a whisper.

*"Speak so I can hear you."* He demanded.

"Yes." She raised her voice.

David raked his hands through the water in the silver bowl with sloping sides in front of him. He did this several times before picking up the white hand towel on the table and patting them dry. Reverently, he picked up the silver wine chalice from the middle of the altar, lifted his chin, and pressed his shoulders back. He raised the cup above his head, briefly closed his eyes, and extended it toward Marilyn.

*"Drink. This is the covenant of your blood that is poured out for the forgiveness of David's mother."*

Her hands slightly shook as she grabbed the chalice, remembering what David said about killing her daughter if she disobeyed. *For Emily,* she thought, and took a sip. The sweet taste of red wine turned bitter in her mouth as David emerged and took the cup from her and lifted it toward the heavens.

"This is the blood that will set me free from the curse of my mother." He took a sip, placed it back on the table, and picked up the matza.

*"One bread, one body, and one sacrifice."* The voice lifted the unleavened bread to the heavens. *"I offer this for the sins of David's mother so she will be forever dead to him."* He handed it to Marilyn. *"Take. Eat as a sign of your willingness to offer your body as a living sacrifice."*

For Emily, she obediently took the bread and consumed it with one bite.

David picked up the water basin, along with the towel, and placed them on the window sill behind him. He picked up the chalice, drank the rest of the wine, placed it beside the basin, and stepped around the table to Marilyn.

"You look like a goddess in my mother's wedding dress." David captured her hands and gazed over her body. "I must say, you wear it much better than she does."

Marilyn followed his eyes to the corner where a skeleton in a red wig sat dressed like a Southern Belle in a gown identical to one she was wearing. The portrait of the woman that once hung above the fireplace in the sitting room now hung on the wall directly above the chair of bones.

"Don't you think so, Mother?" David's robe swished against the wood floor as he made his way to the corner. "What's the matter, cat got your tongue?"

Marilyn wondered if these were his mother's real bones or fake ones. Whether they were or not it didn't matter, she still found it disturbing and repulsive.

"You see, my mother was this loving and caring woman around her friends, but behind closed doors she was a monster. You met my twin brother, Daniel, such a caring and gentle soul. Do you know what mother use to do to him?"

"No." She remembered what the voice said about speaking when asked a question.

"She ignored him. Locked him up in the basement like an animal and said there was no way she was going to let the world know she gave birth to an idiot. Oh, she clothed and fed him, but she never cuddled him. She called herself lucky because she had another child to make up for the one that was stupid."

Marilyn thought about the kind and gentle soul she met in the basement that had taken care of her daughter. By the world's standards he was special, slow, and stupid. To her, he was the embodiment of all that was good. He was the spirit of love, joy, peace, kindness, and gentleness. Perhaps, when it was all said and done, they were just angels among us. To remind the so-called normal people what attributes they should strive for in this life-time.

"Do you know what my father did about it?"

"What?"

"Absolutely nothing. He was a weak alcoholic and let mother do whatever the hell she wanted just to keep the peace. Eventually my father left because he couldn't take it anymore. As time passed, my mother got older, weaker, and I became her caregiver. Do you know what I did?"

"No." Not wanting to hear the answer.

"I made her trade places with Daniel."

The soft curvatures of David's face became hard and drawn. She wanted to look away from his dark demonic eyes before they sucked the very light out of her soul, but she didn't for fear what her defiance would cost her.

*"That's when I took control."* The strong authoritative voice emerged. *"And put our mother into submission. The number one rule was to keep sweet at all times and, if she didn't, she would be denied the bare necessities of life such as food, clothing, and shelter. One day, we just completely forgot about her, left her with her thoughts, and she withered away to nothing and died."*

"Today, just like mother took the place of Daniel," David strolled toward Marilyn. "You will take the place of my mother and atone for her sins. This way, I can be free to marry my beloved Rebecca, raise your daughter as my own and have the family I always wanted."

The thought of him raising her daughter made her sick to the stomach. She wanted to fight back but was afraid he would make good on his promise of Emily taking her place. So, she kept quiet like a lamb to her slaughter.

He gently picked her up off the floor like a bride on her wedding day, carried her across the threshold and laid her upon the altar. She stared at the parasite in front of her wishing she would've obeyed the 'Keep Sweet' mantra. Perhaps if she had, maybe it would've bought her more time to change her fate. However, she would never know because time had run out and it was too late.

A waiting stillness came over her as David lightly caressed the side of her neck to the valley between her breasts, traveled over her stomach, and gently smoothed the skirt of her dress over the sides. Reverently, he stepped to the foot of the altar, slipped the sparkling beaded silver slippers from her feet, and let them drop to the floor.

A lump formed in her throat as he stood beside her, reached inside his cloak, and pulled out a white pearl-pummeled dagger. The handle was made of two silver, intertwined cobras, their bodies splitting apart to form the cross guard with fanged, hissing heads. Marilyn closed her eyes in defeat, knowing the snake had won.

*"According to this woman's own free will, she sacrifices herself for the atonement of our mother's sins, sparing the lives of her own child and our beloved Rebecca, ending this lifelong curse."*

"So be it!" David emerged, raised the dagger toward the heavens, took a deep breath, and lifted his chin in the air.

A silent scream gathered like storm clouds in the pit of her stomach as a loud sound rippled through the room. Marilyn opened her eyes with the scream pounding in her chest to the peals of thunder. A flash of lightning lit up the room. In the midst of the moonbeam that shone through the window, David's eyes grew wide with disbelief as he glanced down at the dark stain appearing on his robe. Marilyn scrambled off the table while he teetered in mid-air like a building on the brink of collapse. Her hands flew to her mouth as the table buckled under his weight and, with a crash; he took her place upon the altar like a dumb lamb to the slaughter.

She glanced to where William was standing in the doorway of the bookcase aiming his gun for a second round. The pounding of her heart pumped out a reservoir of tears. The salty waterfall cascaded over her cheeks while David grabbed the hem of her garment as if it was going to save him. She looked down and stared into his eyes, watching the life fade from them. She briefly glanced over at the skeleton in the corner and back at David. It was then she realized the absence of a mother's unconditional love, in life as well as in death, was one of the greatest destroyers in a child's life.

The silk skirt slipped from David's fingers like a final curtain as she made her way toward William. She gazed into his eyes and with each step the spark of turquoise ignited their heartbeats into one.

"Marilyn, are you okay?" whispered William.

She pressed the palm of her hand gently against his cheek and smiled with her eyes. She softly kissed his lips, stepped into the warmth of his strong embrace and said, "I am now."

"Marilyn!" Kathryn ran into the secret room with sirens blaring in the background.

At the sound of her own voice Marilyn looked up and saw her sister along, with several police officers, standing in the doorway. Softly, two bright orbs materialized in the room, lingered for several seconds, and made a grand exit out the window. A look of knowing passed between sisters as they stepped into each other's arms. In that moment, they realized the love of two mothers had managed to cross the veil of time to give them the one thing they had lost and longed for—family.

Several minutes later Kathryn stepped away and cried, "Marilyn, Richard's awake. He woke up the same time David kidnapped me and has been looking for me ever since. I just finished talking to him and he's on his way here."

"Oh, Rebec … I mean Kathryn that's wonderful."

"Also, there's a little girl outside waiting to see her mommy."

Marilyn stepped outside where Jim was holding their daughter. A look of relief passed between them as the scream that had entered their life nine months ago had finally been silenced. Jim let Emily down, and she ran across the yard towards her. This time it wasn't an illusion in a field of wildflowers as her daughter's strawberry blonde curls bounced in the moonlight. She knelt on the wet ground while the thunder clapped in applause across the sky as Emily jumped safely into her arms.

"Mommy!" she cried as she wrapped her little arms around her neck and squeezed.

"Emily," Marilyn whispered, held her close, and promised to never let go.

With her daughter safely in her arms, she glanced up, gazed into the moonlight exposure of her sister's eyes, and smiled.

# Epilogue

## One Year Later

**M**arilyn stepped through the half-moon opening onto the  connecting walkway where her rock garden was in full bloom with daffodils, daylilies, and crocus. She paused as a gentle wind tilted their pretty little heads her way. She could almost hear their sighs of relief when she knelt and started removing the weeds that infiltrated their garden. Their stems stood taller, their faces grew brighter, and their leaves became greener, as if they knew they were in for an impeccable spring because the little flower that had been lost had finally come home.

After she finished, she saw the mockingbird perched on the  flowering red maple tree. She waited for it to start squawking, but instead it just silently stared while she passed by. She scanned the backyard looking for its predator, but the black cat was nowhere to be found.

She slightly smiled, nodded her head, because their children were safe and all was right with the world.

She made her way toward the pond where Emily and Auntie K were picking flowers. She sat on the bench under the willow, thankful it was more than an illusion. It was nothing short of a miracle that they had survived the ordeal of David Sawyer. Sometimes, she could still feel the lump in her throat and the silent scream in the pit of her stomach as she lay upon the altar to be sacrificed. But, at the sound of a gunshot and memory of her daughter running safely into her arms under the moonlight, the feeling evaporated.

After their rescue, Kathryn and Richard had stayed with her for several weeks before returning to Madison. One day, out of the blue, she got a call stating they were moving to West Virginia, and they wondered if she knew a good realtor. She sold them five of her ten acres. Several months later, they contacted O'Conner's Development, and started building their house. They had a couple of setbacks, but hopefully by the end of the month, everything would be settled, and they would bridge the gap that had separated them for thirty-six years.

"Penny for your thoughts." William stepped up behind her, placed his hands on her shoulders, and lightly kissed her neck.

"It's going to cost you more than a penny for the thoughts running through my head."

"Well, we'll negotiate later."

"Hey, Marilyn, did William tell you who won the golf game?" asked Richard.

"Honey, did you lose again?" Marilyn placed her hand on William's and looked up.

"What can I say? The guy's a pro." He sat down next to her.

"Well, I guess I better go tell my pregnant wife what a wonderful and talented husband she has, so she can tell my unborn daughter." Richard headed toward the field.

After Richard and Kathryn had gone back home to Madison, within four months she became pregnant and was now due anytime. They were going to name their daughter Rebecca Olivia Rubin. She wanted to honor the memory of her former self, as well as the mother who had given her the strength while being held captive. Just like she had forgiven her mother for pushing her into the arms of a psycho path, she also forgave the young boy who had been responsible for killing her children. She and Richard had contacted the mother she had shunned at the roadside memorial, and together they were able to heal two families that had been brought together by a terrible tragedy.

William got up, grabbed Marilyn's hand, and they made their way to the pond. Six months after he had saved her life, he had asked her to marry him. Some thought it was too soon, others thought it wasn't soon enough. If it had been up to her, she probably would've married him the day after he rescued her. However, she had Emily to think about because of everything she had been through. She needed time to heal, and to throw William into the mix would've been too confusing. They took it slow, and he gradually filtered into her daughter's life. By the time they decided to get married, Emily was so excited because now her mommy wouldn't be alone when she was with her daddy.

After they were married, William moved into her house to keep Emily's life as normal as possible. He decided to turn the VanWyc Estate into a Bed and Breakfast. At first, he wasn't sure who was going to run it but, when the Oates' decided to move from Wisconsin so they could be closer to Kathryn, he asked if they'd be willing to run the place for him. Lillian was the host and loved cooking for her special guests. Garth was the handyman, and he also set up his glass blowing class right in the summer house, south of the gardens. This allowed the guests an opportunity to create a masterpiece of some special memory of their stay.

"Here you go, Mommy," Emily ran toward her with Richard and Kathryn not too far behind.

"Well, thank you, honey," she took the bouquet of wildflowers and gave her a big hug. "They're almost as beautiful as you."

"Aunt Dana, Uncle Jason," Emily yelled as she ran across the yard and jumped into Dana's arms, giving her a big kiss on the cheek.

"How's my girl?"

"Great, do you want to ride the paddle boats with me?"

"Not now, maybe later."

"Okay. Mommy can I go play with Ginger?"

"Sure, she's in her crate on the patio. Why don't you bring her out here so everyone can see her?"

"Alright," Dana put her down and she ran toward the house.

Several months ago, Marilyn made a trip to the Humane Society  so Emily could pick out a puppy. Instead, the lab pup ended up picking her when it ran out of its cage and started wagging its tail. She named her Ginger because of the yellow-brown-red mix of its coat. They had become quite a pair, and once the pup reached its full size, it would be a great protector. After what they had been through with David, she thought it was a good addition to the family.

"So, when are you two going to open your business?" Marilyn asked Dana and Kathryn.

"Hopefully soon," said Dana.

"Once we get the DJ and a caterer lined up, we should be good  to go," added Kathryn.

Dana finally got her opportunity to open the business she always wanted. She had partnered with Kathryn and they were going to call it, *The No Borders Extravaganza.* William had found them a nice piece of commercial property on the outskirts of Shepherdstown, and they were going to design it like a small, indoor shopping mall. It was  going to be a one-stop-shop for all wedding needs; from the ceremony to the honeymoon. They were also adding a small chapel for those who only wanted a small affair. Once the business opened, Marilyn was planning on have a coming home party for Rebecca Hilliard,  alias Kathryn Rubin.

"Well, are you going to tell them?" Jason stepped up behind Dana and slipped his arms around her waist.

"Tell us what?" asked Marilyn.

"We're pregnant," Dana's face glowed with expectancy.

"You're what?"

"Yep, I saw the doctor yesterday and he confirmed what I already suspected."

"You guys certainly didn't waste any time! You've only been married for three months," said Marilyn.

"I wanted my kid to grow up with yours and Kathryn's."

William slipped his arms around Marilyn's stomach and said, "Are you going to tell them or should I?"

"Tell us what?" asked Dana.

"Well, we found out the other day we're having twins. Boy and a girl."

"Are you sure?" asked Kathryn.

"Yes, and we've decided to name them after Ricky and Rachel."

Kathryn was speechless as she looked up at Richard with tears in her eyes. He slipped his arms around her and held her close while he looked up at Marilyn and William. He nodded his head with appreciation, letting them know how much it meant to him, that they would honor the memory of his children. In the sacred stillness, Kathryn stepped into her sister's embrace while tears of joy flowed down her face, knowing her children had found a way back into the fold.

"Well, this calls for a celebration," said Richard, wiping away the tear that slid down his cheek.

"Celebration for what?" asked Lillian, as she and Garth made their way across the yard.

"Well, looks like there's going to be additions to the family," said Richard. "Dana is pregnant. Marilyn's going to have twins, and she's going to name them after your grandchildren."

"Oh!" Marilyn placed her hand on her stomach. "They definitely know we are talking about them."

That's all it took. Marilyn, Kathryn, Dana, and Lillian huddled together and cried. The men just stood back and watched, not knowing what to do. When the women stepped from the circle, Lillian looked at the men standing there with their hands in their pockets.

"Don't you think you boys should get that barbecue started so we can celebrate?"

The three fathers-to-be looked at each other, laughed, shrugged their shoulders, and headed toward the gazebo, Garth tagging along, to do what they were told.

"All this excitement is making me want to go to the bathroom," said Marilyn. "I'll be right back."

She made her way to the house where she greeted Charlie and Violet, Millie and Chester, Kathryn's father, Frank and Daniel. Charlie and Violet were now married and deeply in love. She never saw him happier. Millie and Chester were a great addition to the family, bringing a little flare of the old west into the mix. Frank had become a great part of Daniel's life and they were now best buddies.

After the Hilliard's place went up on the auction block, Kathryn bought it and turned it into an equine therapy facility. She called it Sadie's Touch, in the memory of her trusted mare. As she had promised, the assisted living facility had one less patient when her father moved back into his homestead and spearheaded the program.

Several months after David was killed, Marilyn went to visit Daniel at the group home, where she found him withdrawn and despondent. After several visits she finally talked him into visiting, Sadie's Touch. Once he spent time with the horses and Emily, he was back to his jolly old self, dancing like Michael. She found it rather ironic that the twin brother of the man who was responsible for what happened to her was now a part of her family. She guessed that healing, just like hope, comes in the most unlikely places.

"Danny!" Emily squealed when she ran over and grabbed his hand. "Come on, I want you to meet Ginger."

While they made their way to the pup, William's mother and sister came through the gate along with Zach. She gave them a hug and told them she was glad they could make it. While they made their way toward the gazebo, Zach took off and jumped into his uncle's arms. It was a picture worth a thousand words. The long lost search had ended when Zach's father decided to turn himself in. Abbey no longer had to endure the hell he had put her through because her child was alive and safely in her arms.

Just when she got to the patio, Marilyn was greeted by Jim and Sarah. Who would've ever thought they would even speak to each other, much less share the same space? With a brief hello, she watched them make their way to Emily where Ginger was the center of attention.

She and Jim now had joint custody of Emily. Having her child everyday would've been the ideal situation. However, sometimes life hands you a card that you have to play wisely. Jim's betrayal had paled in comparison to the day her daughter was taken and was downgraded to zero on her emotional scale. She wasn't going to change the fact that his new wife, Sarah, was going to be a part of Emily's life. Once she saw Sarah's willingness to work together for the greater good of her daughter, she found she wasn't so bad after all. Besides, Emily loved her. At first it made her a little jealous because she didn't want the other woman taking her place, but when she realized her love had a positive influence on her child's life, she let it go.

Before she went inside, she gazed across her backyard. Compared to the way it looked last spring, it was a great improvement. Who would've ever thought this year would bloom just like her flower garden into a unique family tree? She realized sometimes family wasn't your own flesh and blood. Sometimes they were the ones who join you at the crossroads of your life. Some only stay for a season and others forever. It reminded her of the song her mom used to sing, 'Make new friends, but keep the old; one is silver and the other is gold.'

She thought about her parents and brother often, and wished they were here. However, whenever she cooked in the kitchen, she remembered her mother's promise to always be there. When she heard one of those 'why did the chicken cross the road?' type of jokes, she knew it was her dad telling her to lighten up and live. As for her brother Dillon; she knew neither time, space, nor death, would ever keep him from having her back.

Ireland was still waiting to answer the questions about her and Kathryn's birth parents. After thirty-six years, they figured it could wait a little longer. For now, they were content watching their own families grow and when the time was right, they would go searching for the answers. It was then she would have a 'top of the mornin' to ya' beer' at the Brazen Head Pub in Dublin for her brother.

Marilyn looked up while a flock of geese honked overhead. She thought about the goose that had fallen from the sky the day she went fishing with her dad. After its comrades fell out of formation to bring comfort before it died, they rejoined the flock where they grieved its passing and moved on. Nature had shown her then to everything there is a season, and a time for every purpose, under the shadows of the moonlight exposure.

# AFTERWORDS
*(A letter to myself)*

I have been thinking about you lately, and all you have been through. Reflect back on your journey, tell me what truths have you learned? Be careful of your choices, give yourself time to think it through, because the decisions you make will either make or break you. You never know what awaits you in the bend of a curve. So expect the unexpected, life is full of surprises. Don't run away from conflict but turn around and embrace it. Listen, with an ear of patience. There's always something to learn. Life is like a river, one moment it is peaceful, the next it's treacherous. Learn to embrace life's ever-changing character.

I've learned to accept all of me, my successes, my failures, the cracks, the blemishes. It's who I am. I have come to rest, just for a moment, nothing to prove, just to be, accepting me for who I am.

*Kathryn Rubin (alias Rebecca Hilliard)*

# ABOUT THE AUTHOR

Sheila DuGantt is a native of West Virginia. First and foremost she is the mother of two great children. She resides with her faithful companion, who looks more like a panda bear than a canine. *Moonlight Exposure* is her first novel. She hopes her readers enjoys the twist and turns as much as she loved writing them. It is her desire through their journey between the pages of the dark and lesser light they realize; sometimes hope comes in the most unlikely places.